Leslie,
Much love to you.
hope you enjoy.

T H E

HEARTS

O F

MEN

11-9-01

VILLARD/
STRIVERS ROW
NEW YORK

STRIVERS
ROW

During the 1920s and 1930s, around the time of the Harlem Renaissance, more than a quarter of a million African-Americans settled in Harlem, creating what was described at the time as "a cosmopolitan Negro capital which exert[ed] an influence over Negroes everywhere."

Nowhere was this more evident than on West 138th and 139th streets between Adam Clayton Powell and Frederick Douglass boulevards, two blocks that came to be known as Strivers Row. These blocks attracted many of Harlem's African-American doctors, lawyers, and entertainers, such as Eubie Blake, Noble Sissle, and W. C. Handy, who were themselves striving to achieve America's middle-class dream.

With its mission of publishing quality African-American literature, Strivers Row emulates those "strivers," capturing that same spirit of hope, creativity, and promise.

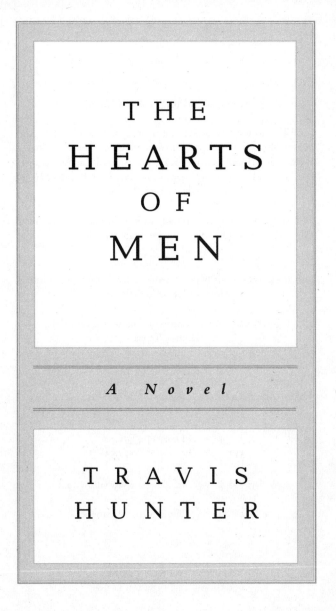

THE HEARTS OF MEN

A Novel

TRAVIS HUNTER

This work was originally published in 2000 by Jimrose Publishing
House, Pine Lake, Georgia.

Library of Congress Cataloging-in-Publication Data
Hunter, Travis.
The hearts of men : a novel / Travis Hunter.—1st ed.
p. cm.
ISBN 0-375-75709-0 (pbk.)
1. Afro-American families—Fiction.   2. Afro-American men—
Fiction.   3. Fathers and sons—Fiction.   4. Atlanta (Ga.)—
Fiction.   I. Title.
PS3558.U497 H86 2001
813'.6—dc21   00-053133

Villard Books website address: www.villard.com

Printed in the United States of America

2   4   6   8   9   7   5   3

First Strivers Row Edition
BOOK DESIGN BY DEBORAH KERNER

Acknowledgments

The Hearts of Men has been through its share of changes, all to make a better novel for you to enjoy and hopefully learn a few things from. I wrote this book with hopes of challenging men to take a more responsible role in life. First off I'd like to thank God, who is and has always been the head of my life. Then I'd like to thank my wonderful mother, Linda J. Hunter, for always being so supportive of whatever dream I let slip out of my mouth. My son, Rashaad, you are the reason that I do what I do. I love you, boy! KaTrina Brown, I love ya. Next up are my wonderful aunts: Carolyn Hunter Rogers, you always keep me pushing for higher ground. Carrie Mae Moses always gives that needed smile. Ethel Hunter (rest in peace), you always kept it real. To my new family, the Browns, especially Preston and Catherine, thanks for the support.

I have to thank the supercool editor and chief of Strivers Row, Melody Guy. You're not only my editor, you're my friend; Carla Sharpe, for giving my book the props that made

Random House my new home; Chandra Sparks-Taylor, for the editing and the support; Carl Weber, for getting the ball rolling and looking out for a brother all over Chicago and New York; my sweet but sharp agent, Marie Brown; my folks at Random House: Ann Godoff, Bruce Tracy, Libby McGuire, Carol Schneider, Tom Perry, Brian McLendon, Amy Edelman, Joseph Sora, Stacy Rockwood, Beth Pearson, Mercedes Everett, Steve Messina, and Deborah Aiges. To those that have been with me for ages: Willie and Schnell Martin, Allean Morton, Sherry Johnson, and Maggie Hardaway; my cousins Ann, David, Sharon, Chris, Lynette, Barry, Ray Ray, Tony (RIP), Gervane, Ron, Darle, and Anthony; my friends, man, it's too many of you to name. You know who you are.

Book clubs: Circle of Sisters, Black Expressions, Soul Expressions, SULA Book Club, and all the rest of you guys. To all the independent bookstores that have shown me love. E. Lynn Harris, Eric Jerome Dickey, and Nathan McCall—thank you for your support.

To the men who gave me the Heart of a Man: James W. Charles, Sr., my great-granddad; Lemuel Hunter, my granddad; Louis Johnson, my dad; Ernest Myers, my stepdad; Willie Earl Rose, my godfather; Dick Hunter, my uncle; James Charles, Jr., my uncle; Fred Rogers, my uncle; Ronald Morton, my friend; Julius Hardaway, my mentor. All of these men have influenced me to become the man I am today. So I'll answer your question now: there's a little Poppa Doc in all of them.

For those of you I didn't mention, charge it to my head, not my heart. Look out for my next novel, *Married but Still Looking*!

THE
HEARTS
OF
MEN

1

Caught with Your Pants Down

t was Friday morning, and Prodigy Banks was running just as late as he had the other four days of the week. After hitting the snooze button for the fifth time, he reluctantly arose at 7:20 A.M., pulling up his tired body and sitting on the side of his honey-oak sleigh bed. He then placed his head in the palm of his hands and proceeded with his morning ritual: trying his best to come up with a good lie to let his supervisor know he wouldn't be in the office that day.

It was not like he was ill; he just didn't feel like going to work, and now he was running out of excuses. He'd lost count of the number of times he'd said his grandfather died. In fact, his grandfather did die, but that was in 1978. After realizing he had already used all of his good excuses, he conceded. He forced himself up and into the bathroom.

Prodigy had never been a morning person, which was why he had to get out of the Army. He realized Uncle Sam's boys really did do more before nine A.M. than he planned on doing all day long. Plus, Simone, his manager and lover, spoiled him. She always covered for his tardiness.

Right now, she was the only one he was kicking it with, sort of. Slowly, Prodigy was trying to minimize his workload of women. He'd been with so many that it wasn't much fun anymore. Plus, he discovered that more than half of the women he dealt with didn't have anything going for them anyway. After sex, there wasn't much left for them to talk about.

Now he was shifting gears by trying to focus on a single relationship that was mentally as well as physically stimulating. His new motto was to screw up, not down, which meant he would bypass the rank and file to focus on kicking it with a woman of power and status. *Rich women need love too,* he thought. He didn't want his intentions misinterpreted, though. Just because he wanted a person who fit his definition of completeness didn't mean he was looking for a serious relationship. He relished his carefree bachelor life, but whoever it was who would be taking care of his physical needs had to bring more to the table than a cute face and a fat butt. And right now, Simone was bringing breakfast, lunch, dinner, and a fat butt.

Maybe that was why, whenever women around the job inquired about him, Simone's name always came up in the conversation. It was as if he was her property. Lately, though, she'd been getting on his nerves. She acted as if his sole purpose in life was to sit around and wait for her to get a moment away from her husband.

Damn that, he thought.

As he stared in the mirror, contemplating whether to give his already bald head a fresh shave, he noticed a white envelope that had been kissed by a set of juicy lips. He opened it and read the contents: *I think it's time that I get a key to your place. Love, Simone.*

"What!" Prodigy said aloud. "She's gotta go!"

He wasn't having it, because not only was she married to some psychotic, pro-football-playing dude who could probably lift a Mack truck, she was becoming a bit too attached.

A key to his place?

Out of the question.

She must be on that crack pipe, he mused.

After deciding he would try to make it to work on time, he showered but opted against shaving his head.

He felt that if he was going to rid himself of Simone, then he'd better not put himself in a position where he would need her assistance to cover for his perpetual lateness.

He remembered his grandmother saying, "Hell has no fury like a woman scorned." And after some of the women that he had dealt with, he now knew what she meant.

After completing his morning grooming ritual, Prodigy decided to wear his tan tailor-made suit. To complete the ensemble, he added a white cotton shirt and brown ostrich-skin shoes with a matching belt.

Since, as usual, he didn't have time for breakfast, he grabbed a Little Debbie snack cake, jumped in his black GMC Yukon, and headed north on Interstate 285. As he bore down on the accelerator, burning rubber along the way, he ran into gridlock traffic on the Atlanta Expressway. From the looks of it, there was no way he was going to be sitting at his desk by eight-thirty.

"Damn! Who taught these nuts how to drive? I'm about to commit road rage." Prodigy turned to his left and witnessed a driver in the far left-hand lane reading a newspaper and talking on a cell phone, with nothing in front of him but highway. Prodigy was infuriated, but all he did was smile and shake his head.

God, give me strength. Good thing today is Friday. I hope Simone

is there to cover for me. I guess I'll have to fire her another day, he said
to himself.

He knew that if Simone weren't there to cover for him, today
could possibly be his last day at GMAC. Because of his habitual
tardiness, he was already in the last stages of the company's disci-
plinary chart, and even that was with Simone's protection.
Otherwise, he would have been out the door a long time ago.

Prodigy really liked his job, once he got there. It was a far
cry from the type of work he used to do. The salary wasn't all
that great, but there were fifteen women to every guy. With a
ratio like that, he'd almost be willing to work for free.

For now, the most important thing was getting to the office.
So, after some creative driving (on the shoulder of the road,
tailgating, passing on the right, and dipping in and out of traffic as if he were a fugitive on the run from the Georgia state
troopers), Prodigy approached his destination. He steered onto
the Dunwoody exit, and shortly thereafter swerved into his
office complex. After entering the employee parking deck at
8:25 A.M., he hopped out of his truck and, much to his cha-
grin, ran into "miserable" Brenda, his ex–booty partner and
current supervisor.

"Good morning, Mr. Banks. I see that you're running late,
as usual," she said, looking at her watch.

"Calm down, I got this," Prodigy said dryly but boastfully,
because today he had arrived to work on time.

"I'm gonna calm you down," she shot back.

He quickened his pace to pass her in an attempt to get to his
desk. He knew that Brenda was still upset with him for leaving
her hanging after Simone was hired more than a year ago. She
was livid when he and Simone started kicking it.

Given half a chance, Brenda would torpedo him with all
sorts of foul words. She reminded Prodigy that every day she
saw him was a day she might snap and break his neck. The

threat really amused him, considering she was only about four feet five inches tall and lucky to be one hundred pounds. And that was soaking wet.

She had a habit of asking anyone who would listen why someone such as Prodigy would play second fiddle to another man over a piece of high-yellow butt, reminding him and everyone else that Simone could never really be his, because of her marriage.

Prodigy just considered Brenda a hypocrite who would often get ghetto on him, calling him everything except the child of God. She would usually say something like: "Ya black ass is gonna burn in hell for all that sinning. But that's the bed you made, and one day you gonna wake up to some hot grits." Or "I hate you, you black bastard!"; that was her favorite one.

He would normally just listen to her, shaking his head. He'd sometimes reflect on their time together, letting her know that what she and he did was also a sin because they weren't married either.

Prodigy could never figure out why she was tripping, because he never thought they had a relationship.

That's just like a woman, trying to make a mountain out of a mole-hill. We never went to dinner or the movies. As a matter of fact, the only place we ever went together was to bed. She never even knew my home phone number. But to hear her tell it, I was her man. Get outta here! he thought.

Despite how wacky Simone was turning out, Prodigy still thought she was more of a woman part-time than Brenda could ever be working time and a half.

"We had sex, no more, no less, and that was all there was to it," he would tell her, trying to avoid belaboring the issue. "Get over it."

The factor that really drove him away from her, other than her being as cuckoo as that damn bird, was she was too much of a fanatic. In the two years he had been with the company, she had been a Christian, a Jehovah's Witness, and a Muslim. Now she was in some new cult that didn't allow her to show her skin on Tuesdays.

"Prodigy! You think that you can do whatever it is that you wanna do, don't you? Keep it up and you'll be looking for a job. You can't keep showing up here whenever you feel like it. This ain't church!" Brenda said snobbishly to his back.

Prodigy knew that Brenda spoke mostly just to hear herself talk, because she knew that he didn't pay her any attention. He reported to Brenda, but Brenda reported to Simone.

Prodigy strolled through the glass doors leading to the mirrored high-rise, acknowledging Brenda with only a wave of the back of his hand. He was thinking that girl needed to lie on a couch and talk to someone with a Ph.D.

It was a good thing that his department was on the first floor, because if he had to wait on those slow elevators he would have met his corporate demise a long time ago. Whenever he did make it to work on time it was usually with only a minute or two to spare.

After arriving at his quadrant and signing in at eight-thirty, he made his daily rounds to greet everyone. It was his charismatic personality, not to mention drop-dead looks, that made many of his colleagues treat him as if he were a celebrity.

He never really thought much of his coworkers' reaction or opinion of him, but it felt good, so he basked in it. Even so, he never let it go to his head, because he still remembered a time when, as a young man, he was teased about his dark complexion and full lips. Bullies in his North Philadelphia neighborhood had given him nicknames such as Smut, Blacky, and Tar Baby.

Now, as an adult, his looks had matured and the names had changed for the better.

As he continued up the corridor, he noticed his wanna-be-black Caucasian coworker, Kevin, standing in the hallway. As they engaged in a little chitchat about the previous night's basketball game, someone interrupted his morning banter with a tap on the shoulder.

"Excuse me," said a honey-complexioned six-footer with a short-cropped haircut. "Is your name Prodigy?"

"Yes, ma'am, that would be me."

At that point he completely ignored Kevin, realizing that he had never seen this flawless figure before, as she was a sight to behold.

He extended his hand to greet her. She grabbed it firmly and held on a bit longer than needed, but that was fine with him.

"It's nice to finally meet you. I'm Gina."

"Finally?" he asked, as he motioned with his head for her to follow him to his work area.

Kevin gave a poor performance of acting like he wasn't listening intently to the conversation.

"Hey, Kev! I'll get with you later, potna! I have work to do," Prodigy said.

"Okay, big guy. Don't do anything that I wouldn't do," Kevin joked as he nodded his head approvingly and walked off.

Prodigy and Gina then walked to his office area.

"What do you mean, 'finally'?" Prodigy asked. "How long have you been with the company?"

"A little more than a year," she answered. "I was at the downtown branch, but I just transferred to this office on Wednesday. Today is my first day here. I was doing the human-resources paperwork, and you know how that goes. But since I've been here, all I hear the women talking about is this Prodigy guy."

"Is that right?" Prodigy said. "Well, as you can tell, they must live some pretty boring lives if all they can seem to talk about is me. But don't you believe a word of it."

"Oh no. It was all good," Gina said as she eyed him seductively from head to toe.

"Look at you," Prodigy said, blushing and shaking his head.

"I'd rather look at you," she said.

After hearing Atlanta women constantly complain about the shortage of quality black men, he thought he had gotten used to their aggressive behavior, but Gina proved him wrong. Every time he experienced such straightforwardness he usually was left a little shell-shocked.

"Have a seat, Gina. Where are you from?" he asked as he walked behind his desk to sit down. He wanted to change the subject because aggressive women were a turnoff. Prodigy considered himself somewhat old-fashioned, believing that the man should be the hunter, not the hunted.

"I'm from Chicago, Southside. And yourself?" Gina asked as she took a seat in one of the chairs in front of his desk, crossing her long, shapely legs.

"Philadelphia!"

"Dang! Is anybody from Atlanta?" she asked.

"Yeah, we have a couple of natives running around here, but this does seem to be the melting pot."

"Sooo," Gina purred, "what brought you down to the A-town, Mr. Banks."

"Long story."

Actually, Prodigy didn't want to think about what had led to his journey south.

"What about you?" he asked. "What brought you southeast to the Peach State?"

"I went to Spelman. I like the city, so I decided to stay."

"Yeah, Atlanta's a nice spot with a lot of beautiful women—present company included," Prodigy said, giving Gina an appreciative nod.

"Oh no, the scenery ain't bad." Gina acknowledged him by reciprocating with a naughty nod of her own.

Realizing she was getting a little too comfortable with Mr. Tall, Dark, and Handsome, Gina stood to excuse herself.

"Mr. Banks, the pleasure was all mine, but I have to be leaving. Maybe we can do lunch sometime."

"No doubt!" he said, standing to shake her hand once again before she left.

"It was nice talking to you," she said.

"Likewise, Gina. Give me a call once you're settled in," Prodigy said, handing her a business card off his desk.

Gina took the card, looked at it, looked back at Prodigy, and winked, leaving no doubt in his mind that it would only be a matter of time before her toes were pointed toward his ceiling.

His quad-mate Debra, who had been listening to every word that was said between him and Gina, peered over the partition.

"Prodigy, you a ho'! You ought to be ashamed of yo'self. Don't you already got a woman, who got a man? Ain't that enough drama for ya? I'ma tell Simone."

"You know, Debra, your life would be so much simpler if you learned the fine art of minding your own business. Now, be quiet! Better yet, go to the break room and get me a bottle of water to go with my Little Debbie," he demanded, already knowing what her answer would be.

"Do I look like one of your little hoochie mommas? Go get ya own damn drink. And you need to stop eating all that sweet stuff early in the morning," she retorted. "One day ya gonna wake up dead."

"My mother lives in Philly! You want anything from the break room?"

"Yeah! Bring me back a man that can last for more than two minutes."

"Look at you! That's how you got all those badass kids, being nasty," Prodigy said.

"Now you mind yo' damn business! Anyway, when you gonna do some work? You ain't done nuttin' since you been here but flirt. Ya lucky Brenda didn't see you. You know she would've started talking in tongues."

Prodigy had learned to ignore Debra over the years. She was more like the sister he'd never had. He went to her with questions that only a female could answer, and she would usually give him an honest reply. Although Debra was always in someone else's business, Prodigy considered her to be one of the cool ones.

After leaving the break room, he went back to his desk to read his e-mail, to check for any meetings. But as usual it was filled with all types of junk mail:

Hi, Prodigy, you look nice today. Latysia.

"Thank you." Delete.

Prodigy, don't wear that suit anymore, it makes me think nasty thoughts. Stacy.

"That's cuz you're nasty." Delete.

Prodigy, why didn't you call me last night? And when are we going to dinner? Remember, you promised. Mishawn.

"Yeah, yeah, yeah." Delete.

Prodigy Banks, you have a mandatory meeting with Craig Botano at eleven A.M. in the blue conference room. Human Resources.

He wondered what his vice president could want with him. He assumed it was probably some corporate mumbo jumbo and continued with his latest project.

As he got his day under way, Jake walked up.

"Yo, P! Did you see that fine six-foot-nine chicken-head that they got in accounting?" Jake asked in his loud country accent as he approached Prodigy's desk.

Debra, disturbed by Jake's outburst, which shook the silence, said sarcastically, "Damn, Jacob! Who you talking to? Prodigy or the people on the third floor?" She gave him a look and continued, "Don't be ignorant all your life."

Her comment pissed Jake off.

"Ah, hell! Sit yo' ass down, Dee. You always got to put yo' two cents in. You know you need it, wit' yo' broke ass," Jake said.

"Just keep it down. Some of us were hired to do a job." Surprisingly, Debra eased back into her chair without much of a comeback.

"That's right! Keep him straight, Dee," Prodigy said, trying to instigate their barrage of retorts. He always enjoyed egging these two on because they sounded like an old, bitching couple living together just for the thrill of insulting each other. Competitively, Debra always got the best of each exchange with her quick ghetto wit.

"What's the deal, dog?" Prodigy asked.

"I want that ass! Hook a nigga up!" Jake was speaking in a tone that he considered a whisper.

"What are you talking about, Jake?" Prodigy asked, pretending to be clueless.

"The new chick. I want that!" Jake said, snorting like a pig in heat.

"Jacob, you look like a beige Buddha. You know that woman don't want you, ya rotten-tooth bastard," Debra said.

"Shut the hell up, Dee! I'm still tryna figure out who in the hell you got drunk long enough to have sex wit' yo' stank ass."

They all laughed at that one.

Jake had a light, damn-near-white complexion. He was about five feet tall with a stomach that hung over his belt. He had a missing front tooth and a chronic case of halitosis.

"Come on, baby. You know I don't roll like that. You gonna have to go for your own," Prodigy said, never turning to face Stinky-winky.

"You on that already, ain't ya? I thought I saw those long-ass legs coming from over this way! Damn, nigga! You already got the finest bitch in the company. Leave some for the peasants."

Debra piped in: "You got that right, peasant! But why she

gotta be a bitch? How would you like it if every time I saw you I called you a jackass?"

"Keep it up, Dee, and I'ma walk around there and hit you right in yo' damn mouth."

"Oh no, don't do that, cuz then we'll have two jack-o'-lanterns walking around here."

"Y'all cut it out and, Jake, watch your mouth. You're in the presence of a young lady," Prodigy said.

"Where she at?" Jake asked with a hint of sarcasm as he threw yet another jab.

"Why you always coming over here starting with her?" Prodigy asked.

"She started it today, P," Jake said defensively.

"Well, both of y'all need to cut it out; y'all bring the property value down over here."

"Hey, P! You remember Brooke, that fine white chick with the sista ass that works in customer service?" Jake asked.

"No, but what about her?"

"Well, she told me to tell Mr. Exotic Deep Chocolate to give her a call. Here's her number."

Debra stood. "If you call that white girl I'll kill ya."

"What you got, elephant ears? I'm talking to Prodigy," Jake said, clearly getting frustrated.

"No, but as big as your nose is you've got to be related to one, cuz that's a damn trunk on your face," Debra said as she sat back down.

"Here, you keep it, but tell her I said hi," Prodigy said, handing Jake back the telephone number.

"No, no, no! I ain't about to get started passing yo' messages. Tell her ya damn self."

"Look here, Jake, I'm gonna have to holla atcha later. I got a lot of work to do. That new girl's name is Gina. Go introduce yourself to her. Tell her I said you're the one I wanted her to meet."

"Oh, you already told her about me? Good looking out, boy," Jake said, as he cracked a raggedy-toothed smile. Then, as if greeting a majestic royal court member or a deity, he grabbed Prodigy's hand and bowed in a show of respect for his putting in a good word for him. "Thank you, Godfather," he said reverently.

"Good luck on your new honey," Prodigy teased as Jake ambled off happily. He stood to observe Debra, who was slumped in her chair, laughing hysterically.

"Oh, you wrong for that!" she said as she wiped the tears from her eyes. "That's what he gets with his ugly self. He needs to find himself a dentist before he hurts somebody with that toxic waste dump he has for a mouth."

"I'll be back. I'm going to the bathroom to wash my hand. Jake kissed it."

"Oh lord, here," Debra said, handing Prodigy some antibacterial hand cleanser out of her purse. "Use this. Go wash it too and hurry up, you might get gangrene."

Returning from his scrub-down, Prodigy pored over some more meaningless e-mail and finished up some paperwork. He then logged off his computer and headed toward the conference room for his meeting with Craig.

As he got off the elevator on the tenth floor, he spotted Simone leaving the conference room.

"Simone! Simone!" he shouted, but the petite, hazel-eyed beauty kept striding hastily around the corner in the opposite direction. Prodigy didn't get a good look at her, but she appeared to be a bit shaken. He sensed something was strange, because it wasn't like her to ignore him like that.

When he walked into the conference room, he got some negative vibes, and his mind began to roam.

Craig, standing in front of a window of the high-rise, greeted Prodigy without turning around.

"Good morning, Prodigy. Please have a seat," Craig said.

Prodigy took a seat in one of the high-back leather chairs, as a listless Craig, who stood silently for about a full minute, continued gazing out the window. Since Craig had called the meeting, Prodigy waited for his cue to speak. The tension in the room was thick as he sensed the odd behavior. Over the past two years, he had never had a bad encounter with his fifty-year-old VP. But now he felt a chasm developing between them.

Craig had hired Prodigy as a favor to a mutual friend, Winston, fondly called Poppa Doc.

"Prodigy, I know you're wondering why I called you here," Craig said as he turned away from the window but still avoided eye contact. "I will get right to the point. We have some time-and-place issues: The hours from eight-thirty A.M. to five P.M. are not the time, and 500 Dunwoody Parkway is not the place, for your impulsive sexual behavior. Now, I know that can be a daunting task for a young stud such as yourself, but it is imperative that you make the distinction between work and play."

Prodigy, at a loss for words, wondered, *What in the hell is Craig talking about?*

He could only figure that since there were so many rules in corporate America concerning sexual harassment, perhaps a female coworker had reported that he approached her in the wrong way. He had always suspected that merely complimenting a person or using a certain tone could be misinterpreted and lead to a formal complaint.

"Damn, Prodigy! What the hell were you thinking about? No, let me rephrase that, because I know what you were thinking about," Craig said angrily, sidestepping his professional demeanor and finally looking into Prodigy's eyes.

"Hold on, CB! What the hell are you talking about?" Prodigy asked defensively.

"Prodigy, when I arrived at work this morning there was an envelope from security on my desk."

When Prodigy heard the word "security," he immediately felt butterflies in his stomach.

What could this be? he asked himself, but kept quiet until he had heard all of the details.

"I thought I knew you better than this," an exasperated Craig mumbled as he reached for a leather binder lying on the conference table. He opened it and pulled out a red-stamped white envelope with the word "security" scrawled on it.

The message read:

> On June 16, 1998, at 1800 hours, I pulled the video from the west-wing staircase that explicitly detailed a male and a female deeply engrossed in a passionate kiss. The female then lifted her dress and turned with her back to the male. She bent at the waist to allow the male, who by now had unzipped his trousers, physical contact. After exactly nine minutes of sexual intercourse, the male leaned back against the wall, allowing the video surveillance device to record his face. The male in the video was identified as Prodigy E. Banks. The female's identity is unknown at this time because her face was not visible to the camera. We will continue with this investigation at your discretion.

After reading the memo, Craig leaned back in his chair and threw up his hands, waiting on a response.

Prodigy was aghast, simply stunned. Figuring today was probably going to be his last day, he decided to try to go out with class, despite the compelling evidence against him.

"Craig, I screwed this up! I know you took a chance on me, and I let you down. Hell, I let myself down. Now, I'm not going to sit here and try to make excuses for my ill behavior. I don't know what I was thinking about when I did that. But before I go, I'd like to thank you for showing me how the other half lives. Now at least I have something obtainable to shoot for."

"What do you mean the other half, Prodigy?" Craig asked curiously.

"This!" he said, panning the conference room that was chock-full of valuables. "Craig, these types of possessions don't happen on my block. Do you know that I'm the only male in my family that has never seen the inside of a jail cell? Don't get me wrong, it's not like I've never done anything illegal. It's just that I think God has another plan for me. I think it's time for my family's generational curse to stop. That's why I feel so bad that I screwed this up. It was sort of my ticket out."

"Prodigy, I can see that you've never been taught the power of positive thinking. Henry Ford once said, 'Whether you think you can or you can't, you're absolutely right.' "

He continued lecturing Prodigy, telling him, "You can see that you need to change your thought process. Start believing that you can achieve things, and then take action. I'm not going to fire you, because I think that you realize your mistake. And, as men of color, we have to look out for each other. God knows the white boys cover one another in more ways than with just sheets. Also, don't let where you came from dictate where you're going. Now, I want you to take the rest of the day off to get some mental rest. And, from now on, you are to arrive thirty minutes before your scheduled start time. That's what I want in return for keeping you on board. And, hell, if Bill Clinton can get a little freaky in the White House and keep his job, then I don't see why you should be terminated. The ball's in your court. Don't make me regret this decision," Craig said.

"Craig, I appreciate the chance, man. And I owe you one."

"That's the way life works, Prodigy. We all need second chances because none of us are perfect. Just don't let it happen again. Now, I have another meeting. Take all of the time you need and tell Poppa Doc to give me a call."

"I'll do that, and thanks again."

Craig packed his briefcase and dismissed himself from the conference room to allow Prodigy time to ponder.

He sat in the soft leather executive chair, swiveling back and forth, replaying the saga of the meeting in his mind. He realized he had dodged another bullet.

What did I do to deserve this treatment? Somebody is trying to tell me something and I'm starting to hear him. I need to get my life in order. I'm a long way from where I came, but I've got so far to go. It's time for some major changes, and the first change is to stop thinking with my jimmy.

After his meditation, he went back to his desk to finish some of the tasks he'd promised to take care of before the end of the week—even though it was already Friday. After he sat down, he noticed that his phone indicated he had four calls.

"Prodigy. It's Simone. Call me on my cell phone."

"What's up, family! This is Jay fo' Liiiiiife. Man, where are you? I need a big favor. Call me. I'm at the spot. One love."

"Hey, boy! This is Poppa Doc. I hope you got your lazy butt up and went to work today. Call me. I need you to help me move a refrigerator. Well, I need for *you* to move it, because you know I ain't moving nuttin'. Oh, and bring me a pack of Kool 100's. I just smoked my last one, and Ethel done hid my car keys, so I can't drive. I'll see you when you get here. Ciao."

Prodigy smiled when he heard his old friend's voice. They had become such good friends over the years. In the past two years Poppa Doc had shown him the reason God made fathers. He believed that if he had had Poppa Doc in his life from day one that he would have been able to move mountains by now. He also felt that he owed Poppa Doc for everything that he was and would become. Whenever he looked at his old father-figure friend, he equated the experience to being in the presence of an angel.

He continued listening to his messages.

"Prodigy, call me at extension 1372. Oh, this is Gina."

Since Gina was a new face in the building, he decided to return her call first. She picked up on the first ring.

"Gina, this is Prodigy. What's up?"

"Hey, how are ya?"

"I'm doing alright. You settled in yet?"

"Getting there! I was calling to see what you were doing tonight," Gina said.

"Nothing! I don't usually hang out on Friday nights, but what's happening?"

"Well, I have tickets to the comedy club in Buckhead. Wanna go?"

"Nah, not really. I just went last night and the same comedians are there tonight. But if you get a minute, you can call me."

"Well, we don't have to do that. Would you like to do something else?" Gina asked.

"I'm open! What do you have in mind?"

"I'll think of something. Where do you live?"

"Stone Mountain."

"Dang. That's far! I live in Marietta."

"If you were walking, it would be far; in a car it's twenty minutes."

"I guess you're right. Give me the directions."

Prodigy gave her directions and his home number.

He then decided to contact his cousin Jermaine, opting not to call Poppa Doc from work because he knew that the old man could outtalk Don King.

After dialing his cousin's number, a blaring voice greeted him.

"What!" his Aunt Nettie snapped as she answered the phone.

"Where's that fool that got my favorite aunt pissed off?"

"Ha ha! Hey, baby! How's my favorite nephew doin'?" Aunt Nettie said, instantly changing her tone after she realized it was Prodigy.

18

"I'm doing just fine, and how's everything with you in the City of Brotherly Love?"

"Oh, everything is going well in Philly, except for that sorry-ass son of mine. You know I should've had one of them, uh, abortions. That boy ain't worth the thirty seconds it took his sorry daddy to make him. Won't work, won't keep this house clean, and now he got this little crumb-snatcher 'round here stinking up the place with his cute little self. But back to that fool, he gonna have to get the hell out of here. I got high blood pressure, and he ain't gonna kill me. Baby, how do you like Atlanta? Yo' momma said she's coming to see you next month. I might fly down there with her if that's all right with you. I ain't never flown in no plane before," Aunt Nettie said as she alternated between ranting and raving to calm and collected.

"Oh, you know as long as I've got a place to put a key you've got a place to sleep. I can't believe you said that," Prodigy said.

"Yeah, you left here and ain't never came back. I don't blame ya, though, cuz ain't nothing in Philadelphia no more. I heard ya got a nice house."

"It's alright. You're gonna have to come check it out. It's a duplex, you know, where one side of the house is mine and the other belongs to someone else. It's sort of like the row houses in Philly but in groups of two."

"Oh, that sounds nice. Hopefully I'll see it next month."

"I'm looking forward to it! And don't you let that knuckle-head son of yours drive you crazy. How old is Jermaine now, anyway?"

"Twenty-four, going on ten. Damn fool. You talked to Ray?"

"Not lately. He's still got a beef, I guess. Is your son there?" Prodigy asked, ready to get off of the subject of his Uncle Ray.

"Unfortunately," she said. "Hold on a second. I love you and I'm proud of you too. Hold on. Jermaine! Prodigy's on the phone. And hurry up, it's long-distance," she yelled to her only son.

Jermaine picked up another phone. "I got it. What's up, my peoples?"

"You. And when did you have a child?"

"I had him three weeks ago. His name is Kahlil. Nigga look just like me."

"Poor fella."

"Whatever, dog! Look here, I need to get the hell out of Philly for a minute. Is that invite still open?"

"Yeah, but what are you gonna do about your son?"

"He'll be straight. Mom's got that. Plus his mom is good people."

"Alright, yeah. You can come down. Now look, I don't know if you heard, but I don't roll like I used to. I don't even associate with people who get down like that. Ya heard me?"

"Damn, you sound country! I'll call you when I'm about to be out."

"Hey! And stop driving my aunt crazy."

"Too late. She been crazy a long time, dog. I'll call ya. One love."

"Peace."

After hanging up with Jermaine, Prodigy thought he might as well end the relationship with Simone, so he gave her a call.

"What's up, lady?"

"Hi. How did your meeting go?" Simone asked anxiously.

"It went alright. I didn't get fired, if that's what you're asking."

"Well, that's good. They're transferring me to the downtown branch, effective Monday."

"Yeah, well at least you're still employed," Prodigy said flatly.

"I know. I thought I was out of here! I almost pooped on myself when Craig put that tape in. I prance my little butt up in the conference room with my notepad, thinking that this was a business meeting. And here I am on video getting my groove on. I'm like, damn! Big Brother done caught me slipping," Simone said in her sexy New Jersey accent, which was why Prodigy was so attracted to her. She reminded him of home. They even knew some of the same people. Even so, he realized there were problems with their relationship. She was married, and he was tired of playing "duck and dodge the crazy husband."

"Damn, he played the tape?"

"Yes! Craig knew it was me but couldn't prove it. I think his old butt was over there getting his thrills at my expense. I had to tell him to turn it off."

"Simone, you know I've got crazy feelings for you, but we are going to have to chill with this so-called relationship," Prodigy said. He wasn't sure if you could label their affair a relationship. As far as he was concerned, it was more like a "sexa-tionship."

"What do you mean, Prodigy?"

"You know what I mean. This fakeness that we are doing: running around, sneakin' and sexin' on stairwells. I'm a grown man, and that's teenage stuff. I can't even take you to the movies without leaving the state. What kind of foolishness is that? So, as of right now, I'm calling whatever this is quits."

"Are you sure?"

"Positive! Bye, Simone," Prodigy said.

"Wait, I mean, can't we meet and talk about this?" Simone asked with a strained voice.

"Nothing else to talk about. I'm out." Prodigy hung up the phone, leaned back in his chair, and took a deep breath.

Although he had made a big decision, he immediately questioned himself.

I just got rid of my total package, he thought. *She's fine, smart, paid. Plus, she got that level-ten coochie. Somebody done slipped me a Mickey.*

2

Not Alone
but Lonely

ork, work, work! That's all I ever hear from you. And, frankly, I'm sick of it. You can have a life outside of that damn Ford plant, Bernard! And now that you've got a little promotion, I doubt we'll ever see you now," Diane screamed at Bernard as he got dressed for work.

"Ain't that a bitch," Bernard responded angrily. "Most people get congratulated on their promotions. All I get is your lip. As hard as I work, the last thing I want to hear before I leave in the morning is your ungrateful ass complaining. Woman, you'd find something wrong with God," he said as he pulled his navy-blue Ford coveralls over his shoulders.

Diane had pissed him off, but she was angry also.

"Well, what else is there to do? I can't get through to you. You have a family, and you seem to care more about that damn job than you do us. News flash: WE DON'T SEE YOU!" she yelled, while gesturing wildly with her hand in his face.

Bernard really went into a tirade then.

"Diane, what would you have me do? Tell my boss, 'Sorry, I can't come to work today because my wife wants me to stay home and hold her goddamn hand.' Nah, but then you'll cry about not having any money. I can't win for losing with you. You said you wanted to stay at home and raise the baby. I allowed you to do that, but now that Brittany's in school you're bored. So, guess who feels the butt-end of your boredom? Me! You need to get a hobby or something. Maybe then you'll stop riding my back all the damn time. I have a little girl to take care of, and I'd rather die than let her go without one single thing because you want me to be Cliff Huxtable. Now, leave me the hell alone," Bernard said, tying his shoes while seated in an overpriced chair that Diane had bought for their bedroom.

"Bernard," Diane said, "there's more to being a man than just paying the bills, you know!"

"Now you're questioning my manhood, huh? Besides, what could you possibly know about being a man?"

"I've been around men all my life, and I know what a real man is supposed to do."

"And what is that, Miss I-sit-on-my-ass-all-day Superwoman?"

"Take care of home, Mr. All-I-do-is-work-sleep-and-shit!"

"You need to be concerned about what a real *woman* does, because you'll never be a man."

"I *am* a real woman, and I'm not trying to be a man."

Trading insults was wearing each of them out, but Bernard angrily launched another assault.

"Look, Diane. It's too early in the morning for this. I know I take care of my home. And if I'm a lemon and you want a lime, then take your ass to a fruit store."

Bernard realized he was letting her get to him, so he decided to mute his end of the conversation by storming out of the room. Even as he left, he could hear her rapidly firing off a soliloquy by swearing at the top of her lungs. She was livid! But then again, so was he.

As he sat at the kitchen table reading the morning news and eating hot grits, scrambled eggs, and crispy bacon prepared by his wife, his precious, sleepy eight-year-old appeared with multicolored beads hanging from her shoulder-length braided hair.

"Daddy! Why were you and Mommy fussing? Y'all woke me up," Brittany said as she climbed on his lap to give him one of her "You mean the world to me" hugs.

"I'm sorry, sweetie. We didn't mean to wake you," Bernard said as he put his paper down and gave Brittany his undivided attention.

Every time he looked at her cute, cocoa-brown face, he was reminded of why he was put on God's earth. His family meant everything to him; they were all he had in this world.

Damn whatever Diane was talking about, he thought.

Bernard realized he didn't spend the time at home that was needed, but he couldn't live with himself if he didn't put food on the table. So something had to give, and right now it was his time.

"But what were you fighting about?" Brittany asked as she soothed his anxiety with her sparkling brown eyes.

"Well, sometimes adults fuss when they can't agree on things," he said as he played with his daughter's braids.

"Do you still love Mommy?"

"Of course I do. And I love you too. Now, go back to bed, I'll tuck you in," Bernard said, looking at his watch.

"Daddy! Why you work so much?"

"So that we all can live a comfortable life. And so that you can have everything you'll ever need."

"Well, can you take tomorrow off? It's Saturday, and I want to go to Six Flags with you."

"We'll see, honey. I just got a new position, and they might need me."

"But I need you too."

"Well, like I said, sweetie, I'll see."

As he held his baby girl in his arms while walking up the stairs back to her bedroom, he realized that unless he put her down he wasn't going to work at all that day. She had that effect on him.

"Okay, sweetie, maybe you can catch a couple of Z's before it's time for school. I'm sorry you had to hear Mommy and Daddy arguing."

"I don't have school today; it's teachers' workday," Brittany said, smiling.

"Is that right? Well, what do you have on your agenda for today?" he asked.

"Shopping!" she said excitedly.

"Oh boy! You're just like your mother. Well, don't spend too much money. Remember, a penny—"

"—saved is a penny earned," she uttered, finishing the sentence for him.

"That's right! Now, go to sleep," he urged. "Daddy loves you very much."

He then pulled the covers over his little angel and kissed her forehead.

"I love you too, Daddy."

Bernard left Brittany's room and headed back to the kitchen to finish his breakfast, which was now cold. After looking at his watch, he decided to skip the morning news. Before bolting out the door, he activated the security system for the house.

He opened the garage and jumped into his ten-year-old Ford Ranger. However, much to his surprise, the engine sputtered and ultimately failed to crank. With more than 250,000 miles on it, he knew it was bound to happen. And now he realized it was time to buy a new truck.

Trying to convince himself it could have been worse, he spoke to the truck as if it were a person: "I guess I shouldn't complain. You've done your job and at least you didn't croak on the highway. You came home to die."

He then jumped out and went back into the house to let Diane know of his change in plans.

"Diane, I'm taking your car to work." He yelled up the stairs in a forceful tone to let her know he was still upset with her for flying off the handle.

Her reply helped to broker a peace treaty, and a truce was declared.

"Bernard! I'm sorry. It's just that I need you. We need you," Diane said, standing at the top of the staircase.

"I know, and I'm sorry too. I'll have to do better. I promise I'll make more time for you guys," Bernard said as he made his way up the stairs and followed her back into the bedroom. He sat on the side of the bed as Diane pulled the covers up to her neck. Bernard leaned down and gave his wife a long, passionate kiss.

Diane was pleasantly stunned, of course.

Damn, she thought, *I didn't know he still knew how to kiss!*

A feeling of relief rushed through her body.

"Thank you, I needed that," she said. "By the way, Brittany is out of school today, and I promised to take her to the mall."

He agreed to make sure they would have a vehicle by noon.

"Is that too late?" he asked.

"No, that's fine. And good luck today. I love you."

"Thanks! And don't spend too much money in them malls. Go to the discount outlets or something," he suggested before leaving for the office.

"Bye, Bernard. I know how to shop," Diane said, pulling the covers over her head.

"I know you do, but you get carried away sometimes. You got clothes in the closet with the tags still on them. When you gonna wear 'em? When you die? One day I'm going to get all that junk together and take it back," he said before turning and walking away.

"I'm waiting on you to take me someplace nice, just the two of us," Diane said as she removed the covers from her head, but Bernard was already halfway down the stairs.

After resetting the security alarm to their country-club-like home, he jetted out of the garage in Diane's silver and gray Volvo, heading for his new position as Ford Motor Company's plant manager. It had been a long time coming, but he had finally reached the corporate level. All those days of working overtime and going to school part-time had finally paid off.

Since not many people were on the road at five-thirty in the morning, Bernard took his time getting to work. He always enjoyed the peacefulness of dawn. As he indulged in the Atlanta skyline, his thoughts drifted to his childhood in South Carolina. Lately, his mind had been finding its way back to the days of Jim Crow laws and hunger. Maybe it was because Brittany was getting to be around the same age he was when his mother abandoned him.

Since his mother left, there hadn't been a day when he didn't think about her, wondering where she was, what she was doing, and if she was still alive. He remembered their good times before her abuse of drugs and alcohol. Like when she would lick her finger and wipe the cold from his eyes after waking him from his afternoon nap, or when she would cuddle him on the sofa during quiet time. They were so close back in those days.

It was her teachings that saved him from his self-destructive behavior, which seemed to trap many of his childhood friends. One of her favorite sayings was "Nothing comes to a sleeper but a dream." Another one was "If you wanna keep getting what you're getting, then keep doing what you're doing."

Then there was the worst experience of all: the last time he saw his mother. She had taken him to church, a mandatory ritual. After sitting and holding his hand tightly for about an hour, she excused herself to the rest room. However, she never returned.

Bernard, who had remained seated until services ended, was approached by a deacon, who told him to go home. The tall man said that his mom had already left. Confused, he began his two-mile walk home on a long, winding dirt road to the black side of town.

He remembered racial slurs and half-empty beer cans that were flung at him as a truck full of racist white boys tried to run him off the road.

When incidents such as those had happened before, his mom was always there to protect him. She would hold him close to her side and give their enemies a look of death, letting them know that if she died, she wouldn't be alone. She was prepared to go down fighting. She never seemed afraid of white people, unlike many of the blacks in the small town of East Dicksville, where she was born and raised.

After the young Bernard arrived at his run-down part of town, he saw his next-door neighbor Mrs. Loula Mae. As usual, she was sitting on her porch, dipping snuff with a big white pot of string beans in her lap.

Mrs. Loula Mae was an extremely heavy-set woman with shiny black skin. She didn't have all of her teeth, and the ones she had were brownish yellow. Her hair was always wrapped in dirty pink rollers, and she always wore a nightgown, no matter what time of day it was.

Mrs. Loula Mae was a cantankerous fixture in the community whom neighborhood kids avoided. It was rumored that the curmudgeon was so bitter because she couldn't get a man.

Ever since Bernard had known her, he had never seen her leave her property. Mrs. Loula Mae was notorious for being the neighborhood bootlegger, selling alcohol out of her home—especially on Sundays. There was always a boisterous crowd trampling inside the feisty brewmeister's home. Despite the amount of traffic, she knew how to maintain order in her home—she'd had several fisticuffs with men, and won.

When he arrived back in his neighborhood from church, Mrs. Loula Mae yelled out to him.

"Bernard! Yo' momma gonna be gone for a spell, and you stayin' wit' me. Go get yo' things and put 'em in the back room."

"Where my momma at?" Bernard asked.

"Gone to see a man about a mule. And, boy, watch yo' tone wit' me," Mrs. Loula Mae ordered.

"I don't wanna stay with you."

"Well, stay where ya wanna stay. You think I care? Yo' momma got you thinking you somebody. You ain't nuttin' special, boy."

"I'm going home," Bernard said, walking toward his house with tears streaming down his face.

"The white man will be there to get the bill money tomorrow, and he don't accept no tears," she said.

The crowd of derelicts in her home roared with laughter at Bernard.

When he entered his home, he noticed that all of his personal belongings were neatly packed in six brown grocery bags. She had left a note atop one of the bags:

Dear Bernard,

I know you don't understand why I had to go, but one day you will. I really hate to leave you all alone like this, but if I stay, I will only bring pain to your life. And I would rather die than to see you hurt. I'm afraid that you'll learn to hate me. The truth is that I can't seem to kick my old habits. And it kills me that you have to see misery so close to home. I know Loula

Mae's house is not any better, but at least she's not your mother. I never told you this, but your daddy died when you were two years old. I started drinking heavily to drown out the memory. When that didn't work, I made another bad mistake; I turned to drugs. Please find it in your heart to forgive me. This may sound a little crazy, but now you can have any mother you imagine. Use your mind to leave this place. You are eleven years old, but you are a man. I know that you will be alright. Never become a victim, Bernard. I love you, and hopefully I'll see you soon. Be good, my prince. I love you so much.

Love always,
Momma

After Bernard read the letter, he waited up all night for his momma, crying until no more tears would flow from his eyes. "Why, Momma?" was all he could say as he looked at a picture of them both standing barefoot on the dirt road in front of their white shotgun house.

Bernard's mom, Susan Charles, was a petite woman, about four feet eight inches tall, with pretty brown eyes.

Her long straight hair was usually parted in the middle with two long braids framing her cinnamon-brown face. The alcohol and drugs had reduced her full figure to a mere ninety pounds.

Susan wasn't the typical drug user, because she had strong moral values and was very expressive. She never had men in the house and always kept their dilapidated home clean. His mom made sure Bernard had a cooked meal every night, although some nights it wasn't enough to fill the neighborhood rooster. Although she had a quick tongue and wasn't bigger than a minute, she wasn't afraid to go head to head with anyone who disrespected her or her only son.

Susan Charles didn't show up, but the white man did. When Bernard couldn't come up with the twenty dollars for the week's rent, he was told to pack up and leave. With only one option available, Bernard swallowed his pride and walked next door to Mrs. Loula Mae's house to apologize and seek lodging.

He asked the evil woman if he could stay until his momma returned.

She looked at him, spit a little snuff on the porch, and said, "You can stay until you eighteen, not until she comes back. Ain't no tellin' when that might be."

"Mrs. Loula Mae, do you know where my momma is?" Bernard asked submissively.

"Yeah, I know! But that be grown folks' business, not your'n. Now, if you gonna stay here, you ain't ever gonna ask me nuttin' about yo' momma ever again. You hear me, boy? I don't like you. The only reason you here is because I owes yo' momma a favor and I always pay what I owes. Now kay ya lil' nasty ass in the back and wash. Supper will be ready in a lil' while," Loula Mae demanded as she alternated between chewing tobacco and spitting while rocking in her chair.

"Yes, ma'am," Bernard said as he fought back tears while wishing his momma would reappear. He was so full of anger that his mind began to roam: *My mom would shoot this fat heifer for talking to me like this.*

He stayed at Mrs. Loula Mae's house for the next four years. He got used to the fights and profanity in the household but never allowed himself to become a part of it. Since he didn't smoke, drink, or swear, the other occupants of the house ignored him because they didn't have anything in common.

They called him weird because he spent his time reading and never talked to anyone. He was never there during the day, spending most of his time at school or at the library. At age fifteen, he started a job at T&M Groceries as a bag boy and used his money to rent a room on the other side of town. He wanted to be as far away from Mrs. Loula Mae's clan as possible.

Although he appreciated her for taking him in, even if she

was paying off a debt to his momma, he still considered her to be a tyrant. All four years he stayed with her, she required that he knock on the door before entering the house.

When he went to inform her of his decision to move and express his appreciation, she interrupted his conversation by throwing up her hands.

"So you got a place, huh?"

"Yes, ma'am. That's what I was about to tell you."

"Well, good. Pay yo' bills, because once you leave you can only come back to drink, and that ain't free," Mrs. Loula Mae said.

"Well, thank you anyway," Bernard said as he lifted his bag over his shoulder.

"You ain't takin nuttin' in that sack that ain't your'n, is ya, boy?" Loula Mae asked as she spat a little snuff in Bernard's direction.

Overwhelmed by hatred, a belligerent Bernard dropped his bag and marched toward the abrasive woman.

"I don't know who did something to you to make you such a wicked woman, but I've about had it up to here with you. I'm not a child anymore and if you want to find out the hard way then keep on. I came to you to thank you for giving me shelter, but you're so stuck on being miserable that you can't even accept that. Now, if you insist on disrespecting me . . . You just need thank my mother for raising me right," Bernard said as the lessons of respecting his elders came crashing down on him.

A stunned Loula Mae decided to back off.

"Have a good life, Bernard." She realized the muscled, six-foot, two-hundred-and-ten-pound teenager was a little too much to handle at this stage in her life.

"If my momma comes by here looking for me, give her this address," Bernard said as he handed Mrs. Loula Mae an envelope containing his new address and twenty dollars. He then proceeded down the dirt road to his new place and new life.

Now he was truly on his own. Even so, there was still no peace for him. Every day was the same basic routine: go to school, work, and return to his boardinghouse. He never stopped awaiting his mother's return and often dreamed they were cuddled on the couch together. Much to his dismay, his dream didn't become a reality.

After graduating from high school at age seventeen, Bernard was offered an academic scholarship to New York University. However, after spending the previous six years without his mother, he didn't want to take a chance of being too far away if she returned looking for him. He didn't believe that Mrs. Loula Mae would share his whereabouts with his mother.

Instead, he took a job at the Socar steel factory as a laborer. Since the love for his momma lingered in his heart, he regularly sent a Mother's Day card to Mrs. Loula Mae's house in hopes that his momma would drop by and ask about him. After three years at Socar, he was laid off. With nothing to keep him in South Carolina, he moved to Atlanta.

After hearing that Atlanta offered many opportunities for blacks, he bought a one-way ticket on Greyhound and headed west.

Upon his arrival in Atlanta, he found a boardinghouse, rented a room near downtown, and accepted a job as a dishwasher at a small family-owned soul-food restaurant. Eventually, after filling out numerous job applications, he was hired at the Ford Motor Company plant, where he continued to work to the present day.

Because of his tough upbringing, his family's security had become an important part of his life.

After Bernard finally left for work, Diane was unable to go back to sleep. Her mind was racing. The conversation with her husband revived thoughts of intimacy and his compassion.

She was in such a good mood with a renewed sense of

romance that she whipped through her morning cleaning duties. She awakened Brittany and let her help with breakfast.

After all of the chores were done, they dressed and waited for their transportation to arrive. Bernard had a couple of his coworkers drop off a new truck for Diane and Brittany to tool around town in for the day.

"Mommy, is this Daddy's new truck? It's da bomb."

"No, sweetie, it's just a loaner."

"Let's buy it for him. I'm tired of that old beat-up thang he's been driving since before I was born. My friends be busting on me whenever they see me in that."

"You got some money?" Diane asked.

"Yeah, but not enough for this!"

"Well then, what are you talking about *us* buying this truck for?"

"Ah, Mommy, you know what I mean!"

Once they hit Interstate 85 North, they visited all of the discount malls and outlets throughout the city, trying on different clothes. To Diane's pleasure, Brittany was starting to develop her own personality, and she no longer wanted her mom to pick out her clothes.

Brittany would hit the mall and head straight for the boys' section. She idolized the hip-hop artist Da Brat and tried to imitate her dress. Diane didn't mind, as long as she didn't pick up the singer's hip-hop vernacular.

As exciting as the day had been, Diane couldn't keep her mind off the morning's episode with Bernard. It had been more than a year since they had made love. She missed being held in her husband's strong, masculine arms. She knew Bernard still loved her, but somewhere along the way, working, going to school, and being exhausted had impacted his role to make her scream and crawl walls while in the throes of passionate lovemaking. She missed the way he used to make her feel sexy.

Every so often she would get in the mood and try to make her move, but to no avail. Bernard always found an excuse, such as that Brittany might hear them or that he was too tired.

After a while Diane got tired of trying. She figured when he was ready he would approach her. Unfortunately, he wasn't making a move in that direction.

She wondered if it was because her five-feet-five-inch frame had picked up a few pounds over the years. Nevertheless, Diane still maintained a sculpted figure.

She rationalized that after having a kid and being in her early forties it was normal for her to gain weight. Although Bernard wasn't looking, Diane still had her fair share of stares from other men. She refused, however, to react to their lust. Her big brown eyes would light up any room she happened to be in, and her cocoa-brown skin was as smooth as paper. She kept her shoulder-length sandy-brown hair pulled back on her head.

This morning's kiss had rekindled a flame, and she made up her mind that she would do everything in her power to put the spark back into her love life.

After Diane and Brittany depleted their spending budget, they decided to have a mother-daughter lunch at Applebee's. Diane ordered a chicken Caesar salad with a side order of chicken fingers, and Brittany chose Buffalo wings and fries.

As they waited for their food, they decided to engage in a game of knowledge.

"Brittany, what's the capital of Washington, D.C.?"

"It doesn't have a capital because it's not a state yet."

"Yet?"

"Not now, but I got my people working on it," Brittany said, as they burst into laughter.

"Girl, you're too much. Do you have any plans for tonight? You know I have to ask because you're so last-minute about everything."

"I know, I'm just like my mommy. But to answer your

question, no. It's Sierra's weekend to spend with her dad, and you know that's my best friend in the whole wide world."

"Would you like to spend your weekend with your grand-parents?"

"Yeah! But wait, Daddy's taking me to Six Flags tomorrow."

"Oh yeah? When did he tell you this?"

"This morning after y'all woke me up with all that noise."

"Alright, young lady! You're getting too comfortable."

"Sorry, Mommy."

"Well, I plan on doing something special for your daddy tonight. How about spending time with your grandparents? You and your father can spend all day tomorrow together."

"That's fine, since I have the best grandparents in the world. I'm sooo lucky, plus Granddaddy always gives me lots of money. The last time I was over there he gave me twenty dollars."

"Oh yeah! What did you do with it?"

"Secret, can't tell ya. Saving for something."

"Well, I better give them a call to see if they're free. I hope your daddy paid this Sprint bill."

Diane dialed her parents' number.

"Fuller residence!"

"Hello, Momma! How ya perkin'?"

"Hey, girl, I was just thinking about you. I was watching the news, and they said today was gonna be one of the hottest days of the year. They advised people to stay inside. I remember you saying you were taking Brittany shopping today. You make sure my baby drinks plenty of water. I don't want her out there de-hydrating," Ethel Fuller said to her daughter.

"Already taken care of. She's drinking bottled water as we speak," Diane said.

"Well, what about you? I need you around too."

"Oh, I'm fine. If I take one more sip I just might pop. What are you guys doing?" Diane asked.

"I'm sitting here looking at CNN. They're talking about the heat wave here in Atlanta. Three people have already died."

"Yeah, it's pretty hot out. Where's Daddy? He's not outside doing the lawn, is he?"

"No. He's downstairs watching those baseball games. You know he still thinks he can play."

"Yeah, Daddy is still holding on to his youthful days. Well, tell him I said hi. I wanted to know if you guys could keep Brittany tonight."

"Sure, sweetheart. You know you don't have to ask us that. Just bring her on over. Are you and Bernard going out?"

"No. We just need some quality time together, you know, just the two of us."

"Okay! Well, we'll see you when you get here."

"Do you need me to bring you anything?" Diane asked her mother.

"No. Just hurry and get out of that weather," Ethel said.

"Will do. And we'll see you in about an hour."

"Okay. Bye-bye, darling."

"Bye, Momma."

Later that afternoon, Diane dropped Brittany at her parents' house.

Diane decided to head back out to pick up some personal items. She went into Victoria's Secret and purchased a black camisole with a matching thong. Then she went to Chats Wine Cellar and picked up a bottle of 1970 Johannesburg Riesling. After that she stopped by Marshalls to buy an assortment of scented candles. For her last stop, she went to the grocery store to gather items for Bernard's favorite meal: filet mignon with all the trimmings. Tonight would be a special night for both of them.

3

I'm Poppa Doc

oday was not a good day for Winston L. Fuller, known to all his friends as Poppa Doc. A second opinion from a well-respected doctor confirmed his diagnosis of lung cancer.

After he left the hospital, he sat motionless in the parking lot, meditating over his medical condition. He realized he had to come to grips with it; he had a way of doing that. No matter what curveball life threw his way, he always responded with a grand slam.

As he made his way onto Georgia 400 to get to the Country Club of the South community in Alpharetta, he wondered how the news about his health would affect his wife, Ethel. He figured she'd surely take the news much harder than he had.

He tried to figure out how to inform her without turning her into a nervous wreck.

Maybe I shouldn't tell her, he thought, but that idea disappeared in the wind.

Over the years they had become a unit, and he often relied on her for support. However, she was known to be a super-emotional woman who often made matters more difficult to tolerate.

Her usual response to crises was "Oh Lord God! Lord! Jesus Christ!"

But when things were really bad she turned into Florida Evans and chanted, "Damn! Damn! Damn!"

Even so, he knew he couldn't keep the truth from Ethel, his wife of forty-six years. It was as if she had an internal polygraph device that enabled her to determine if he was lying.

Although Poppa Doc was slightly depressed when he first heard the news, he was not one to let anything get him down. Comparatively, he was the pillar of the family; she was like a feather in the wind—gentle yet fragile.

He knew this would be a tough battle for both of them, but despite her vulnerability he was certain they would pull through together.

As he maneuvered his silver late-model Mercedes 500SL toward his house, he gazed at the beautiful homes with their magnificently manicured lawns. Each was situated on golf courses and lakes. He marveled at the progress black people had made during his lifetime.

He remembered a time when advancement appeared to be only an illusion that eluded blacks.

As a youngster growing up in a small town in south Florida, he never thought he would see the day when he would be waving at little black children playing in front of their own homes valued at up to $1 million. He was proud of the accomplishments. *This is how it should be when families work hard. They deserve to be blessed with all the luxuries that life has to offer,* he thought.

He was glad his son, Michael, had talked him and his wife

into moving to Atlanta after they both retired from their jobs with the state of New York, even if his motives were questionable.

Atlanta gave Poppa Doc the feel of the country life that he missed from his childhood and the vibration of the city, which he experienced in the past forty years while living in New York. With both skyscrapers and farms in the Atlanta area, he was enamored and sold on the idea.

As Poppa Doc pulled into the long, curved driveway leading to his seven-bedroom estate, he saw his son's car. A feeling of uneasiness invaded his body because Michael had become such a disappointment. And Poppa Doc was not in the mood for him today.

As much as his family loved him, there was little anyone could do to alter Michael's shiftless behavior. Living from pillar to post didn't seem to bother him one bit.

He started out as such a good kid by earning excellent grades and never getting into much trouble. His sister, Diane, on the other hand, was the mischievous one. But surprisingly, she was now a very dependable person, married with a beautiful little daughter.

Michael's life took a 180-degree turn. He decided he preferred a lifestyle more like that of Super Fly. At thirty-three, he'd had three kids by three different women, while not even owning a pot to piss in or a window to throw it out of.

As Poppa Doc turned the ignition off, his cell phone rang.

"Hello!" Poppa Doc answered.

"Winston, how'd it go?"

"I'm gonna be fine, I'm in the yard. Let me come in the house, then we can talk."

"But what did the doctor say?"

"Ethel, I'm on the way in the house right now."

"You can tell me now. I've been waiting all morning."

"Did you not hear me? I'm in the yard. Bye!"

Before he could put his key in the lock, Ethel had barreled to the door, opening it fiercely.

"How'd it go, Winston?" she said, rubbing her hands together nervously.

"Good lord, woman. Let me get my foot in the door first."

Ethel stepped back and allowed him to make it to the foyer before resuming her inquisition. "Well, you have both feet in now. Tell me how it went."

"Ethel, calm down. I'm just fine. Don't I look like a million bucks?" asked Poppa Doc, putting on a fake smile as he walked past his wife to sit at the kitchen table.

"Yeah, you look fine, but what did the doctor say, Winston?"

She followed her husband into the kitchen and sat beside him.

"Well, he said it looks like lung cancer," Poppa Doc said. He felt as if he had betrayed himself. He knew he couldn't keep anything from her.

"Lord, no! Say it isn't so! Winston, we need to get another doctor to check you out," Ethel said frantically as she stood and began to pace the floor. Pain was written all over her caramel-colored face. She sat back down and stared into space.

"Now, Ethel, this is the second doctor I've seen, and he said the same thing the first one said. There is no need to keep running around looking for doctors to tell us what we already know. I have it, and we'll deal with it. We are not going to worry about this thing. We are going to follow the doctor's orders and that's that. Whatever comes, comes. Okay?" Poppa Doc said as he held his wife and best friend in his arms. He wiped tears from her moist brown cheeks and kissed her forehead. After all these years, he was still as affectionate and as attentive as the day they met.

"Okay, Winston," Ethel replied, wiping her nose with the tissue that he had just handed her.

"Didn't I tell you that I would never leave you?"

"Yes, but Winston—"

"Hey, hey! No buts! That's what I said, and that's what I meant. Now, where's Michael? I need to talk to him."

"He's in the basement watching TV."

"TV! That boy's life has enough drama. Why does he feel he needs to be entertained?"

Seeing where this father-son confrontation might be headed, Ethel tried to shift gears from one emotional roller coaster to another.

Since Poppa Doc and Michael were not on good terms, Ethel cautioned, "Now, you don't need to be getting upset, so just go lie down and talk to him tomorrow, okay?"

"Tomorrow, hopefully he'll be somewhere else. I'm tired of that boy using us. We were responsible for him until he was eighteen years old. He done conned us out of another fifteen years."

"Oh, Winston! Please don't start that again. Not now."

"Ethel, I love you with every bone in my body, and when I married you, I said that I would rather die than to let any man take advantage of you. He's a man now and he's taking advantage of you, and it's killing me. Now I know that it's hard to sit by and let your kids go without, but sometimes that's what they need in order to grow—especially a man. Ethel, believe it or not, every time you give him something, you take something away from him. He has to learn to handle himself out there because we won't always be here for him. It's time he stands on his own and becomes accountable for his actions. His life is way too easy for the position that he placed himself in. When his kids need something, who do the mothers call? Us, not him! And do you want to know why? Because they know they cannot depend on him for anything. Well, that has to stop. If he's going to be a trifling bum, then I'm not going to contribute, and as of this day neither are you.

"Don't you see, Ethel? We've been giving that boy the fish instead of teaching him how to fish. Don't you feel proud when we have dinner at Diane and Bernard's house? Well, you could have that same feeling with Michael if you just let him grow up. Now, let my arm go. I need to talk to the boy," Poppa Doc said as he headed downstairs to the basement.

"I know, Winston, but everyone needs help sometimes," Ethel said.

"And we've been helping him since day one. Every time I put some pressure on Michael to stand up and be a man, you run to his rescue. Now we have a thirty-three-year-old baby on our hands. Ethel, hold out your finger," Poppa Doc requested as he extended his pinky finger.

Ethel dropped her head and complied. When they had first started dating, they made pinky promises that they vowed never to break. It was something special that they shared, and they took their promises to each other very serious.

"Ethel, do you like the man that I am?"

"Of course! You're a good man."

"Well then, promise me that as of this day you will no longer interfere with the way I handle Michael."

Tears rushed down her face. She knew that her baby would be leaving for good. She always felt a need to take care of him because they had a special bond that only mothers share with their sons.

While her husband had worked to make a living for the family, Ethel stayed home and took care of the kids.

Although Diane was seven years older than Michael, she always was independent like her father.

So when Ethel needed a hug, she went to Michael and he came to her. As far as she was concerned, Michael would always be her baby.

Ethel interlocked pinkies with her husband and made a heartfelt vow: "I promise, but go easy on him. He's just a baby."

Poppa Doc answered her comment with an astonished look that said, "No, you didn't!"

As Poppa Doc made it downstairs, he could sense his anger growing. However, he always managed to control himself. Michael was playing a game of pool, and the music was blasting.

"Grab a stick and take your whipping like a man," Michael said, smiling from ear to ear with his hair in braids that stuck up like each of them had a toothpick hiding in it. Other than the braids, he was the spitting image of his father.

"I can do that. And speaking of a man, when do you plan on being one?"

"Oh, come on, Dad! It's not a good time for one of your lectures."

"Son, I can't think of a better time. And you need to remember where you are. This is my house. You don't have one. You're just a visitor, which means you play by house rules. Now, rack up the balls and turn that crap off."

Michael walked over to the entertainment center and turned the music down.

"Once again, you're not listening. I said off."

Poppa Doc was a very distinguished gentleman, who stood about five-feet-ten. He was very slender, with gray hair, always spoke in a calm manner, and never seemed to get upset about anything. His son's lackadaisical approach to life was the one thing that pushed him close to the edge.

Poppa Doc believed that many young males didn't take their roles in society seriously enough, and he blamed men for most of the world's problems. So he was especially hurt when his own son turned out to be a slothful womanizer. Poppa Doc accepted part of the blame because he was caught in the middle of trying to appease his wife while trying to raise a responsible young black male in a white man's world.

Whenever he had spanked Michael, Ethel would comfort the youngster. Whenever he had grounded him by withholding privileges, she would restore them. When he said no, she said yes.

"Dad, how'd it go at the doctor's office?" Michael asked, trying to change the subject.

"I have lung cancer, son, but that's not the issue right now."

"Wait, wait, wait. Lung cancer! Dad, that's serious. What are you . . . ?" Michael said as he thought about life without his father. He had never had to think about that before.

"I'm concerned about your life. You are thirty-three years old, and you have nothing. And I'm not talking about material possessions, either," Poppa Doc continued, dropping three balls on the break. "As a man, you should have at least three things: a legal income, a place to house your children, and the ability to make intellectually sound decisions. Son, do you know the difference between being a father and being a daddy?" Poppa Doc asked as he blasted another ball into the corner pocket.

"There is no difference. It's only a matter of what you prefer to be called," Michael answered.

"Oh, but that's where you're wrong, son. Although I find it hard to call you anything other than a sperm donor, a father creates a child and a daddy takes care of his child. Any fool with a working penis can make a baby, but it takes a man to be there to raise it. Son, you are only adding to the statistics—the ones that say black men don't take care of their children. Now, I didn't leave you to fend for yourself, so why would you leave your kids out there like that? And I must say that is not characteristic of a Fuller. My daddy was about the poorest man you could ever meet, but he was rich with character and he was there for us until the day he died. You carry my father's name, son, and that's nothing to play with. So, if you don't plan on getting your life together, then you better see about getting a name change."

"Dad, I love my kids, but I can't deal with their mothers."

"Son, when you were a little boy I had the same issues. I

didn't take a stand, and that's why you're in the position you are in now. Your mother fought me tooth and nail on every issue when it came to disciplining you and your sister, but especially you. So believe me when I tell you that you have to be the man and do what's right for your kids regardless of what the mothers say. You see, son, women are very emotional creatures and think with their hearts. As a man, you need to think with your head and not that lil' one that's got you in all this trouble."

"Dad, things aren't like they used to be. Women these days are way too argumentative. It's a no-win situation with them."

"Son, you ain't dealing with nothing that hasn't already been dealt with. Now, you put the blame on everyone else except where it really belongs—you. These are the mothers of your children, and I have yet to hear you say anything good about any of them. All you seem to come up with is some trivial juvenile nonsense. Look at your damn self in the mirror sometimes. Never mind what their problems are. We all have imperfections. You of all people should know that. Now, you need to make it right with all of your kids' mothers and become someone they all can count on. The only way you can do that is to change your attitude. If you do that, then your actions will follow. You have to lead by example, son."

"I love my kids, and I have been having a hard time dealing with the fact that I can't do for them the way I would like, but—" Michael said before being cut off by his father's stinging words.

"You can do for *you* like you want to. So don't sit up here and tell me that you can't. Once you bring children into this world, you don't count until they are taken care of. You're so concerned about looking good. For what? To get some more women pregnant so you can have more babies that you don't plan on taking care of? To hell with that car and those fancy clothes you seem to worship. You have children who need their father, and you're sitting around here trying to look cute.

When's the last time you've seen little Winston?" asked Poppa Doc, concerned especially about his only grandson because he was going to be a man too one day.

Although he spoiled his granddaughters, especially Brittany, since she visited the most, he was partial to little Winston.

"Samantha got a restraining order on me," Michael said, trying to sound like a victim.

"Damn, boy, what did you do to that woman?" Poppa Doc asked as he stopped shooting pool to peer into his son's eyes.

"Nothing!" Michael lied.

"Oh, she just called the police and got a restraining order on you for nothing," Poppa Doc said sarcastically.

"She said since I hadn't sent them any money then I didn't need to come around."

"I guess you think I'm crazy, because I've never heard of a restraining order being issued for nonpayment. But she is right for not wanting you around. Son, you don't have anything positive to bring to that child's life, so you may as well stay away. But you're gonna fix that, Michael. You hear me?"

"Why do you always have to blame me? Why couldn't she have done something?"

"Because you're the man, which means you're the head of the family, which means you're responsible no matter who did what. Do you think your mother and I could have made it forty-something years if we bailed out at the first sign of discomfort? When two people have a child, they engage in a partnership, like it or not. And any partnership is about sacrifice and understanding. If she's not being understanding, then that means you have to be even more understanding. I told you that a woman is of a different breed, boy. Do you know what your momma said to me before I came down here to talk to you? She said, 'Go easy on him, he's just a baby.' You believe that? A thirty-three-year-old baby! Nothing worth having is easy, son. Pick up your Bible and read Genesis 2:24. Son, you have to leave here. Go out there and take your dignity back. Get your own house and be your own man," Poppa Doc said as he leveled his stick and pocketed another ball.

"When do I have to leave?" Michael asked, hoping it wouldn't be that night.

"Son, today is Friday. You have two weeks, and I don't mean go stay at one of your lady friends' houses. I mean go get your own place and keep it," Poppa Doc said as he pocketed the eight ball. "Damn, boy, did you even get a shot? You're way too easy to beat. You need to get serious, Michael. I love you, but I'm not proud of you. Make me proud of you before I leave this earth."

4

A Day
in the Life
of Prodigy

ou moved that refrigerator by yourself, boy? What's your girlfriend's name: Stingy?" Poppa Doc said as he chuckled and handed Prodigy a sixteen-ounce bottle of water. "Come on 'round here and sit down and tell me some of them lies of yours."

"Now, you know I don't lie on Fridays. Where's Mike?" Prodigy asked as he took the much-needed Crystal Springs bottle and followed his old pal into the entertainment area of his basement.

Poppa Doc removed his glasses, sat in his favorite recliner, and kicked his feet up. "I don't know where he is. I got on his case today about being so damn shiftless, so he's probably somewhere having a pity party. What's been going on with you, youngster? How's work?"

"Uh-oh, what'd you hear?"

Poppa Doc raised both palms up and hunched his shoulders

49

as if he was clueless. Prodigy didn't know it, but Craig had already called and informed Poppa Doc of the woman-on-the-stairwell incident.

"What? All I asked was, 'How's work?' You know the guilty will tell on themselves."

"Everything will be alright. I had a little scare, but I think I'll make it through the fire without losing my boxers."

"Talk to me."

"Well, have you ever heard of the saying 'getting caught with your pants down'? That actually happened to me."

"Yeah, yeah, I heard about that NC-17-rated video you put out. Boy, why didn't you tell me you wanted a job in the porno business? I could've made some money off of you."

Prodigy gave a little embarrassed smile and shook his head. He was thinking that nothing got by this guy.

"Well, I decided to make some changes in my life."

"What kind of changes?"

"First of all, I stopped seeing Simone, because that situation wasn't right. She's married and—"

"Is that the one you were with when that eye in the sky took a peek at you?"

"Yep, that's the one."

"Have I ever met her before? You know, you got so many damn women, you should make 'em wear hats with their names on them."

"Yeah, she came over with me to watch Mike Tyson eat up on Holyfield."

"Oh yeah, I remember her. I sat down and talked a good while with her. Yeah, boy, she was finer than frog hair, but I didn't know she was married."

"Yeah, but she claimed she wasn't happy at home and the whole nine."

"That's dangerous territory. If she's not happy at home then that's her problem, not yours."

"You're right and that's one of the reasons I gave her her walking papers."

"Well, let it play itself out, but sometimes women don't go away as easily as we would like them to. Now, about this getting to work on time, boy, what's your problem? Don't you know people are just waiting on you to screw up? When you do things like that, you make every other young black male a suspect. I don't know about that generation of yours. You cry about not having a job, then when you get one, you don't wanna go to work. Some of y'all don't even show up on payday," Poppa Doc said, shaking his head.

"I got you, I got you," Prodigy said, trying to stop his old friend before he started one of his hour-long tirades.

"Prodigy, I sure hate to bring up things that I do for people, but I put myself on the line for you with this job. Don't make me lose face. So from Monday on, you have your ass at work early!"

Prodigy didn't answer; there was nothing to say. He just stood up, straightened out the legs of his baggy FUBU jeans, and grabbed a pool stick.

"Let's shoot a game before you have a heart attack."

Poppa Doc laughed. He knew that he had gotten his message across. "All them damn sticks you see over there and you gonna go and grab mine. Give it here."

As Prodigy reached over the table to hand Poppa Doc his stick, he gave his old friend a wink and a nod, just to remind him that he was really appreciated.

"What's the series?" Prodigy asked, while opening the wooden case to the chalkboard that kept a tally of their wins and losses.

"I don't know, but whatever it is I'm whipping your butt."

"You've got to be kidding me, you're not that old. You should still be hurting from that last slaughter. As you can tell by this," Prodigy said, pointing to the marking under his name that had him in the lead. "You lost the last game, old fella, so get the rack."

"Oh, you gonna count that? I was drunk."

"Yeah, yeah, whatever. Any excuse will do. Get the rack."

"Damn, boy, I ain't know you'd do me like that. But just to show I'm still a nice guy, I need to ask you not to take these whippings personally, because you ain't winning nothing tonight. I played Michael today, and he didn't even get to lift his stick. Boy, I'll tell you, I'm cooking with grease. You sure you want some?"

"Well, I'm about to put your little fire out. Do you wanna put a little friendly wager on the game to make it interesting?"

"Make it easy on yourself."

"Alright. Loser pays the winner's way into the Gentlemen's Club and picks up the tab."

"Boy, you ain't said nothing but a word. When are we going?"

"Tomorrow night, that's if Mrs. Ethel will let you out."

Poppa Doc didn't answer, just gave Prodigy one of those looks that said, "What she doesn't know, she can't fuss about."

"Look here, I wanna run something by you," Poppa Doc said as he racked the pool balls. "A friend of mine has started this after-school program for kids between ten and sixteen, and they need volunteers. I was wondering if you'd like to volunteer in the afternoons for one or two days a week."

"Sure, you know I love the kids."

Poppa Doc cocked his head to one side as if straining to hear. "Speaking of kids, is that my little Britt-Britt that I hear?"

"Hi, Granddaddy, can I come down?" Brittany asked from the top of the stairs.

"Yeah, come on down and hug my neck," Poppa Doc said as his face lit up like a Christmas tree. It was plain to see that this little girl meant the world to him.

"Hi, Prodigy, when are you going take me for another ride

in your truck?" Brittany asked as she pulled herself away from her granddaddy and walked over to give Prodigy a hug.

"Whenever you want, sweetheart, just say the word and I'm there."

"Granddaddy, I'm staying over tonight."

"Good. That means I can win some of my money back in checkers," Poppa Doc said, referring to their late-night games that were played for a quarter.

"You can try your luck. I'm going back upstairs with Grandma; I just came down to say hi. Grandma said that I could help her finish cooking. Bye, Prodigy," Brittany said as she waved her little hand.

"Bye, sweetie, and be good."

"I'll be up in a little while, Britt-Britt. Let me finish whipping up on this boy."

"Okay," Brittany said as she turned and walked back up the stairs.

"Back to this youth thing, go ahead and tell them to count me in," Prodigy said, thinking that this would be a good opportunity for him to help some kids.

Poppa Doc cracked a smile. "I already did."

"You think you know me that well, huh? Well then, you should know that I'm about to put it on ya like you owe me money, and don't give me no loose rack. I gotta watch you. You get a couple of balls behind and start cheatin'."

"Boy, shoot the damn ball and stop all that whining."

They shot pool, drank beer, and talked about a bunch of nothing for another hour. Then Prodigy's cell phone gave a double ring, which meant it was being forwarded from his home phone.

"Just a second, Poppa Doc . . . Hello."

"Answer your door. I'm outside," a female voice said.

"Who's this?"

"Who do you think it is?"

"Look, don't play," Prodigy said, ready to hang up the phone because he didn't recognize the voice.

"This is Gina, and I'm standing on your steps."

"Oh, I'm sorry. I lost track of time. I have my calls forwarded to my cell. I'll be home in about a half an hour."

"Where are you?"

"Alpharetta."

"And you think you can get to Stone Mountain in thirty minutes? Anyway, what am I supposed to do for thirty minutes? You don't have a key hidden under a flowerpot or something, do you?" Gina asked.

"Yeah, but if I tell you where it is I'd have to kill you. Are you hungry?"

"Starving."

"Then why don't you go and get some Chinese food or something. I'll give you the money for it when I get there. Some people invite you over to work and don't feed you," Prodigy said, giving Poppa Doc the wrinkled-lip treatment.

"Thirty minutes, okay?"

"I'll see you in a few."

"Where's a good restaurant around here?"

"Just check up on Memorial Drive, you'll find something."

"Hurry up."

"I'm leaving now. Bye."

"Poppa Doc, I gotta run and I know you're glad, because I was just about to make my comeback. When will you have all of the information on the youth thing?"

"Is everything alright?"

"Oh yeah, just had some company come over that I forgot about."

"Well, you're behind six to two, so looks like the Gentlemen's Club is on you, the door and the tab. Call me tomorrow, I should have something for you by then."

"I'll do it. I'll call you after I wake up."

"Yeah, you do that. It'll be good for you to help out those kids, because to reach one is to teach one, or whatever the hell that saying is."

When Prodigy pulled up, Gina was sitting in his driveway in a white BMW Z3, swaying her head to Maxwell's "Fortunate." He knocked on her window, but she threw up a hand and shook her head, never looking up, as if to say, "Don't disturb this groove." He stood there and shook his head, giving her a moment, then she snapped out of her Maxwell trance and stepped out of the car looking like a sho-nuff dime piece. She wore one of those Erykah Badu head wraps and a long sundress that had all kinds of different colors in it—it fit loose but tight enough to show you she had enough body to make you say ughh, nah nah nah nah. "Sorry to keep you waiting. You look nice," Prodigy said, as he snuck a peek at her goods.

"Thank you. Did you forget I was coming over? I mean, we just talked right before you left work."

"Nah, I didn't forget, I was at my old friend's house and he was holding me as a conversation hostage. Come on in, it's seven-thirty and it's still hot out this piece."

"Oh, it's not that bad."

"You can stay outside if you want, I need manufactured air."

"I agree. I got shrimp fried rice and pepper steak. I didn't know the place, so I didn't trust them with anything exotic," Gina said, as she handed Prodigy the bag.

"Yeah, that cool. Make yourself at home. I gotta run upstairs right quick and shower. I feel sticky."

"Take your time. Did you wanna go out somewhere? It's still early."

"It's up to you, I'm a homebody, but I'm open," Prodigy said as he ran upstairs and into his room.

As Prodigy disappeared up the stairs and around the corner,

Gina took in the sights of the eye-catching duplex. Her first impression was that a woman had decorated or he had a gay friend. She walked around his living room, feeling the Italian leather of the navy-blue sofa, checking out the exquisite artwork that hung from the colorful walls and noting how tastefully they were matted and framed. She noticed a picture of Prodigy and an older gentleman sitting on top of the huge projection-screen television in an elegant hand-carved frame, and assumed that the older man was his grandfather. There was a chalked painting of Prodigy and a very pretty middle-aged woman, who undoubtedly had to be his mother.

Gina kicked off her shoes, pulled one of the overstuffed throw pillows to the hardwood floor, and sat down to find some music. Her mother always told her that she could learn a lot about a man by looking at his home and his taste in music. If that was true, then Prodigy was a very complicated individual. His music selection went from George Howard to George Michael, from Mystikal to Pearl Jam, all the way back to Nina Simone. After finding the *Life* movie soundtrack, she thought about letting Maxwell finish his number on her but changed her mind, deciding to let Trina Broussard do the wailing this time. As Trina's soulful voice filled the room, Gina found herself wishing that she and Prodigy shared this home, then quickly caught herself and picked up a photo album with pictures of Prodigy when he was younger.

"I see you found something to entertain yourself. My old friend smokes, so I had to get that smell off me. Sorry about that," Prodigy said, as he came back into the room wearing sweatpants, sweat socks, a T-shirt, and Nike flip-flops. He pulled up a pillow and sat down beside her on the floor.

"Oh, you're alright. You were so cute when you were a baby."

"Yeah right. You don't have to lie. Every baby's not cute, and I was one of the ugly ones."

"No you weren't, but speaking of ugly, I'm going to kill

56

you," Gina said as she reached over and grabbed his neck in a playful choke hold.

"What are you talking about?" Prodigy said as he grabbed her hands.

"I'm talking about that little fat boy that you sent to harass me. What's his name, Jake? He came up to me in the cafeteria and said, "I got a new Lexus, you wanna ride?"

"I said, 'Excuse me?' 'I'm the guy that Prodigy told you about. My name is Jake.' He's standing there looking up at me, breathing that horrible breath in my face. I lost my appetite."

Prodigy let Gina's hands go, leaned his head back onto the seat of the sofa, and laughed until tears appeared.

"What did you tell him?"

"I just said, 'Thanks for the offer, but I'm gay.' "

"What did he say then?"

"The fool said, 'For real?' and kept following me. Finally I had to be rude and tell him to go away."

"You shouldn't have said that, because most guys fantasize about having two women."

"Oh God," Gina said as she shook her head. "This place is nice. Who decorated?"

"I did."

"Yeah right. I find that hard to believe. Men don't think like this."

"Well, it's true. I mean, I don't have any of my own creative taste here. It's all out of magazines and model homes that I visited."

"Well, I must say I'm impressed."

"Thank you."

"Hey, I was going through your DVDs and I saw *Enemy of the State*. I've never seen it. Do you wanna stay in and watch that?"

"Sure, if that's what you wanna do, but let's eat first," Prodigy said as he handed her a twenty-dollar bill. She waved him off, got up, and walked into the kitchen to microwave the Chinese food.

They ate and got settled in to watch the movie. Prodigy watched about ten minutes of it, then he was out like a light. He must have slept for the rest of the movie, because a naked Gina awakened him—kissing him in spots that made him think that he was having a wet dream, but he wasn't, this was live and in color. He adjusted his eyes to take in her Amazon-like body. *Damn, she's fine as hell.* She pulled him to his feet and led him upstairs to his bedroom, without hesitation. That made him a little suspicious. *How did she know where my bedroom was?* Oh well, now damn sure wasn't the time to be asking questions. He stood up by the dresser and undressed while she crawled on the bed, rolled onto her back, and began to masturbate. *Damn, I like her freaky ass,* he thought.

Prodigy made his way to the bed to join her, but she stood up and took the long way around to his side of the bed, allowing her picture-perfect silhouette to bounce off of his walls. She stood over him and leaned down to kiss his lips, then his chest, and then she worked her tongue all the way down to his knees. By now Prodigy's jimmy was harder than forty dollars' worth of jawbreakers. After teasing him for what seemed like forever, she found her way to his sweet spot and commenced to give him the best oral pleasure known to man. It was so good, Prodigy felt like he owed her something, so he pulled her on to the bed and positioned her where her cookie was staring him right in the face and drove her crazy, sixty-nine different ways. She moaned, he groaned, they sounded like two little Master P's.

After a few hours of hot sex on a platter, Prodigy found himself lying there, in a pool of sweat, trying to think of a way to get rid of her. He always lost interest after sex, especially when it came so easily. But he never asked a woman to leave. He would usually just lie there and pretend that he was interested in all that gibberish that she was talking, and once she left he conveniently lost her number.

As a matter of fact, he was normally a little offended when he ran across a woman who seemed to think that all men wanted was sex. *Of course we want sex, but we tend to categorize you if you give it up too early. You can't make a whore a housewife. And if you gave it up on the first night, then what else is there to look forward to?* he thought.

Prodigy cherished the part of the relationship when the chase was on, when he had a chance to wonder who that person really was. But most of the women that he'd been coming in contact with didn't even bother to run for the chase to begin. So there he was once again, staring at the ceiling fan, watching it go around and around. Thinking that the fan looked like his life, moving fast but not going anywhere.

I wish Gina would shut the hell up. She's been babbling about a bunch of nothing since we finished. Prodigy hadn't responded, not so much as a grunt. He was hoping that she would take the hint.

And they say men change after sex; at least we don't feel so comfortable that we are willing to share everything we know about ourselves the minute after an orgasm, he thought.

"Prodigy, are you falling asleep on me?"

"No, ma'am."

"Then why aren't you talking to me?"

"I like to listen. You learn more like that."

"Well, let me ask you a question. How many men can a woman have before you would call her promiscuous?"

"Depends! How old is this young lady?"

"Let's say she's twenty-six."

After a few seconds to ponder her question, Prodigy answered, "Well if she's twenty-six, then I'd say eight, and that's being generous."

"How'd you come up with that number?"

"Well, let's say she started getting her groove on at about

seventeen. I'd give her two young boys during her teenage years, before she realizes that thing between her legs is special. Then I'd give her three boyfriends during her early twenties, all of whom she thought that she was in love with. Then I'd count that time she got drunk and had sex after one of those breakups, but swore that she would never tell. And I got to give her a slick talker who just talked the panties off her. And me!"

"You?"

"Yeah, I've probably got it one time," Prodigy said as he gave her a wink. "Naw, I'm just kidding."

Gina popped him on his arm and said, "Prodigy, how old are you?"

"Twenty-eight!"

"And how many women have you slept with in your twenty-eight years on planet Earth?"

"A lot!"

"Aren't we vague."

"Don't mean to be, just never sat down and counted—but it's been quite a few."

"Do you consider yourself a whore?"

"Never thought about it like that."

"But if I gave you that same answer that you just gave me, then I would be a ho' fa-sho, right?"

"Absolutely."

"Why?"

"Because there's a double standard that's been around since the beginning of time. A guy with a hundred women is a hero; a girl with a hundred guys is a zero. You see, sweetheart, women are held to a higher standard than men when it comes to social behavior. You're always supposed to conduct yourself as a lady. Hell, somebody has to have some morals."

"That's foul. So how do you look at me now that we've had sex on the first night?"

"You alright. You're an adult who made an adult decision.

So no, I don't look down on you, if that's what you're asking," Prodigy lied. *Tramp, how in the hell do you think I look at you, when I just met you less than twelve hours ago and now we're knocking boots like dogs in an alley? You just found out how old I am,* he thought.

"Good answer," Gina said, as she slid her head under the covers to get things started for round two, but she was interrupted by the ringing telephone.

"Damn, it's three o'clock in the morning. Who's calling me at this hour?" Prodigy grumbled as he reached over to grab the cordless phone resting on the nightstand. After checking the caller I.D. screen to make sure it wasn't Simone, he hit the talk button.

"Probably one of your many lady friends, making a booty call," Gina said, but he ignored her.

"Hello!"

"You have a collect call from an inmate at the Fulton County Jail. Caller, state your name."

"Jermaine."

"Press one to accept this call, Press two to . . . Thank you. Do not use three-way calling or your call will be disconnected," the computerized voice stated.

"Yo, what's up?" Prodigy asked as he got out of the bed and walked into the bathroom for some privacy.

"Yo, yo, yo. P-man, what's the haps, baby? Did I catch you at a bad time?" Jermaine said, sounding like he was at a party instead of jail.

"Naw, man, you alright. Well, welcome to Atlanta. I see that you've already met Officer Friendly."

"He was kind of friendly, compared to those assholes in Philly. No knots, no bruises, and he didn't even cuff me until we got to the station," Jermaine answered.

"When did you get here? I thought you was gonna call me with some flight dates."

"I got here tonight. I was trying to surprise that ass, but not like this."

"Oh yeah, well, consider me surprised. What they get you for?"

"Some ol' bullshit. You know they be targeting niggas at them airports. They set a two-thousand-dollar bail for me. Can you come scoop me?"

"Yeah, I can get you, but I'm gonna have to call around first and get a bondsman."

"How long do you think that will take?"

"Shouldn't be too long."

"Oh yeah, I forgot you done squared up and got a job, so you wouldn't have no bondsman in the Rolodex. Call Uncle Ray. I know he got people on his payroll that can handle this. Hold on a minute, P." Jermaine dropped the phone. Prodigy could hear him talking to what sounded like a female guard. "Alright, dog, they just told me they got to hold me for at least six hours, so I'm about to take my ass to sleep; I'm tired. Hey yo, P, you got a VCR?"

"Yeah, why?"

"Cuz, I want you to record *Jerry Springer* for me, that's my shot. And since they got a hold on me, I might miss it. It comes on at home at nine. What time does it come on here?"

"Nigga, I don't watch that shit. You in jail and you're worried about some damn *Jerry Springer.* You done lost it," Prodigy said, annoyed that his little cousin took jail so lightly.

"Ahh, nigga, you sound like my momma."

"Well, Momma knows best. I'll see you in a couple of hours."

"A'ight, peeps. Don't forget me, dog. I don't know anybody down this piece, so hurry up before I be up in here for murder. I already had one altercation with this gold-tooth, perm-wearing cat with broken English."

"Yo, dog, behave yourself and I'll see you in a few. I'm out!"

"One!"

As he hung up the phone, Prodigy wondered what he had gotten himself into by allowing his hardheaded cousin to come down here and stay with him. But then he realized that if Poppa Doc hadn't taken the time to show him the right way, then that could've just as well been him sitting up in some jail. So he decided that he would try to lead by example, and maybe, just maybe, Jermaine would open up to a new way of doing things. Prodigy walked out of the bathroom and noticed Gina sitting up on the bed, looking at him with accusing eyes and her lips all twisted up as if she was saying, "Go ahead and give me the lie."

"What?" was his answer to her look.

"Who was that? And why did you have to go and hide in the bathroom? That was so rude."

"If you think it was rude, then I apologize, but I do need to take care of some—"

Gina cut him off. "What! Are you asking me to leave? That must have been your other little hoochie on the phone and she's coming over. You don't have to lie. All you had to say was 'Gina, you have to leave,' " Gina said as she slowly got up from the bed with the sheet wrapped around her. "You're a trip, Prodigy."

Prodigy stood there reading her face, which was telling him that she really wanted to go off but she thought that she would look like a fool. He leaned on the bathroom door and stared at her as she went on.

"Now that you got what you want, you think you can just treat me any ol' kinda way. That's foul. You played me." Gina dropped the sheet and slid on her dress.

After she had gathered all of her belongings, shaking her head and sucking her teeth, she stopped at the bedroom door and looked down as if she was really hurt.

"What do you mean I played you? I haven't done a thing to you," Prodigy said.

"You come up with a lie at three in the morning, talking about you have to go take care of something. Come on, Prodigy, what do I look like? I was born at night, but not last night."

"Gina, what makes you think that I have to lie to you? You're giving yourself way too much credit. And what do you mean, I got what I want? You woke me up, with your ass hanging all out. Be careful going home," he said calmly. He was glad that her insecurities showed up so quickly. She saved him a bunch of drama that, based on her little performance, was bound to happen.

"I hate guys like you," Gina said as she snatched her keys from the dresser, in the process knocking over a rust-colored ceramic vase that his mom had given him. As the vase crashed to the hardwood floor, she must have realized that she was acting a bit irrational, because she dropped her Coach bag and turned to him.

"I'm sorry. I'll get you another vase. It's just that I really like you, and I heard about Simone, and I thought that maybe you were talking to . . . Well I'm sorry," Gina said, flustered as she bent over to clean up the broken pottery.

Prodigy just stood there and wondered why women were so emotional. *A whole other set of expectations is there after they drop their panties,* he thought.

"Listen, I don't like drama and I don't like explaining what goes on in my life to every Tom, Dick, and Harry. Just because you get something in your head, that doesn't mean that it's a reality," Prodigy said as he picked up her bag and handed it to her. "Don't worry about the vase. I'll clean that up."

"I know, but I thought that I was more than just any ol' body. Is that all I—" Gina began, but Prodigy cut her off with a wave of the hand.

Right at that moment, Prodigy decided that he'd take a break from dating. Take a break from women, period. He needed some time to himself. First Simone, then this, and all in less than twenty-four hours. In the last two years all types of crazy things had happened to him because of his dealings with quick and crazy women.

A woman named Theresa slashed his tires because she saw him at the movies with another girl.

Another girl, named Liz, spray-painted FUCK YOU BATSTARD on his garage door. He was glad that she kept her nonspelling ass away.

Annette, his last girlfriend, threw a rock through his window with a note attached telling him that she hoped he died of AIDS, just because she thought that he had another girl in his house when he wouldn't answer his door. When in all actuality he was next door helping his neighbor move some furniture. Needless to say, he quickly took an AIDS test and prayed that the results came back negative. When the test arrived with the negative sign, he popped open a bottle of Cristal.

So this incident really wasn't anything in comparison to the other things that had happened, but something struck a chord, so he said enough was enough. In essence this was the chick that broke the playa's back, so Prodigy was pulling himself from the game. *I quit,* he thought.

"Look, let's talk tomorrow. I'm tired and I have a lot on my mind. Call me when you get home," he said as he walked her downstairs and ushered her to the door.

"Prodigy, do you accept my apology?"

"Sure. Call me when you get home. Bye." Gina tried to reach back and give him a good-bye kiss, but he inched back and shook his head. The look he gave her told her that this was her last visit. He closed the door and watched out of his bay window as her taillights got smaller and smaller then finally disappeared around the corner and off into the early-morning darkness.

Prodigy plopped down on his love seat and turned the

television on, but he left the volume all the way down. He needed to think. *My mom raised me to be respectful to all people,* he thought. "Kill 'em with kindness" was what she would say when he came home with news that someone had mistreated him. But his uncles wouldn't have any of that kindness mess. They would say go kick their asses and don't you come back here with any excuses. Growing up, Prodigy got real good at fighting, but he never liked it. He hated hurting people. Even if he was justified in doing so, he would always feel bad. Just like now. He wondered why.

Prodigy's mom had help in raising him; she had one sister and two brothers and they all had something to do with the grooming of Prodigy Banks. His mother and his Aunt Nettie, Jermaine's mother, still lived in Philly. She'd always played bad cop to his mom's good cop. In other words, she would whip his butt and his moms would pet him up. His Uncle Herb was in a federal penitentiary out in Texas, on some ol' bullshit. He'd been a member of the Philadelphia chapter of the Black Panther Party in the late sixties and early seventies and had built up quite a reputation with the authorities for his y'all-can-kiss-my-black-ass attitude. Once J. Edgar Hoover did his thing on the Panthers, his uncle joined the MOVE group and changed his name to Herbert Africa. He got arrested on a drug possession charge and was given a one-to-three-year sentence; that was almost fifteen years ago. Why was he still in on a one-to-three after fifteen years? Some ol' bullshit. After the arrest of the wrongly imprisoned Mumia Abu-Jamal, the authorities had a pissing contest and wanted to prove that they were bigger than Africa, at least the name. So if you wore the last name "Africa," more than likely they got you for something. Prodigy could still smell the flames from when then-mayor Wilson Goode gave the order to bomb the block that the MOVE members lived on.

Prodigy's other uncle, Ray, was in the car business, the

stolen-car business. He moved down to Atlanta to take advantage of the natives' carefree lifestyle. Once the cars were stolen, he then sold them to his connection overseas.

Prodigy was always good with numbers, so Ray had invited him down to take over the financial side of his six-figure crime organization. Prodigy was making extreme sums of money, but then his conscience did a back flip on him when one of the workers stole an old lady's car.

That night Prodigy was watching the news and saw that someone had pulled this old lady from her car and left her stranded in ten-degree weather holding a small child. The way that the news reporter described how the crime had occurred, he knew that it was some of their people. He stayed up all night long thinking about that old lady and baby.

When he arrived at the chop-shop location the next day, he saw the car. Prodigy went through the information that was in the glove compartment, found out who the car belonged to, and returned it. He drove right up to the house, parked it in the driveway, and walked away. He was halfway down the street when an old man pulled up behind him and offered him a ride to get out of the freezing-cold weather. He accepted. The old man asked Prodigy what he was doing out there in the cold. He told him that he was returning something that didn't belong to the person who took it.

That car belonged to a lady named Ethel Fuller. And the man who picked him up out of the cold was Poppa Doc.

Criminals are always paranoid, so after his Uncle Ray found out what Prodigy had done, he shut down his operation for fear of Poppa Doc going to the authorities. Uncle Ray also stopped speaking to Prodigy. That really hurt, because they had been so close, plus his Uncle Ray was the only male influence that he'd had growing up. His Uncle Herb was always away in prison and his dad was killed in a Philadelphia gang war two weeks before he was born. It had been almost two years since he last talked to Uncle Ray. Prodigy had tried to call him a couple of times, but Ray's tone of voice told him that he didn't have any words for him. Prodigy got the point and left him alone.

"Somebody better be dead." That was Uncle Ray's hello, which was said in that old raspy voice of his.

"Did I wake you up? This is Prodigy."

"No, I'm—what's that word you use when people move at night?"

"Nocturnal!"

"Yeah, that's me. What's up, nephew? How's life in the fast lane?" His tone said that he had buried the hatchet. Nothing formal needed to be said.

"Nice and slow! And you?"

"Prodigy, I can't complain. I got a pretty woman lyin' next to me and all of my bills are paid. So I'm doing just fine. Did my daughter call you?"

"No, is she in town?"

"Supposed to be, doing some hair show or something. Called me last night to get your number."

"I see that you still have it, being that you gave it to her. It's been a long time. Good to hear your voice."

"Yeah, I agree. It's been too long."

"Your other nephew is in town, but he's locked up."

"What they got him for?" Ray asked flatly. Prodigy found it sad that no one in his family thought it was a big deal when someone got arrested. He used to be the same way, just wondered when his time would come. By the grace of God, it never did.

"You know."

"What? Some ol' bullshit?"

"Whatever it is, they got a six-hour hold on him."

"They must have him for something alcohol- or drug-related, if they got to hold him. You need some money?"

"Nah, I can handle that part, but I need a bondsman."

"Here, take this number down. The guy is an asshole, so just ignore him, and tell J-man to call me when he gets his ass out. I don't want him down here fucking up what you're trying to do. I never told you this, Prodigy, but I'm proud of you. The day that you took your stand and did what you did, you stopped being a follower and became a leader. You've got principles and you're more of a man than I'll ever be. But you still can't whip my ass and you owe me twenty dollars. Call me if you need anything," Uncle Ray said as he hung up.

Ray surprised Prodigy with his comment, because since he'd left his organization, he thought that Ray hated the ground that he walked on.

A million and one things ran through his mind on the way to pick up his institutionalized-ass cousin. How would he tell the person he used to do major dirt with that he wasn't going to put up with his shit? Finally Prodigy stopped the continuous chatter in his mind and decided that he would just lay down the rules; if Jermaine didn't like them then he was free to head back to Philly or go and stay with Uncle Ray.

When Prodigy arrived at the bail bondsman's, the short fat white man his uncle had warned him about wanted him to prove that he was the child of God.

I'm not the one locked up, he thought. After signing what seemed like his life away, they headed over to the jail. After another hour of sitting on hard, graffiti-covered steel chairs, out came his thugged-out little cousin, Jermaine, wearing a white tank top, royal-blue Polo sweatpants, and some Allen Iverson sneakers.

"What up, my nigga? Let's ride," he hollered, obviously happy to be free.

"Not so fast, hotshot. I have to take your picture and get some information from you," Short-and-Fat said.

"Yo, P. Who dis clown?" Jermaine said, pointing at the bail bondsman.

"I'm the clown that got you out of that living hell. Now, if you'd like to go back in there, I can arrange that," Short-and-Fat said in his "I've had it up to here with you dumb niggers" southern drawl.

"Slow down, son. I didn't know who you were," Jermaine said, trying to put the bail bondsman at ease.

"I ain't cha damn son. Just stand by that wall while I take a Polaroid. Then sign these papers and you can be on your damn way," the bail bondsman said as he snapped the picture and shuffled through the papers.

"So, P, I see you got me a real personality case here."

"Whatever works. He's getting you out and that's all that matters, right? Ignore him."

"Yeah, I guess you right, but he still a dickhead." They were talking loud enough for the bail bondsman to hear them.

"Excuse me. What was that?" Short-and-Fat said.

"You know what? I tried to be nice to your little Humpty-Dumpty-lookin' ass, but you ain't trying to hear that. And I guess you think you can come out of your mouth talking to me like you talk to all of these other country cats. That's not happening, dog. Now, you can take the money and shut the fuck up or we can call somebody else. Because another hour or two in jail ain't gonna mean a got-damn thing. It's up to you, Doughboy."

Short-and-Fat was obviously not used to anyone talking to him that way, because he turned red as a beet. "Let's just sign the papers and be done with it," he said, and not another word left his lips before he hurried to his car.

Once they were outside in the jail's parking lot, Prodigy thought that now was a good time to let Jermaine know the laws of the land.

5

Noodles

verything was perfect! Diane's dining room table looked like she had peeled it from the pages of *House Beautiful* or *Elle Decor* magazines. She placed candles sporadically around the room, which gave the place a subtle romantic vibe. The filet mignon was cooked to perfection; the escargot was sautéed in butter, garlic, and wine and baked to a golden brown. The broccoli was simmering in a cheddar cheese sauce. Fresh white lilies were placed in the center of the cherry-oak dining room table, while Anita Baker rhythmically hummed in the background for the operator to get her baby on the line. Diane poured the Johannesburg Riesling in their crystal glasses and lit the scented candles.

She decided against the black camisole that she had just purchased from Victoria's Secret. She was feeling a bit naughty and needed to feel her husband, so in his absence she put on one of his white dress shirts, which hung right below her love box, one of Bernard's silk ties, thong underwear, and some black pumps. She sat there and waited, half naked, for her husband to bring it on home to Momma.

Bernard had just called from the cell phone in Diane's car to say that he was on his way. After ten years of marriage, Diane knew that the kitchen would be the first place he would venture into, and since their dining room adjoined the kitchen, he couldn't help but see her, all made up, hair looking nice, nails and toes done.

Diane heard the garage door open and looked up just in time to see her silver and gray Volvo turn into the driveway. She felt like a sixteen-year-old waiting on her first date. It had been a long time since they had been intimate.

The garage door went back down. When the door leading to the house cracked, there was a double beep from the alarm and Diane heard Bernard sigh as he dropped his bag and closed the door behind him. Then there was nothing. The toilet flushed as he mumbled something inaudible. A minute later he came back out and called out Brittany's name, then Diane's. But Diane didn't answer.

Bernard said, "Hello. Anybody home?" which sounded like he had come across an unlocked door in an unfamiliar area. He made his way down the hallway and into the kitchen. Diane still said nothing as she crossed her legs and twirled a single white rose around and around. As he opened the refrigerator door, he looked at his wife and did a double take.

"What the . . . ?" he said.

"Why don't you close that refrigerator door and come and find out."

"I think I'll do just that," Bernard said as he closed the door, walked over to where she was sitting, and pulled her to her feet. He positioned her arms up and around his neck, then he placed his own arms around her waist. He kissed her soft, then hard, one of those long, deep, passionate kisses that had "I love you" written all over it. Diane felt herself getting weak, her knees trembled, but Bernard held her close and steady. He moved her hair out of her eyes and said, "Thank you. All of this looks nice. How much money did you spend?"

Diane managed a soft "Twoddles," which was their way of saying, "I love you too." Then she said, "Don't be tacky" in reference to his inquisition about the cost.

Bernard looked at the food and moaned in a way that said everything looked lovely. He blew out the candles and said, "I sho am hungry, but the food can wait." He picked her up, carried her upstairs to their bedroom, and placed her on their king-size bed, which Diane had covered with red and white rose petals.

She lay down on her back, watching her husband undress, fingering the single rose that she still held.

He said, "You look fabulous. I'm gonna take a shower, keep it right there for me."

"I'll do that," Diane said as she took a naughty bite at him from across the room.

"The place looks nice, you look nice. I like coming home to this."

"Wasn't anything to it. I thought about you all day and how much you mean to me, to us. And this is my way of apologizing for the things that I said. Bernard, you're all man and I'm sorry that I ever questioned you in that way."

"Where's my baby girl?"

"At my parents'."

"Be back in a minute."

"Take five minutes. I smelled you ten minutes before you turned into the subdivision," Diane said, and they laughed together for the first time in a long time.

Diane lay across the bed while the shower washed the Ford funk off of Bernard's body and tried to remember the last date they'd made love. She couldn't.

Bernard stood in the doorway of the bathroom, naked as the day he was born. He had put on a few pounds around the midsection, but his strong handsome presence still made Diane's nipples hard.

He walked over to her and gently kissed her neck. He unbuttoned the shirt she was wearing, picked up the hot oil she had strategically placed on his dresser, and rubbed it all over her body. His strong hands sent surges of electricity through her. He kissed her breasts; his tongue made little circles around her swollen nipples. He took one into his mouth and sucked it gently while he massaged the other one with his thumb and index finger. His lips made their way up to her neck.

Ohhh damn, that's my spot, she thought.

Bernard's tongue found its way to part her lips. She sucked it deeper inside of her mouth. He turned her over and slid his tongue all the way down her back until he came to where her legs formed a V. Her legs parted automatically. His lips and tongue mixed with her love juices; he licked, sucked, and kissed as Diane's legs shook uncontrollably. She pulled him up so that she could feel him inside her, but his penis was like a wet noodle. She massaged it, rubbed it. She rolled him over so that she could try something else, but he stopped her.

He sat up on the side of the bed and stared out the window up at nothing.

"Baby, what is it?" Diane said as she sat behind him and rubbed his back and neck.

"I don't know. We've never had this problem before. I hope this isn't what I think it is."

She wanted to tell him that it had been so long that his little pecker probably forgot how to operate, but she figured now was not a good time for jokes.

"Oh, it's probably nothing," Diane said. "We'll try again later."

"I'm sorry, Diane. All that you went through to make this night special, and I come up limp."

"That's alright. Let's go eat," Diane said, but she was really let down. Her body was craving some loving.

All throughout dinner, Bernard was distant. He responded to all of her questions with one-word answers. And while they watched the movie *The Best Man* (Diane figured a little romantic flick with a touch of humor would lift his spirits) he seemed to have his mind on another place and time. No doubt thinking about his nonperformance, he apologized a million and fifteen times. She told him not to worry about it, that they were married and therefore they had the rest of their lives to try and try again.

Midway through the movie, Bernard got up and went upstairs. Diane thought that maybe he was going to the bathroom and that he would return, but he never did. After the movie was done and the rest of the wine gone, she joined him in bed. When she curled up next to him, he stiffened. She decided that now was as good a time as any to give it another try; hell, she was still in the mood. She reached around and grabbed his stuff. But Bernard was not in the mood and showed it by grabbing her hand firmly and placing it back on her thigh.

He then got up, went down the hallway into the guest bedroom, and closed the door.

Diane lay there for about ten minutes before she got up and headed to the guest bedroom herself. She wanted to apologize for pushing the issue, but the door was locked. She decided to give it a rest and returned to her empty, cold, rose-petal-covered bed and tried to sleep.

Bright and early Saturday morning Diane was awakened by the sound of a screaming telephone and much-too-bright sunshine. She turned to see if Bernard had rejoined her in their bed, but no luck.

That Johannesburg Riesling had done a number on her. She didn't realize that she had had that much to drink, but her dry mouth told a different story. She picked up the phone and heard her daughter's happy voice on the other end of the line.

"Hey, Mommy. Can I speak to Daddy?"

"And good morning to you too, sweetheart," Diane said as she sat up on one elbow.

"I said hi. Can I speak to Daddy?"

"It's *may* I speak to Daddy and yes you may. Hold on, little girl." Diane put the phone down and went to wake up Bernard. But the door to the guest bedroom was open and he wasn't there, so she yelled downstairs for him to pick up the phone. Silence. Diane walked downstairs and looked around, but he was nowhere to be found. She called outside into the yard and noticed that the borrowed truck was gone. She picked up the den phone.

"Hey, sweetie, your daddy must have run to the store or something. You want me to have him call you when he gets back?"

"Yeah, he said he was gonna take me to Six Flags today."

"Oh yeah, that's right. Well I'm sure he'll be back in a little while. Are you being a good girl over there, or are you driving your grandma and granddaddy up a wall?"

"I'm being good. I won ten dollars from Granddaddy last night, playing checkers."

"You tell Daddy to stop having you over there gambling. Let me speak to him."

"He's gone. Went to get Michael."

"Where's Michael?"

"I don't know."

"Let me speak to Momma."

"Hold on. Grandma, telephone!" Brittany yelled to her grandmother.

"Hello."

"Hey, Momma, what's going on with Michael?"

"Samantha called over here about six o'clock this morning saying that he was beating down the door."

"Why didn't she call the police? He needs to learn his lesson. That's the third time that he's done something like this. You know what it comes from, don't you?"

"No, but I'm sure you are gonna tell me," Ethel said, having heard it all before from her daughter.

"No! That's a word that he rarely hears. He's not used to that word, since no one ever says it to him. He loses it when he hears that word, just like he did when he was a child. I hope he goes to jail. Out there harassing women all times of morning!"

"Don't say that, that's your brother. I know he's not perfect, but give him a chance."

"Momma, that's all Michael ever gets is chance after chance. He'll never learn if he keeps getting all the chances in the world. But I know talking to you about your baby is a waste of time, so could you have Daddy give me a call when he gets in?"

"Don't get all upset. How was your dinner last night?"

"It was nice, and thank you for keeping Brittany for me."

"Oh, don't mention it. That's my baby. Winston done bought her another bike. He said the other one was too small for her."

"You and Daddy are gonna spoil my child yet."

"That's what grandparents do: spoil 'em and send 'em home."

"Yeah, you see what spoiling Michael got you, a thirty-three-year-old bum."

"Alright now! Is Bernard coming to get Brittany? I don't think she slept a wink last night. Talking about that Six Flags."

"He's not here, but he should be back before too long. I'll have him come get her when he gets in. Love you, Momma."

"I love you too and I'll tell your daddy to call you. Bye-bye."

"Bye, Momma! And I'm sorry if I yelled."

"It's okay, I don't pay you no mind."

Diane had been asleep for the last four hours. She guessed her body needed it. Last night she didn't get any real rest, thinking about Bernard and their non–sex life. But something didn't seem right. She didn't hear Bernard come in, and Brittany hadn't called since early this morning. Usually she rang the phone off the hook. Maybe her daddy took her to Six Flags like he'd promised, but it seemed like he would've come home first, or at least called to tell her something.

Diane picked up the phone to call her parents' house, but she didn't hear a dial tone. Just as she pulled herself up from the sofa she heard the doorbell ringing. *Damn, I look a mess,* she thought. She peered through the peephole and saw her mother and Brittany.

"Hey, Momma, hi, sweetheart," Diane said, searching their faces to see if anything was wrong. In the six years that they had been living out in Fayette County, her mother had never come out there calling before. The trip was about a forty-five-minute drive from her parents' Alpharetta home.

"Girl, what's wrong with you? We've been trying to call you for more than an hour."

"I didn't hear the phone ring," Diane said as she checked the phone again. Still no dial tone.

"It didn't ring. It was busy. Far as I know someone could've knocked you over the head and been gone."

"Wait a minute, Momma," Diane said as she walked into the garage, returned with her cell phone, and called her own number. Busy. Then she remembered.

"Oh, Momma, I'm sorry. I left the phone off the hook in my room this morning when Brittany called. I came down-stairs looking for Bernard and I didn't go back upstairs to put it back on the receiver. Have you spoken with your daddy, sweet-heart?"

"No. He told me a tale. He said he was gonna take me to Six Flags and he didn't. Lashay and Christina are already gone and I gotta stay home," Brittany said as the tears made their way down her honey-brown cheeks.

"Lawd have mercy, this chile has been wailing all morning. Where is Bernard?"

"I haven't seen him this morning. He was gone when I woke up. Let me try him at work. He better not be there." Diane sent Brittany upstairs to put the phone back on its cradle and called Ford.

"Bernard Charles, how may I help you?"

"Bernard, your daughter is here crying. She said you promised that you would take her to Six Flags today. You could've at least given her a call to let her know that your plans changed, but I see that once again you're more concerned with your job. I hope you have a good day."

"Wait a minute. I never told Brittany that I would take her, I told her that I would see. I found out last night right before I left work that I would have to work this morning."

"You mean to tell me, as big as Ford is, they couldn't find anybody else but you. I find that hard to believe."

"Diane . . ."

"You volunteered, didn't you? I guess that overtime means more to you than your promise to your child. Bye, Bernard."

"Diane, we'll talk about this when I get home. I'm in the middle of a conference and you call up here with all that noise about something that's not really that important. Tell Brittany I'll take her tomorrow."

"No, Bernard, I won't give you another opportunity to let her down. It's Saturday and her friends are going today, not to-morrow. I'll take her."

"Why couldn't you take her in the first place?"

"Because she wanted you to take her. She's always with me. She wants to spend some time with her father. Is that so wrong?"

"We'll talk when I get home, I have to go. Bye."

Diane hung up the phone and told Brittany that she would take her to Six Flags.

"Brittany, go to your room and change that shirt, I'll take you. Momma, would you like to join us?"

"And walk around in that hot sun? I'll pass."

"I really don't want to go, but I hate it when she gets her hopes up and he doesn't come through."

"Now, if the man has to work, then you can't fault him for that. Somebody has to pay the bills around this nice place that y'all have."

"Momma, that's all that man does is work. Even when we go on vacation, he takes his computer and stays online working all night. It's like he's here, but he's not here."

"Diane, sit down. As a woman you have to learn to be a little more understanding and supportive. Bernard is a good man. He's not out in the streets all times of night. Your family has this lovely home and he loves you guys more than he probably loves himself. So give him some time, he'll come around."

"When, Momma? This has been going on forever. Work, work, work."

"You can't make him into the man you want him to be to suit your needs, you have to accept him for who he is. Has he ever hit you?"

"No!"

"Cheated on you?"

"No!"

"What about let you guys go without food, shelter, clothes?"

"No, no, and no, but it's more than food, shelter, and

clothes, Momma, it's the mental neglect that's driving me up and down the walls."

"It's a remarkable thing, the mind is. If you let it control you, it will drive you up the wall, but if you commit to happiness, then your mind will find a peaceful place. All those years your daddy was on the road with his job, who do you think kept you and your brother? I did that, because that was my role. We all have a role to play. Play your role, Diane."

"What's my role, Momma? Should I sit around and wait for Bernard to tell me what to do? Or should I just wait until he has a minute in his schedule to fit us in? This is not a knock on you, but I'm not as docile as you are. It's not in my character to sit around and not voice my opinion when I feel like I have a point to prove."

"Be careful, Diane. Sometimes you win the fight, but you lose the war. I'm gonna get on back to my side of town, but think about what I told you."

"I will! I love you, Momma."

"I love you too, baby."

Just as Ethel was getting up to leave, Poppa Doc and Michael walked in the house, both of them looking like they were ready to kill someone.

"What's wrong?" Poppa Doc said, looking around the room as if someone might be hiding.

"Nothing, we're fine. What's going on?" Diane said.

"Ethel left me a message saying she couldn't find you. You alright? Where have you been? Where's Britt-Britt?" Poppa Doc asked, still looking behind doors and out the window.

"Everything's fine, and I was here asleep, but I left the phone off the hook. That's all. Brittany's upstairs."

"Put that phone on speaker," Poppa Doc said as he dialed in to retrieve his messages. Ethel's frantic voice came on the line, sounding worried out of her mind.

"Winston, we can't find Diane! I've been calling her for over an hour! Something done happened, I can feel it! Somebody must have cut her phone line! Lawd save my baby! I'm on my way out there! Call the police!"

They all laughed at Ethel's dramatic performance over nothing. Even she laughed. Michael was standing over by the entertainment center going through CDs.

"Diane, let me borrow this Lucy Pearl."

"No."

"Please."

"No."

"Aw, come on, Diane, I'll bring it back."

"No."

"Ma, tell Diane to let me borrow this CD. I'ma bring it back."

"You see what I mean, Momma? He doesn't even hear that word," Diane said, proving her point to her mother.

"What word?" Michael asked.

"*No!* The word that Samantha was probably saying when you were beating down her door this morning. That word."

"You need to mind your business. Nobody asked for your comments."

"Alright, boy, what did I tell you about respecting people's houses," Poppa Doc said as he walked over and got right in Michael's face.

"Daddy, she started it."

"Boy, you are almost sickening, thirty-three years old and still giving me five-year-old answers. Put that CD back. Didn't she say you couldn't borrow it? You are gonna learn one way or the other to respect other people's property. You don't have any of your own, so you leech off of other people. Go get in the car, you getting on my damn nerves."

"Daddy, I—"

"In the car, son. Or you're gonna have to find you a ride home. I'm not telling you again."

6

Take Her
or Leave Her

rodigy didn't get a chance to pay Poppa Doc for losing the bet on their pool game.

He doesn't need to look at any naked women anyway. This is the steroid generation, one slap in the face with one of those hard 36DD implants might be a little too much for his old ticker, he thought.

Instead of the Gentlemen's Club, Prodigy found himself sitting in his living room, face-to-face with someone who he never wanted to meet.

Prodigy had just come home from serving a couple of his homies up something nice on the basketball court. After six games in a row, all he wanted to do was hit the shower and fall asleep while watching *Cops.* He was looking forward to catching up on some Z's. Between dealing with Gina and trying to free up Jermaine, he had only managed to keep his eyes closed for three hours in the last two days.

Once Jermaine was free, they talked and talked about those long Philly nights. And how their childhood games went from Dixie Doorbell (when you would ring someone's doorbell, then run away) to Snatching Pocketbooks (when you just flat-out robbed any lady who had a purse). That happened to his Aunt Nettie one time and she caught the guy and gave him a black eye, then she held him until the police arrived. Jermaine told Prodigy that the reason he had to leave Philly was that he got tired of defending Prodigy.

Ever since Prodigy could remember, he'd rolled with this guy named Tyrone, whom everyone called Ty. Ty was Prodigy's ace, his partner, his homie, and whatever synonym you could find for the word "close." Wherever you saw Prodigy you saw Ty, and vice versa. They were closer than most brothers could ever hope to be.

One day this crackhead named Lisa came by Prodigy's house, banging on his door like she had lost her mind. He was hesitant to answer, figuring she just wanted to borrow the VCR or something else that she didn't have any intention of returning. He opened the door and Lisa told him that Ty had just been shot. Prodigy asked her who had shot him; she said that she didn't know. It never crossed his mind that his friend might be dead. Prodigy threw on his Timberlands and raced down to the block where they all hung out. He knew that Ty was there, because he had just left him standing in front of Mr. White's store only five minutes before. He was shooting dice with some guys who pulled up in a white Monte Carlo.

When Prodigy arrived on the block the police had already arrived and Ty was covered with a blanket. Prodigy remembered asking the policeman if he thought he was going to make it, and that racist pig said with a sinister smile that he hoped not. Prodigy turned and walked back home filled with hurt.

He went through his stockpile of weapons, bent on a little

revenge, but Prodigy's mom blocked his door. She said that if he left, she was afraid it might be a few more mothers crying that night. She suggested that Prodigy give Tyrone's mother a call to inform her of her son's tragedy. He returned to his room, sat on his bed, and cried like a baby. He stopped crying long enough to make the call that every mother or father never wants to get, but it was that call that changed his life. She was so calm.

"Miss Rachel, Tyrone was killed," Prodigy blurted out before he could make up his mind on how to say anything.

"Where is he?"

"Down on Vernon Road."

"Hold on, Prodigy. I have another call."

She clicked over, then came right back.

"Prodigy, that was the police telling me that my son is dead. I have one in jail, one in college, and now one dead. Do you have any relatives outside of Philadelphia?" Rachel said, and he could hear the pain in her voice.

"Yeah, my uncle lives in Atlanta."

"Then go and stay with him. I don't know who killed my son, but it could've just as easily been you. If you will do me that favor then I'll be forever grateful to you. You guys have been friends for so long, I don't think that I could take seeing you without seeing him. Will you do that for me?" she said, crying uncontrollably now.

"Yes, ma'am. Miss Rachel, I'm sorry."

"Me too, baby, me too. Take care and live a long life for me, will you?"

"I'll try."

"That's not good enough for me. You do it."

"I will," Prodigy said as he held the phone in his hand. All of the moments that he and Tyrone had shared ran through his mind.

Damn, I don't even remember being on this earth without him. We played ball together, we boxed together, and we even went in the Army together on the Buddy Plan to assure that we had the same duty stations. Damn, I'm gonna miss my dog, Prodigy thought.

Prodigy turned to his mother, who was standing in his doorway crying as she listened to his conversation with Tyrone's mom. He told his mother that he was leaving Philadelphia. She released a smile that lit up his room like a chandelier. With so many of his childhood friends dead, Prodigy's mother said she had a feeling that his time was coming, even though he was in his second year at Temple University. She also expressed her concerns about Atlanta; she thought that he was jumping out of the fire and into the flame. Knowing the types of things that her brother Ray was into, she made him promise that he would never have anyone make a call like the one that he had just made to Ty's mother. With that, he called his Uncle Ray and told him that he was on his way. Ray was thrilled, since he had been trying to get Prodigy to come down to Atlanta for some time.

Jermaine had informed Prodigy that those ignorant nuts in Philly had put Prodigy's hasty departure together with Ty's still unsolved murder and started a vicious rumor that somehow he'd had something to do with it. Prodigy thought that their assessment was ridiculous, and wanted to call Tyrone's mom to see if she had heard it, but Jermaine said that he saw her one day in the Gallery Mall and she gave him a hug and told him to tell Prodigy to call her sometime.

Now, when Prodigy pulled up into his driveway, he noticed that his front door was open. He made a mental note to introduce his foot to Jermaine's butt. He had just passed Jermaine as he was turning onto his street. Jermaine flagged Prodigy down and introduced him to some little chicken-head that he'd met during his brief incarceration. She was the desk clerk who'd processed him into the jail. They said that they were on their way to catch a movie.

As Prodigy got out of his truck, he could have sworn that he saw a shadow of a person standing in his living room window. He pulled his .40-caliber Glock pistol out of his door panel and got out of the truck, ready for whatever. When he opened the screen door and made his way into his home, he looked into the living room; the shadow belonged to a six-feet-five, high-yellow brother with muscles everywhere. He walked over to Prodigy and extended his hand, which didn't put Prodigy at ease one bit. Prodigy didn't shake his hand, but asked, "Who are you and what are you doing in my house?" He held his gym bag in one hand and his Glock in the other. The light-skinned guy's eyes were on only the Glock.

"I think you know who I am, and your cousin let me in. He's a nice young man. I told him that I would wait outside, but he insisted that I wait inside. He probably thought that we were old Army buddies. Put your gun down. We have enough of our black men killing one another as it is. If I meant you any harm, do you think I would be sitting in your house in some dress slacks and a silk shirt? Looks like you've been shooting some ball. Where do you play?"

"Run n' Shoot. What can I do for you, dog?"

"I play there sometimes. It's too damn crowded and they cry too much for me."

"What can I do for you?"

Light-skinned walked over, looked out the window, and asked, "You screwing my wife?"

"What!"

"Are you having sexual relations with my wife?"

Prodigy looked into Light-skinned's eyes to see where he was headed with his question, but found nothing but a blank stare. Prodigy could tell that a conversation was all he wanted.

"I already asked you one time now, I'm going to ask again: Who are you?" Prodigy dropped his bag and released the clip out of his gun.

"My name is Anthony Campbell, I'm Simone's husband. May I sit down?"

I must be slipping. I'm surprised I didn't recognize him from the pictures that she kept in her office, he thought.

He looked a little closer, and sure enough it was Anthony. He started to put the clip back into his gun and pop him one, maybe two, as big as he was, but Anthony was right about the black-on-black crime thing.

"Go right ahead. Sit down. You've already let yourself in. You want a brew?"

"Naw, I'm cool."

Prodigy walked through the living room and into the kitchen and grabbed a bottle of water. It's a good thing Anthony didn't want a beer, because all twelve of them were gone.

Damn, Jermaine is an alcoholic, he thought.

He closed the fridge and returned to chat with the curly-haired brother sitting on his love seat.

"So, Mr. Campbell, what can I do for you? First off, how did you know that I was in the Army?"

"I know plenty about you. Simone thinks she's slick. She told me that you were her cousin."

"Her cousin, where did she get that from?"

"Well, apparently she wanted her cake and her ice cream. I've been aware of my wife's infidelity for sometime now. Hell, I've been cheating since day one, but she doesn't know that. I play pro football, I'm always on the road. I married for tax purposes, not love. Now that I'm on the back end of my career and looking at retirement next year, I'm looking for a little more than a tax break out of my marriage. Do you see where I'm going with this, Prodigy?"

"I think I do. So you're saying if I am seeing your wife, then I need to stop seeing her."

"No. I'm saying if you are seeing her, which you are, that you need to make a decision. Either take her or leave her."

"Take her where?"

"Prodigy, my wife thinks she has it all together, but she doesn't. She couldn't last a week on her own. She wouldn't know how to adhere to a budget if her life depended on it. I feel responsible for her like you would a child, more than anything else. She has gotten used to our lifestyle, and she would probably crack up if I took it all away from her. She makes pretty good money, but nothing like what I bring home. Now, she doesn't know that I know what she's been doing for the last year, and I'm not sure if I'm going to tell her. Talking is a key component to any relationship. We don't talk, which leads us to where we are now. I take full responsibility for our predicament. At one point, I didn't want any communication between us so I would be free to do whatever I wanted to do without all the questions."

"Well, I think she did her share to put the relationship where it is today. It takes a big man to do what you're doing and go about it the way that you're going about it."

"Well, don't give me no credit that I don't deserve. Prodigy, I used to be a violent man. A couple of years ago I wouldn't have cared if I hated Simone. If I found out that she was cheating, I would have done somebody some bodily harm. But that's neither here nor there, I came to talk to you, man-to-man, to give you an opportunity to stake your claim. What's it gonna be?"

"You seem to be a good man. Simone had me thinking that you were crazy. But, dog—I know you may find this hard to believe, considering the circumstances—you got a good woman and I wish you guys the best. You don't have to worry about me. You've respected me enough to come to me like a man, so I'll extend to you that same courtesy," Prodigy said as he stood. Anthony reached out his hand again; this time Prodigy gave it a firm handshake.

"Prodigy, you're an a'ight dude. Hopefully I can put this thing behind me. I got this big-ass ego, ya know. I constantly gotta fight to keep it in check."

"Me too." They both chuckled.

"You think I'm soft for coming over here talking to the man that's banging my wife, don't you?"

"To tell the truth, I only wish that I could handle the situation with as much class as you have, if the shoe were on the other foot. This could've easily been an ugly scene."

"Yeah, it could've. And it almost was. I was looking at the picture of you and this older dude," Anthony said as he pointed at a picture of Prodigy and Poppa Doc. "He looked so peaceful and happy. I thought, *I'll never find that peace if I keep on handling every bad situation that arises with violence.*"

"Once again, I feel you." Prodigy showed him to the door. "Yo, dog, how'd you get here? I didn't see a car outside."

Anthony looked at Prodigy and shook his head. "I'm seeing one of your neighbors; my car is at her house in the garage, where no one can see it. That's how I knew where you lived. I've seen Simone's car over here plenty of times. I was creeping and she was too. She has to stop; I'll probably never quit. You hold it down, Prodigy, and anytime you wanna test your b-ball skills on a real player, call me. You know my number."

With that Anthony walked down the street and turned into a yard just three houses down from Prodigy's. He was definitely playing with fire. He imagined that some of those nights when he and Simone were in there getting busy as a beaver, Anthony was right down the street.

I could have gone to sleep one night and woke up dead. Damn!

Prodigy showered after Anthony left and fell into a comalike sleep. He woke just in time to catch the eleven o'clock service at church. He woke Jermaine and told him that they were going to church. Jermaine looked at him like he had said a foreign word or something and claimed that he didn't have any clothes to wear. Prodigy left it at that, but told him he had exactly one week to come up with some, because next Sunday his face would be in the place.

Prodigy pulled a tailor-made suit from the closet, a gray one, threw on a gray linen pullover shirt and black alligator shoes with a matching belt, and mentally prepared himself for the traffic fight that was surely waiting for him at New Birth Baptist Church.

Once everyone was seated, Reverend Ernest Myers preached about the wandering eye. And how single people didn't think that they were sinning by having sex. Prodigy liked coming to his church, because the pastor always seemed to be talking about some of the things that he was currently dealing with. At times he could've sworn that the pastor was talking directly to him.

Prodigy sat next to Mrs. Ethel and Poppa Doc. They always saved two seats, one for him and the other one for whatever date happened to stay over on Saturday night.

Today Prodigy showed up alone and planned on keeping it that way for a while. They had been saving him a seat since he met them two years ago, but he had just started using it last year.

After church they would always go to a nice restaurant, and he and Poppa Doc would always fight over who was going to pay the bill. Poppa Doc usually won. He would start telling Prodigy that he was making his heart hurt. Then he would turn and wink at Mrs. Ethel to let her know that he was only acting. She would just shake her head and say she was flattered that at her age men still wanted to fight over her.

Normally after Sunday dinner Prodigy would go home, but he needed to talk to Poppa Doc. Plus he needed to get some information about the youth mentoring program from him. So he found himself following the Fullers back out to their Alpharetta estate.

Once they arrived, Prodigy went down into the basement while Poppa Doc changed into his Sunday after-church clothes. His official old-man gear: cut-off khakis, a white T-shirt, dress socks, and sandals.

Prodigy gave Poppa Doc the 411 on all of the happenings in his life that had taken place since the last time they saw each other, just two days before. He told him how Jermaine made his grand appearance at three o'clock in the morning straight from the city hotel, and how Simone's husband just showed up in his living room and acted like they were old buddies.

Prodigy prepared to be bombarded with a bunch of "I told you so's," but Poppa Doc surprised him. He said that Prodigy should take all of his blessings, multiply them by two, and pass them on to everyone he could.

"So, Poppa Doc, tell me what I need to do for this youth thing."

"Well, first of all you have to be at the center tomorrow at six P.M. I told them you were coming, so don't be late. Does six o'clock give you enough time?"

"Yeah, that should be plenty."

"This thing is important to me because I like helping people. Our people need to see their people doing good. It's as important as air or water. So make me proud."

"Wait. What will I be doing?"

"Hell, I don't know. Whatever it is, it's better than almost getting your ass kicked in your own house by some broad's husband."

"Oh, I knew this was too good to be true."

"You damn right. I hope you learned your lesson. You got off easy this time; the next time you might not be so lucky. You better start using that bald head of yours for more than a hat rack. Now, tell me about this young cousin of yours and why he wasn't in church today," Poppa Doc said with a frown face. He felt the pain in his heart with Prodigy just as he would his very own children.

"He's a misdirected young man. He'll give you the shirt off of his back, but he can't keep a job to save his life. Oh, and he claimed he didn't have any church clothes, so that's why he was absent today. But next Sunday you can save those two places for us, because he's coming."

"You mean he *won't* keep a job, and having no clothes is a poor excuse. Tell him that the Bible says come as you are. What type of experience does he have?"

"Fast-food restaurants. I told him to get him a real job and to stop settling for that minimum-wage stuff."

"Now, wait a minute. McDonald's, Burger King, Wendy's, those are all multimillion-dollar corporations. And you have to remember not to put your life's objectives on other people. It's about personal fulfillment, not what anyone else thinks. If he's happy doing the fast-food thing, then that's all that matters."

"Yeah, but I know he can do better. The only reason that he works fast food in the first place is to cover up those illegal funds."

"What do you mean by illegal?"

"He's a hustler. I had some reservations about letting him come down here, but after thinking about what you did for me, I couldn't help but give him a chance."

"I understand, but you know him better than me, so if he deserves a chance, then give it to him."

"I think he does, but changing him won't be easy."

"It will be impossible for you to change him; he'll have to do that himself. Do you remember when I first met you?"

"Yeah, I remember."

"Do you know why I didn't call the police on you but instead picked you up out of the cold and helped you find a nice job?"

"I never asked, and you never told."

"Character, I liked your character. Sure, some people do some things and their conscience gets the best of them, but not everyone would have had the courage to bring that car back to the house, knowing what could happen to them."

"Well, there are some things in life that you just can't sit by and let happen."

"I can dig it. And that's what I'm talking about. Now, this cousin of yours, I want you to take him with you when you go to this youth thing. You never know what might trigger someone into changing."

"I don't know, Poppa Doc, he's a little rough around the edges. Jermaine might have the kids up in the place selling weed."

Poppa Doc grunted and shook his head. "You know, the sad part about it, he probably thinks that's cool. We don't need the militias to kill us anymore, because we do that to ourselves. Can you name me one person that tried using crack cocaine and was a better person for doing it? You know any crackhead home owners? I don't. So tell me, why would someone even try a drug that has such a track record of destruction?"

"To escape their miserable existence. That's all I can think of."

"And you're exactly right. Prodigy, we've got to stop this genocide. That's what I have dedicated my life to."

They were silent for a moment, no doubt thinking about the tragedies that had touched both of their lives. Then Bernard walked in.

"Hey, Pops, how ya perkin'?"

"Bernard, what brings you over this side of town?" Poppa Doc said as he stood to shake his son-in-law's hand.

"Oh, just needed to ride and clear my head."

"What's up, Bernard?" Prodigy said, even though he felt that Bernard never cared too much for him. In the two years he had known him, they had never sat down and had a conversation. Bernard was never rude, but always short and laconic. Like right then! Prodigy spoke, but Bernard just nodded his head.

Poppa Doc said, "Sit down and take a load off ya feet. How's my babies?"

"Well both of them are good and mad at me right about now, that's why I had to take a ride."

"Why are they mad at you?"

"Brittany thought I said that I would take her to Six Flags, and of course Diane's mad about me working so much."

"Yeah, lil' Britt-Britt talked about Six Flags all night long the other night. So you say y'all had a communication gap, huh?"

"I guess you can call it that. I'll make it up to Brittany, but that daughter of yours, man, ain't no pleasing that woman."

"Well, I'll tell you like I told Michael, a woman is a different breed. Now, Diane is my daughter and I'll die for her right now, but she has that women's logic. So just give it up, Bernard, find you a place in the basement and go to sleep."

"I don't know, Pops, can't live with 'em, can't kill 'em."

"Unless you're O.J.," Poppa Doc said.

"Get off of O.J. That man didn't kill anybody," Prodigy said.

"You *would* think he was innocent, wouldn't you, Prodigy?" Bernard said snobbishly.

"That's an old issue, tired and discussed too much," Prodigy answered.

Poppa Doc said, "Prodigy and I were just talking about how messed up some of our people are and don't even know it."

"Yeah, a bunch of parasites. He should know," Bernard said, looking at Poppa Doc but talking about Prodigy.

"I should know what?" Prodigy asked.

"How messed up some of our people are. You know, users, people that prey on others. People like yourself."

"What do you know about me? Have you ever sat down and tried to get to know me? No! But you can sit here and act all high-and-mighty and judge me."

"I only go by people's actions, and you're a thief. I work every day, all day, for what I have, and for someone like you to come along and try and take what I have is grounds to be called a thief. That's not judging, that's a fact."

"I don't steal. Get your facts straight before you get diarrhea of the mouth again."

"Okay, y'all cut it out. Now, both of you are guests in my house, so act like it. Apologize, both of you," Poppa Doc said, hearing enough.

"For what, calling it like it is? Pops, I done told you that you can't save the world. Some people are givers and some people are takers. He's a taker, and I can't and won't apologize about his actions."

"You're wrong, Bernard, and you will apologize or you will see yourself out."

"Naw, he's your family, I'll leave." Prodigy stood up. But Poppa Doc stood also and placed his hand in front of him to restrict his movement.

"You're family too. Bernard, apologize right now or come back when you're ready to," Poppa Doc said, looking over at Bernard, who was still seated.

"Prodigy, I apologize to you," Bernard said halfheartedly.

"Uh-uh, like a man. Stand up and shake his hand."

Bernard stood up like he was told, walked around the table, and gave Prodigy a weak handshake.

"Prodigy, it's your turn," Poppa Doc said as he turned to face him.

"Bernard, I apologize if I offended you in any way. And I'm

sorry for disrespecting your home, Poppa Doc," Prodigy said. He shook Bernard's hand like it was supposed to be shaken. They said the words to pacify Poppa Doc, but Prodigy felt like he had gained a new enemy, and he was sure that Bernard didn't feel any better about him.

To hell with Bernard! Prodigy thought.

Poppa Doc looked at his watch and said that he was getting sleepy. He walked both of them out to their vehicles. Everyone noticed that Bernard had a brand-new Ford Expedition, parked right behind Prodigy's truck.

Bernard said, "Prodigy, how many miles you get to a gallon in that truck?"

Prodigy was still a little heated with him, and so it was his turn to be short and curt. "Don't keep up with it," he said.

"Well, you should. Gas prices are pretty high, especially for these tanks that we've got."

"I'll keep that in mind," Prodigy said as he gave Poppa Doc a quick handshake. He got in his truck and drove off, thinking, *This cornball has a lot of nerve calling me a thief one minute and wanting to talk about trucks the next. With that cheap-ass, spraypainted vanity plate. BERNARD'S TRUCK. Please!*

7

The Beginning
of the End

iane and Bernard had been pretty much like two ships passing in the night since she got mad at him for not taking Brittany to Six Flags. Sometimes Bernard felt like he had two kids to raise. He guessed Diane was playing a little "get back at him" now, because she had just started working at the church in the evenings. She didn't ask his opinion one way or the other, just came home one day the week before last and told him that she had a job. She walked in one evening and told Bernard that he needed to adjust his work schedule so that he could be at home in the evenings with Brittany. Told him it was time that he learned the other half of being a father. That was the most she'd said to him in the last three weeks. And to tell the truth, Bernard liked it that way.

If all she can fix her lips to do is fuss, then I'd rather have the silent treatment. It's a lil' more peaceful 'round here when she gets like that anyway, he thought.

He thought Diane only seemed to care about what she wanted, and that was not the way he intended on operating.

Bernard thought that Poppa Doc had spoiled his daughter way too much, and since they'd been married, Diane had expected Bernard to pick up where he left off. Initially he did take on that role of giving her anything she wanted. But after years of being unappreciated and taken for granted, Bernard went on strike.

Brittany had Bernard out on the deck in this hot sun while she played in her Barbie playhouse. He tried everything within his power to get his little girl to come in the house. He even told her that they could take her toys in the basement, which was normally off-limits to everyone except him. But his baby girl insisted on being outside, so outside it was.

Bernard thought that Brittany was trying to see how much she could get away with. She knew that he felt guilty about the Six Flags incident and was eating it up. Plus he always had a hard time telling his only child no.

That's why he couldn't believe that Diane went off like she did. She should've known that he would never intentionally let his baby girl down.

Just as soon as Bernard felt like he was about to have heatstroke, Brittany popped her little head out of the pink and white dollhouse.

"Daddy, I'm ready to go get the ice cream now."

He didn't remember promising her any ice cream, but since he was in the doghouse and had a little making up to do, ice cream it was.

Once they were outside and in Bernard's new truck, Brittany hit him with a thousand questions.

"Daddy, can I have ten dollars?"

"For what?"

"I'm saving for something for my birthday."

"Me and your momma are gonna buy your birthday presents. Did you make your list?"

"Yeah, but this is something special, just for me, that I want to pay for."

"Well, okay, I can't argue with that, birthday girl. Three more weeks and you'll be how old?" Bernard asked as he reached in his pocket and pulled out a ten-dollar bill.

"Nine."

"God almighty, girl. You're getting old. I'm going to have to buy you a walking cane for your birthday. Put you in the old girl's home or something."

"Uh-uh, I'm staying with Momma. Daddy, how much money do you make a week?"

"Why?"

"Because!" Brittany whined.

"Well, honey, that's pretty personal. Tell me why you need that information?"

"Daddddeeee. I just wanna know. Can you tell me, please?" Brittany said as she folded her crisp new ten-dollar bill and put it in her little pink see-through purse.

"Brittany, I don't want you running around asking people how much money they make. That's rude. Do you hear me?"

"Yes, Daddy, but I—"

"No buts. You got your ten dollars; now, no more talk about money."

"Momma mad at you, Daddy."

"Is she? She'll get over it. What about you, are you upset about me not taking you to Six Flags?"

"Momma told me not to say nothing to you about Six Flags, but why didn't you take me? 'Shay and Christina's daddies took them, and by the time me and Momma got there, they had already left."

"Brittany, I didn't say that I would take you, I said that I'd see. You know that I have to work on Saturdays sometimes, don't you?"

"You always work, Daddy. I like it when you're at home."

"I like it too, baby, but I can't make any money for all of your nice presents if I stay home all the time."

"You don't have to stay home all the time, just sometimes."

"Okay, I'll do better."

"Promise?"

"I promise."

They pulled up to the Dairy Queen's drive-through window. Brittany ordered a vanilla Heath sundae and Bernard ordered a plain old ice-cream cone. He had to admit, hanging out with his little girl felt good. They weren't ready to go home just yet, so they put the Expedition on the expressway. They drove down to the Sweet Auburn section of town and got out to walk around. Bernard showed her Martin Luther King's childhood home, then they went to The King Center, and after their little history lesson was done they headed down crowded Peachtree Street to grab a bite to eat at the Hard Rock Cafe near Underground Atlanta.

Sitting down talking with Brittany, Bernard learned all about her friends and interests. It wasn't until now that he realized how much time had gone by and how Daddy's little girl had grown. She didn't own up to having a boyfriend, though. He was happy to hear that news. Bernard thought he would have flipped his lid.

Diane was right: I needed to spend more time with my daughter. She's growing up without me and I live with her, he thought.

After they got their tummies full, they decided that it was time to call it a night. Brittany called home several times during their little outing, trying to catch Diane, but she never answered the phone. Brittany kept hitting redial on the cell phone, because she wanted all of them to have a family day.

Bernard assured her that this would not be the last opportunity that they would have to spend some time together as a family.

By the time they made it back out to their Fayette County home, it was near dark. Diane's car was in the garage, and when Bernard saw it he got a sinking feeling in his stomach. Stress! He didn't say anything to Brittany, but every time that she'd pushed the redial button, he'd prayed that Diane wouldn't pick up.

They walked into the house and Brittany ran up to her mother like she hadn't seen her in ages. They hugged and told each other how much they missed each other in that whole five or six hours since they had last seen each other. Diane said a dry "Hi" to Bernard and told Brittany to go get ready for bed.

Brittany walked over and gave her daddy a big hug, and asked him if he could tuck her in after she took her bath. He said that he would.

Diane said a sarcastic "Don't make her any promises that you can't keep."

Bernard ignored her.

Diane's not happy unless she's unhappy, Bernard thought. He told Brittany to give him a holler when she was ready to be tucked in.

Bernard walked over to the den and plopped down onto the sofa. He must have made some "I'm tired" sound because Diane walked into the room, looked at him, and shook her head.

"What's your problem?" he asked.

"I can't believe you can give Ford fifteen, sixteen hours a day, and you spend four or five hours with your daughter and you're huffing and puffing."

"I'm not huffin' or puffin'. You just need something to complain about. And true to form, if you can't find anything to fuss about, you make up something. Diane, leave me alone."

"Bernard, do you feel like talking?"

"No!" Bernard said, frustrated with his wife because time had taught him that talking to her meant agreeing with her. And he had just had a good day with his daughter and he didn't want to ruin it by arguing with Diane.

"Why are you getting so upset? I only asked if you wanted to talk. It's a yes-or-no question," Diane said as she sat down beside him.

"And I said no. And I'm not getting upset. You see, Diane, that's just it—I will not let you get me upset today with all of your whining and complaining. Now, if you want to sit down in here and enjoy a television program with me, then get comfortable. But if you wanna fuss, get lost."

"Bernard, are you interested in how I've been feeling lately?"

Didn't I just tell her that I didn't want to talk? This is exactly what I'm talking about. She doesn't give a damn if I'm in the mood for conversation or not. Selfish ass! Bernard thought.

If he didn't respond to Diane when she wanted to talk, then that would always lead to an argument. She would start yelling at the top of her lungs, so Bernard got into the habit of saying that he would talk just to keep the peace. He decided to pacify his wife again tonight.

"Diane, how have you been feeling lately?" Bernard asked, not really caring what her answer might be.

"Don't ask if you really don't care." Diane knew her husband well. She could tell by his expression that he wasn't interested in what she had to say.

"Diane, how have you been feeling lately?" Bernard repeated.

"Like I'm not being loved the way I feel I need to be loved."

"And how do you need to be loved, because we don't want Diane to feel any discomfort. So tell me how you need to be loved."

"Well, I need to be held sometimes and told that I'm special.

I need to be kissed, caressed, and I need to make love to my husband sometimes. I haven't felt that in a while," Diane said in a soft voice.

"Well, Diane, are you interested in my needs?"

"Bernard, we're talking about my needs right now. Why do you always try to turn things around?" Diane whined in a louder voice.

"Diane, when we got married it stopped being me and you. It's about us. And what you're feeling has something to do with us, not just you."

"But I'm the one that's hurting; you couldn't care less."

"If you believe that, then you really haven't been paying much attention to me over the last ten years. Just like I've always said, it's all about you, Diane."

"How could you say that? I'm always trying to come to you to talk. If it were up to you, we'd never talk."

"No, you come to me to listen to your gripes and complaints. Do you know why you have two ears and one mouth? So that you can listen twice as much as you talk. You should try it sometime," Bernard said.

"*You* should try it," Diane snapped back. "You've always got to get the last word. Well, it's not about the last word, it's about understanding!" Diane was already starting to yell.

"You want everyone to understand you, but you don't take the time to understand anyone else. Like I said, Diane, it's all about you. You should try a different approach, maybe you'll get different results."

"What do you mean a different approach?"

"Diane, you act as if the world revolves around you. You think the grass doesn't get green until you get up in the morning. You'll always be unhappy until you learn to take less and give a little more. Now, I've got to get some rest. I have a job."

"What about our lovemaking? Are you no longer attracted to me?"

"On the outside you're pretty as a rose; it's the inside that turns me off."

"Oh, so now I turn you off."

"Diane, if you think you can keep putting a man down and calling him all kinds of names, then turn around and want him to be all hugged up against you, talking 'bout 'I sho do love you!' then you have another thing coming."

"I say some things when I'm upset, but you do the same thing."

"You don't act a fool then turn around and want someone to treat you like your butt don't stink," Bernard said.

"I guess everything that I did three weeks ago was for me too, huh?"

"Yes! You wanted something. You didn't just do that because you'd like to see me eat a nice meal by candlelight. You did that for a reaction. Now, don't get me wrong, I appreciated it, but you only do stuff like that when you want something. Pay attention to yourself sometimes, you'll see."

"What about you, Bernard? When will you do something nice for me? You don't pay me any attention. You come in the house and go straight to the basement and fall asleep in the chair. Do you know I can't remember the last time that we went to bed together?"

"What? Everything I do is for your comfort, but the more I give, the more you want. When you were pregnant with Brittany, you said that you didn't want to work while you were pregnant and I worked two jobs so that you could stay at home. But then, just like now, you complained about me not being home. You wanted a bigger house, so I worked overtime so that we could get a nicer place, but that wasn't good enough for you either. I'm at a loss. I'm confused. What does it take to make my wife happy?"

"Balance," Diane said, and walked away without saying another word.

Ten minutes later Brittany called for Bernard to tuck her in. He trotted upstairs and into her room. He kissed his little princess on her forehead and told her that he'd really enjoyed himself today. She asked him if he remembered his promise about spending more time with her. He told her that he did and pulled the sheets up. After they said their prayers, Bernard turned her night-light on. As he was leaving Brittany's room, Diane was leaving theirs. She was all dressed up. He asked her where was she going.

"I'm going over to the church."

"Diane, it's eight o'clock in the evening. Since when did you start going to church this time of night?"

"We're going into the prisons tomorrow and we need to discuss some things about the ministries; now, move, Bernard. It's not like you're going to miss me," Diane said as she walked around Bernard and trotted downstairs.

"Okay, just try to make it home before five o'clock, because some of us have to work."

Diane was walking away but Bernard heard her mumble under her breath, "God knows we don't want you to be late for the big Ford plantation."

He thought about what she had said for a second and started to let her know that it was that Ford plantation that was paying for everything they had. And it was that Ford plantation that was paying for that car she was about to get into. But he let it go. He felt good letting it go.

Bernard took a shower and put on his pajamas. He walked into Brittany's room, lay on the floor, and went to sleep.

8

I Got Your Back

Prodigy was running late again, but it wasn't the job this time. He was supposed to pick up Blake about thirty minutes before.

Today was Brittany's birthday and Poppa Doc was throwing a big shebang for her at his house. Prodigy promised his little homie that he would take him for getting a good conduct report for a full week.

Blake was a kid from the youth center. He was only six years old, but that little rascal was something else. The whole youth center was off the hook; the little kids up in there were crazier than all of Bellevue put together. Prodigy had tried to get Jermaine to come, but he kept telling him that he didn't have the patience for all of those badass kids.

Whatever!

Poppa Doc didn't tell Prodigy that it was going to be like a second job. They called what he did youth counseling. But sometimes, some of the kids on his team needed him after-hours, so he found himself putting in just as much time at the center as he did at GMAC.

Prodigy had gotten pretty close to this little Blake guy. He saw so much of himself in the little guy and he couldn't help but gravitate toward him. Blake was the youngest kid in the entire center. Actually he should not have been there. The program was for ten-to-sixteen-year-olds. Blake came to the center every day with a kid named Trevon, from his home near the projects. And since there wasn't one person in the entire center who could resist his charm, he stayed.

Blake was a little comedian in the making. He followed Prodigy around all day saying things like: "Mr. P, when you gonna hook me up with a girl? I see how all these ladies around here be sweating you. Hook ya little homie up with the ones you don't want. I seen Mrs. Lanatha rubbin' on ya bald head the other day. I'm 'bout to cut all mines off. I wonder if she'll rub on it for me. You know I like older girls." The boy was only six years old. Prodigy had to take a couple of the kids home every night because most of their daddies were missing in action and a lot of the mothers didn't have cars or had something else going on.

Blake's daddy was another MIA, and his mother went to school during the day and worked at night. So Blake spent most of his time with his Aunt Cathy.

Every night when Prodigy was passing the drug dealers, addicts, and prostitutes who were fixtures on the corner of Blake's street, near the violent East Lake Meadows projects, he found himself saying a silent prayer that none of the fools standing on the corner would send a stray bullet through Blake's first-floor bedroom window.

Prodigy finally made it over to Blake's house and saw his tooth-picklike body sitting outside in the heat, crying. When Blake saw Prodigy's truck pull up, he ran and jumped in before Prodigy could shift to park.

He hopped in, looking a bit nervous and trying to hold back his tears, so Prodigy asked him what the problem was.

"He hit me in my face and took my chain," Blake said, showing Prodigy a little cut under his left eye.

"Who hit you?" Prodigy asked, as he touched his little friend's caramel-colored face.

"Barry!"

"Who's Barry?"

"This dude that's always messing with me. He's bigger than me and he's always taking my stuff. I'm tired of him; one day I'ma get me a gun and shoot that fool's brains out. I swear I am," Blake said, losing the fight with his tears.

Prodigy didn't like to hear his little friend talking about guns so casually and he told him so. "Blake, if you have a problem with someone you deal with it without guns. And if they come at you with violence then you go and get someone that can handle it. Are we clear?"

"But he—"

"It's not up for discussion, Blake. Are we clear?"

"Yes."

"Now, stop crying! When did this happen?"

"Just now, at the playground, while I was waiting on you. He told me that I couldn't come out there anymore until I was ready to fight. I can't beat none of them up. I'll be glad when my momma move us outta here," Blake said, looking like life was over.

"Okay, little homie, show me where the playground is," Prodigy said as he parked his truck and jumped out.

They walked around to the back of the building where the playground was located. There were about ten guys hanging around the swings. Prodigy asked Blake to show him which one of the thugs had taken his chain, but Blake wasn't giving him up. So Prodigy walked over to the one talking the loudest and asked him who'd taken his little partner's chain.

"Who wants to know and what's it to ya, strange man?" a tall lanky guy with about thirty-two gold teeth said as he stood up.

"I wanna know. Because I'm getting it back," Prodigy said calmly.

"Well, everybody out here got on chains, so maybe if his little punk ass wanna point out who got it, then I might be able to get it back. I ain't making no promises, though," the tall lanky guy said for the amusement of his friends.

Prodigy looked at Blake, who looked away. He was understandably afraid of the bigger boys and realized that he had to live there long after Prodigy left.

"Look here, fella, my little friend ain't talking, so I'm gonna ask you who took it, and if I don't get a satisfactory answer then I'm taking yours, comprende?" Prodigy got in the tall boy's face, close enough for him to smell what he'd eaten for breakfast.

The tall boy backed up a step, and just as he was about to say something that would've gotten him a severe beat-down, a familiar face stepped out from around the side of the building.

"P-man, what up, folk? I saw ya truck out front. What brings you to my 'hood?" Steve asked as he walked over to where Prodigy was standing.

Steve was one of Uncle Ray's workers a couple of years back when they did the hot-car thing. Prodigy had always liked Steve. He thought that Steve had principles, yet he could get off into some of the illest of things if the opportunity presented itself.

Prodigy shook his hand, gave him a frat-brother-like hug, and said, "One of these soft-ass nuts took my little man's chain and hit him in his eye."

"Who yo' homie?" Steve asked, looking around for a new face.

"Little Blake over there," Prodigy said as he pointed at Blake, who was looking like he would rather be anywhere but there.

"You must be hittin' his momma."

"Nah, I met him over at the youth center."

"You done left the bank?"

"Nah, I still work there. I go over to the center after work and do some mentoring."

"Damn, folk, you got two jobs?"

"Basically."

"Yo, P, if times are hard for ya, I got some work. Just say the word."

"I appreciate the offer, but I'm straight."

"Youth center. That's right up yo' alley. The way all of those kids used to be hounding yo' ass over at the shop. Nigga, you shoulda been a teacher or somethin'," Steve said.

"You know how I do," Prodigy said.

"They always fucking wit' lil' Blake 'round here. They only do that to make his ol' fine momma come out here and slap one upside they knotty heads. Little horny bastards." Steve turned to the crowd and asked, "Who took his chain?"

No one said anything, so he asked again. "I said, who took Blake's shit?" Again, silence. "Okay, P, ain't nobody man enough to speak up, so you can just take any chain you like. Get a nice one too."

Prodigy smiled and walked over to the tall boy with the loud mouth, who by now had taken a seat on the bottom of the sliding board. Prodigy stood over him, pulling him to his feet by the thick gold chain that was dangling from his neck.

The tall boy started to say something, but Steve stopped him. "Shut the fuck up! You had yo' chance to talk."

Prodigy told him to take it off, and the tall boy reached for a small one that had a gold *B* as its charm. Prodigy took it and handed it to Blake, then told the boy to give him the other two. The tall boy looked to Steve to see if he was going to say anything, but all he got was "You heard him, muthafucka, hurry up. I told y'all little asses, what comes around goes around, didn't I? Now, if I hear of any of you bastards fucking with Blake again, I'ma bust a cap. And if ya think I'm playin', try me. Now, this nigga right here's name is Prodigy and he ain'ts ta be fucked wit'. So when you see him around heah, show some respect."

Prodigy asked Steve which one of the boys was Barry, and just as he guessed, it was the tall loudmouth with all the gold teeth.

"How old are you?" Prodigy asked Barry.

"Eighteen," Barry mumbled.

"Don't you think you a little too old to be hitting on a six-year-old?"

"I was just playing with him," Barry said, looking down at the ground.

"Look at me when I'm talking to you." Barry lifted his head up and Prodigy nailed him with a hard right hook that dropped him on his skinny little bottom. He looked like he was thinking about getting up, but quickly changed his mind.

"Next time you wanna play with somebody, call me," Prodigy said, as he stood over Barry. He grabbed Barry's shirt to pull him to his feet.

Prodigy tossed Barry's two chains back at him. They hit him in the head, then fell to the ground.

Prodigy stepped away from Barry and walked over to where Steve and Blake were. "Yo, Steve, I need a favor."

"You name it, baby, and it's done."

"Make sure these thugs find someplace else to hang out. I

damn near ran over someone's kid coming in here today. Now I see why they play in the streets—the playgrounds are taken."

Without a second thought, Steve turned around and shouted, "Move out and don't none of y'all bring ya lil' black asses 'round here no mo'! Bye," Steve said as they silently filed out.

"Blake, you gotta learn how to fight, lil' man," Steve said.

"You know what, Steve, fighting ain't happening. Let these kids be kids."

"Look who's talking, a bald-headed Rocky Balboa. It ain't even been five minutes since you done coldcocked somebody and you talking about nonviolence. I hear ya, Martin Luther."

"Oh, I was just playing wit' him. Isn't that what he said he was doing with Blake?" They laughed a little, but both of them knew nothing was funny.

"I don't know what I'm talking about. These lil' youngstas don't even know how to get 'em up no mo'. It's all gun play. But lil' man still needs to learn how to throw them thangs, cuz you ain't always gonna be there to knock a nigga out for him. Ya heard me! So teach the boy a jab or two, he'll be a'ight."

"I feel you. So you the man around here, huh?"

"Nah, man, I ain't shit. I just come around to collect my loot and then I'm out. This place is fucked up, dog. That's why they call it Lil' Vietnam, and that's why those kids act like that. They ain't ever been taught to love. Don't know love, can't show love. I'll probably have to pop a cap in one of them lil' fools that I just ran off, you watch. So you say you still at the bank? Let's set up a quick robbery—I'll give you half the score," Steve said, half joking.

"It's not a bank, it's a finance company, and you know better than to come at me with that nonsense."

"Just checkin', baby, just checkin'," Steve said.

"So what's up with you these days, Steve?"

"I'm into pharmaceuticals. Here, give me a call," Steve said, handing Prodigy a business card from Big B Drugstore with his pager number typed on it.

Prodigy smiled, shook his head at Steve's terminology for his drug sales, and took the card. "I see you're still crazy. But I'm gonna have to holla at you later."

"P, how ya uncle doin'?"

"He's straight. What about your people?"

"All is well, my man. Look here, don't be no stranger. Holla at me sometimes. You got the number, use it."

As Blake and Prodigy walked around the building to his truck, Prodigy noticed Blake's little chest was sticking out a tad bit farther than before. He smiled and was happy for him. Blake was an only child and had no one to stand up for him, but that had just changed. Poppa Doc would've said that Prodigy handled that situation totally wrong; but he figured, sometimes you have to fight fire with fire.

As they were about to get into the truck, Blake's mother, Nina, was standing in her doorway and called out for them to come over.

Prodigy had met Blake's Aunt Cathy before and had talked with Nina on the phone daily for the last three weeks, but this was his first time actually meeting her. As he approached, he couldn't help but notice how beautiful she was. She looked like she was mixed with some culture from an exotic island. She seemed out of place in this dismal environment. She stood about five feet eight inches tall, with long, jet-black hair that was pulled back in a ponytail. Her cinnamon complexion was flawless, and she had the whitest, straightest teeth that he'd ever seen on any human this side of the Mason-Dixon line. And those dark brown eyes were hypnotic.

Blake spoke up. "Momma, I thought you were sleeping."

"I was, until I heard all of that racket out back; and what happened to your eye, young man?"

"Nothing," Blake lied.

"Nothing? Okay, nothing. Well, take nothing in the house and put some peroxide on it," Nina said, then turned to Prodigy. "So I finally get to put a face to the voice of that man who has my son wanting a bald head. Do you have time to come in for a soda or something?" Nina asked.

"Sure," Prodigy said as he walked into the two-bedroom apartment. Their place was spotless. It also seemed out of place. It was as if you put a Bentley Azure in a junkyard. And their apartment was nice and cool, unlike all of the other homes on the block, which had their windows heisted and a fan blowing the hot air in. Nina had pictures of Blake going through his different stages of life, in custom African frames sitting over a makeshift fireplace. There was an oriental-like throw rug over the tile floor.

Prodigy took a seat on the cream-colored couch and waited for his beverage. Nina returned, handed him a fruit punch, and sat in a chair across from him.

"I thought Cathy said that you would be here at five. You're a couple of hours early."

"Oh no, I called last night and asked if it would be alright if I came by a little earlier so that Blake could make him some extra cash working on my lawn."

"Cathy didn't tell me that, but that's Cathy. Her mind comes and goes. You must have money to give away, because this is about the laziest child that I've ever seen. Isn't that right, Blake?" Nina said to her son, who had just taken a seat beside Prodigy on the couch.

"No. I do stuff around here."

"Like what?"

Blake smiled and said, "I clean up."

"Whatever! Mr. Banks, I—"

"Prodigy! Call me Prodigy."

"Okay, Prodigy, I have some reservations about letting my

son go somewhere alone with somewhat of a stranger. I know that—"

"Ah, Mom, you said . . ." Blake started, but Nina held up a finger and he was instantly quiet.

"I understand, and I totally agree with you. As a matter of fact, I would worry about you if you weren't at least a little concerned," Prodigy said. "But he's in good hands. And you're more than welcome to join us."

"No, I—"

"Here, take my home, cell, and pager numbers. Just in case you start missing him like y'all mothers do."

Nina took the paper that Prodigy had scribbled all of his numbers on and said, "I saw you guys out the window a few minutes ago. What was that all about?"

"Somebody took his chain, so I got it back."

"Who took his chain?"

"Some little knucklehead, but we got it back. It's a done deal."

"Well, thank you. He's always running in here crying about something, but then before I can turn around good, he's back outside."

"He's a little boy and that's how little boys are. Are you sure you don't want to join us? Poppa Doc makes a mean potato soufflé."

"Nah, I don't wanna spoil his fun by having Mommy around, and I have to study for this exam that I have early Monday morning."

"Mom, can you come, please? I'll help you study like I did last time," Blake said, dropping to his knees and putting his hands together, begging.

Prodigy and Nina looked at each other and shook their heads. They both knew that Blake had a way of getting what he wanted.

Nina asked Prodigy if he was sure, and he said of course.

Fifteen minutes later they all piled into Prodigy's truck and headed back to his place.

Once they pulled into his driveway and got out of the truck, Blake ran around the house and came back frowning and complaining about how many leaves he had to rake for ten dollars. Nina looked at Prodigy and gave him an "I told you so" look.

"Blake, how much do you think you should be paid to rake those little bit of leaves?" Prodigy asked.

Blake did a quick survey of the yard and calculated. "Umm, twenty dollars for the front and back. And you're helping. How long do we have before we have to leave?"

"If we start now we can get a good two hours in before we need to start getting ready."

"Alright, twenty dollars and you have yourself a deal."

"Twenty if you do it alone. If I help, then I'm cutting down half of your work so you get half the pay," Prodigy said as he looked over at Nina, who was shaking her head and mouthing, "Lazy."

"Aw, come on, Mr. P, I think I should get that extra ten just cuz it's so hot out here."

"Okay, you little swindler. I'll get the rakes. Do you know how to rake?"

"Yeah, I rake all the time."

"Blake, stop telling tales," Nina said as she sat down on the front step.

"I ain't telling no tales, Momma. I raked the dirt at Grandpa's, I put them lines in it."

"Okay, dirt raker, you go ahead and get started. I'll go let your mom in the house to get her out of the hot sun."

Prodigy opened the door and almost lost his mind.

Jermaine was laid out on the floor in his underwear and a T-shirt, drunk. The smoke detector was screaming for everyone to leave the house. Jermaine had left some grease on the stove, and the house was full of a suffocating dark gray smoke.

If Prodigy hadn't come home when he did, Jermaine would have surely been cooked to his final destination.

Prodigy rushed in the kitchen and turned off the stove. He took the hot pot out of the back door and threw it on the ground. Jermaine stumbled into the kitchen and asked, "Did my french fries burn up?"

Nina turned on the ceiling fan and started opening the windows to let the smoke out. Prodigy snatched Jermaine up by his T-shirt and thought about punching him in his face, but after seeing the condition that he was in, he told him to go to bed.

Shoes, CDs, and clothes were everywhere. But Nina didn't seem to mind; as a matter of fact she went right into cleanup mode as if the place were hers.

Prodigy liked that. She seemed really nice and down-to-earth.

Between the both of them, Prodigy and Nina got the place looking halfway decent again. Prodigy yelled out the window to tell Blake that he was on his own. He told him that he would give him a tip if he did a good job. Blake smiled and raked even harder.

Nina asked Prodigy if he minded if she played a CD while she straightened up, and he told her to make herself at home. Carl Thomas provided the tunes while Prodigy cleaned the black soot from his white kitchen cabinets with a bottle of Tilex. Nina tidied up the living room.

9

You Wanna Fight?

Prodigy, Blake, and Nina stopped at Lenox Square Mall to pick up a gift for Brittany. Since Prodigy didn't have a clue what to buy for the birthday girl, he asked Blake.

"Blake, what would a girl want for her ninth birthday?"

"Me," Blake said, with a smile.

"Alright, boy, stop showing off," Nina said.

"I should've known not to ask you. Nina, what do you think?" Prodigy asked.

"Do you know what she's into? Birthdays should be for fun gifts, things that make you smile."

"Okay, but you just complicated things. I don't know what Brittany likes. Why don't I just give her some money?"

"That's such a male thing to do. What's the budget?"

"Oh, I don't know, about one-fifty," Prodigy said, not wanting to be too cheap, but not sure if he'd overdone it. Nina didn't indicate one way or the other. She just reached out her hand and Prodigy handed over the plastic.

"Oh, you wouldn't happen to know her size, would you?" Nina asked.

Prodigy looked around the mall and found a little girl that looked to be about Brittany's size. "About that size," he said, pointing to the little girl.

"Why don't you guys find something to do for the next forty-five minutes. I'll meet y'all back here at the food court at five-thirty."

"Cool, let's go to the arcade, Mr. P, and play that football game," Blake said.

"What, Madden 2000? You can't see me on that game, boy," Prodigy said, but he knew he didn't stand a chance with the little crumb-snatcher.

"We'll see. I'ma beat the taste out of your mouth!" Blake said, nodding his head. "It's on."

Nina shook her head as if to say, "Oh my God. Boys will be boys," and walked off. Prodigy and Blake headed in the opposite direction.

One hour and about ten losses later, Prodigy walked out of the arcade with Blake on his back into the food court to find Nina sitting at the waterfall with two neatly wrapped gifts, sipping a banana smoothie.

"Sorry, I lost track of time," Prodigy lied. "What did you get?"

"I found this cute little Lady FUBU shorts set and a gold bracelet that she can add charms to. And I got it all for one hundred and thirty-one dollars. But we still have to get her a card. I would've got one but I didn't want you guys waiting on me," Nina said, handing Prodigy his card and credit card receipt, signed "Nina Banks."

That was about the most considerate thing that he'd heard

from a woman in a long time. He intentionally stayed in the arcade longer because he assumed that she was like most other women in a mall with a credit card.

Blake said that he needed some new sneakers, and Prodigy promised him that he would get him a pair after his next progress report. Nina protested and said that although she appreciated his generosity to her son, she would be doing all of the buying for Blake.

"Sorry, Blake," Prodigy said, as he shrugged his shoulders.

When they arrived on Poppa Doc's street, cars were everywhere. They parked at the end of the block and walked up the long, winding driveway. Blake caught another piggyback ride from Prodigy. Nina shook her head and told him to stop spoiling her baby.

Once they made it to the house, you could hear the thump of music playing in the backyard and the smell of the grill. So they followed the beat until they reached the food.

Prodigy was talking to Nina and Blake and wasn't paying much attention to where he was walking. He turned the corner and bumped right into Bernard.

Bernard looked at him, said something snobbish under his breath, and shook his head as he thought, *What the hell is he doing here?*

Prodigy ignored him like he always did.

Nina looked as though she wanted to ask what had just happened, but Prodigy's lack of response made her let it go.

Diane was the first to greet them, and she gave Prodigy an uncharacteristic hug.

"Hey, boy, I haven't seen you in a month of Sundays. Where have you been?" Diane asked.

Prodigy wasn't used to this type of treatment from her. Usually she was pretty distant toward him, sort of how Bernard used to be before he showed his ass in Poppa Doc's basement a couple of weeks ago. Prodigy played it off as if her behavior was nothing abnormal.

"I've just been working and doing some mentoring over at this new youth center. This is my friend Blake and his mother, Nina," he said, as he introduced them.

Prodigy felt good to have a job and to be doing something positive that could change someone's life for the better. He thought back to just a couple of years ago, when he would have had to scramble or get creative when someone asked him what he did for a living.

"Yeah, I heard that you were over there doing some wonderful things. You know, Daddy raves about you all the time, but don't tell him that I said that."

"He'd just deny it anyway. Is Michael here?" Prodigy asked, changing the subject. He wasn't really comfortable talking to Bernard's wife at such length, even if it was a party.

"I haven't seen him, but he'll probably show up later on. You know that boy is going to be late for his own funeral."

Diane shook Nina's hand, pinched Blake on the cheek, and commented on how cute he was.

"Prodigy, you're going to have to keep this young lady around so that I can do like they did in the old days and arrange a wedding for this little handsome fella and Brittany," Diane said, assuming that Nina and Prodigy were a couple.

"So, Nina, where did you meet Prodigy?" Diane asked, but before Nina could answer, "The Electric Slide" came on. Diane told her to hold that thought, and rushed off to the area where all of the old folks were simultaneously moving to the music. Mrs. Ethel was even out there sliding.

Brittany was radiating with beauty. Her long, braided hair went every which way as she ran over to greet Prodigy and his guests. She was wearing an all-white shorts set. She gave Prodigy a hug at the waist and introduced herself to Nina like a little lady. Prodigy realized that she and Blake were about the same age, so he asked her if she could take him to play with her and her friends. She agreed and grabbed Blake's hand, and they were off on their merry little way. Blake shot a quick look back at Prodigy and nodded his head, like "Thanks for the hookup." Prodigy gave him a wink back; Nina saw what was transpiring and playfully punched Prodigy on the arm, then shook her finger at Blake.

"I don't know about you, Mr. Banks. You have my son trying to be a little player," Nina said.

"Don't put that on me. I couldn't have possibly taught that little cat all those moves in less than a month. Somebody else is to blame for that one."

"Well, stop encouraging him," Nina said, smiling and shaking her head.

"I don't know. The way that he has women pulling on him, he might be able to teach me a thing or two," Prodigy said.

"Oh, I'm sure you have your share of women pulling on you," Nina responded.

"You'd be surprised," Prodigy said, thinking about how silent his telephone had been lately.

Poppa Doc walked over to where they were standing and introduced himself. "Winston Fuller! I'm this here boy's daddy," Poppa Doc said as he took Nina's hand and kissed it, looking at Prodigy like he was saying, "Eat your heart out."

Nina turned to look at both of them to see if she noticed any resemblance. She didn't, but she didn't say anything.

Poppa Doc, still holding Nina's hand, saw what she was doing and said, "I know he's not as good-looking as me, but we won't hold that against him."

"Nina, he left his glasses in the house, so please forgive him," Prodigy responded.

Mrs. Ethel walked over to fill the punch bowl and to give Prodigy a hug. As Prodigy was hugging her he glanced over her shoulder at Poppa Doc and returned his eat-your-heart-out look. Poppa Doc turned his head and waved him off.

Prodigy introduced Mrs. Ethel to Nina.

Poppa Doc said, "Ethel, I'm trying to find out what would make a beautiful woman like this young lady here wanna hang out with the likes of this knucklehead?"

"Oh, honey, don't pay him any attention. Prodigy's a good boy and just as sweet as he can be," Mrs. Ethel said to Nina. "It was nice meeting you, but I have to run and get these kids' plates ready."

"Do you need any help?" Nina asked Mrs. Ethel.

"No, chile, you enjoy yourself. Winston just used my baby's birthday party as an excuse to have him one and he hasn't lifted a finger," Mrs. Ethel said, looking at Poppa Doc, who looked the other way, smiling.

"So back to you, Nina. Are you okay? I mean, you hanging out with this guy is bad for your image."

"He seems to be alright," Nina said as she looked up at Prodigy.

Prodigy already liked her style. She was elegant and beautiful, with a good sense of humor and a touch of street smarts.

"Now see, I can save you some time. He's trying to woo you. Don't let him fool you," Poppa Doc said, and Prodigy could tell that he had already had one beer too many.

"So he's faking me out with all that gentleman stuff, huh?" Nina asked, enjoying his company.

"Yeah that's all a game. He's worthless and you can't believe a word he tells you. He calls me and says that he's coming over, and I see him a week later. Can't shoot pool to save his live. Owes me money and won't pay me. And that's just the small stuff. Come here, let me tell you the kicker," Poppa Doc said, as he pulled Nina away from Prodigy, all the while looking at him like he was about to give away some big secret.

"Now, wait a minute, if this is your son, then who taught him all of those wooing ways?" Nina asked.

"You know kids don't listen no mo'. I tried my best, but he just hardheaded. No, I'm just kidding, this is my boy," Poppa Doc said, rubbing Prodigy's head like he was a four-year-old at a T-ball game.

"You have a lovely home here," Nina said, changing the subject.

"Thank you, we enjoy it. I'll make sure that Prodigy gives you a tour before you guys leave. But right now the night is still young and I feel like dancing. Now, I don't accept no no's, so let's leave this bad-looking fella over here by himself while we dance the night away. He's making us look bad anyway," Poppa Doc said as he grabbed Nina's hand and led her to the dance floor.

Prodigy was left standing alone by the refreshments. He took a seat and watched them do that corny Electric Slide over and over again.

How long are people going to be doing that boring-ass dance? he wondered.

Blake ran over in his socks to where Prodigy was sitting. He was breathing hard, like he had just finished a mile relay. He got some fruit punch.

"Blake, where are your shoes?" Prodigy asked, sounding like a father.

"Oh, they got this big ol' air balloon thing that we're jumping up and down in and you got to take your shoes off. I thought *you* had a bad house, but this is a mansion," Blake exclaimed, as he ran back off to play. He was obviously having a good time.

Out of nowhere, Bernard appeared behind Prodigy.

"I don't remember seeing your name on the guest list," he said.

Once again Prodigy ignored him. He was there to have a good time, and he wasn't about to play his games.

"How could you show up at my daughter's party? You come around here hugging on her and bearing gifts like you're some damn family friend."

"I am a family friend. You're the only one around here that has a problem with me," Prodigy said.

"Brittany is my daughter, and until she's eighteen, I say who her friends are, and you're not one of them."

"Man, what is your problem?" Prodigy said, and sat in his chair looking straight ahead.

"You are my problem, and everyone like you."

"What's that supposed to mean, Bernard?"

"I hate takers. I've been working since day one, young man. And I've never taken anything that didn't belong to me in my life. So when people like you come around, it sickens me to my stomach. Every time I see you, I think about my daughter and my mother-in-law being left stranded in the cold, while you and your criminal-ass friends rode around town like everything was hunky-dory."

"You know what, Bernard, if I was as ruthless as you try to make me out to be, do you think that I would still be putting up with your shit? Besides, I didn't take the car, I returned it."

"It doesn't matter if you pulled the trigger or not, you're still guilty as sin."

"I tell you what, you keep harping on something that happened damn near three years ago. I'm done with explaining myself to your uptight ass."

"Son, you have a lot to learn about life. When you have children you'll understand things a whole lot better and you might see where I'm coming from."

"I already see where you're coming from, Bernard. What happened was wrong, and I did everything that I could do to make it right, except kiss your ass."

"You don't need to kiss my ass, that's not what I want."

"Then what do you want, Bernard?" Prodigy asked.

"I want you to stay away," Bernard said.

"That ain't happening," Prodigy said flatly.

"Then you better be prepared, because one day I might not be able to control myself when I see you," Bernard calmly threatened.

"Then you're gonna have some problems!" Prodigy shot back just as calmly.

"You think I'm playing with you, don't you?" Bernard asked.

"I don't give a damn what you're doing!" Prodigy said, no longer interested in the diplomatic approach.

Bernard stormed around the refreshment table toward Prodigy. Prodigy stood up. It seemed like right now was the culmination of nearly three years of frustration on both of their parts. They were almost nose to nose. But today would not be the day for them to prove how ignorant they could be, because Poppa Doc walked between them with Nina following on his coattails.

Poppa Doc sized up the situation, and not wanting any drama at his granddaughter's birthday party he said, "Prodigy, I need for you to go in the kitchen and get some ice. Take Nina with you and show her the house."

Bernard looked at Poppa Doc like he was crazy for letting Prodigy go into the house by himself. "I hope you have some hidden cameras in place or a good insurance policy," Bernard said as he walked away.

Nina looked at Prodigy, as if to ask what that was supposed to mean, but he told her not to worry about it and grabbed her hand, leading her toward the house.

"Bernard, give it a rest. I sure would hate to kick you out of your own daughter's party, but I'll do it. Now, I told you a hundred times to leave it alone. If you don't like Prodigy, then just don't say anything to him, but I'm about tired of this shit," Poppa Doc said, as he caught up with Bernard.

"It's very difficult for me to be in the same place as the man who snatched my daughter out of a car and left her on the side of the road to freeze to death. Anything could've happened to her out there," Bernard said.

"He did not snatch Brittany out of the car. He wasn't even there."

"That's what he says. If he didn't do it, he had something to do with it, and that's enough for him to be my enemy for life," Bernard said, fuming.

"I'm sorry to hear that, Bernard. You have to remember that my wife was in that same car, and I love Brittany more than life itself. But I got over it and you should do the same. It does nobody any good for you to act up every time that boy comes around. He's a good kid. You should try to get to know him and I believe you'll feel the same way."

"I doubt that. I really do."

"Does it make you feel better to hate him?"

"In a way it does. I just don't understand that generation. They have ten times more than I had growing up and probably twenty times more than you, but they act like the world owes them something."

"Whose fault do you think that is? It damn sure ain't theirs. Kids can't raise themselves; somebody had to neglect their responsibility somewhere."

"I never had a daddy, and I haven't seen my mother in over twenty years. So I'm not buying that."

"Bernard, you're an exception, and you've done good for yourself and your family, but pointing fingers is not the answer. Now you have to learn how to forgive and forget."

"I'll work on forgiving, but I'll never forget."

"That's a start," Poppa Doc said. "Now, let's enjoy this party.

Hey, and look here! I want us to have a sit-down tonight and establish some dialogue."

Prodigy walked Nina through the house, looking at this and that. She complimented everything from the carpet to the crystal. Once they made it to Brittany's room and Prodigy told her that Brittany didn't even live there, Nina couldn't help but be jealous. She dropped her head and wondered when would she be able to provide a place like this for her son. She leaned against the door and closed her eyes. Prodigy walked over to her and touched her shoulder. He didn't know what the problem was, but he wanted to let her know that everything would be alright.

"I'm sorry. It's just that things are really hard for me right now. I'm working full-time and going to school full-time, to try and give my son a nice place to lay his head. But right now it's sacrifice time, and it's not easy by a long shot. I'm always broke, and this home just seems like a fantasy."

"Is there anything that I can do?" Prodigy asked.

"I'll be alright. It's nothing."

"Are you sure?"

"Yeah. Let's go get that ice."

They were walking down the stairs with Prodigy in front of Nina. She started laughing. He stopped midway down the stairs, turned to her, and asked her why was she laughing.

"Are you sensitive?" Nina asked.

"About what?"

"Your peanut head," she said, laughing.

"Oh, you just gonna talk about my head. Okay airbag lips."

"Oh no you didn't!" Nina said, covering her lips.

"Just kidding! You have nice lips."

"Oh, now you wanna flirt!"

"Complimenting is not flirting."

"Well, thank you anyway, peanut."

Once they were in the kitchen, Nina sat at the table while Prodigy filled the cooler with ice.

Nina said, "I hope I'm not getting too personal, but what's the deal with you and that light-skinned guy? It looked like you guys were about to get physical."

For some reason Prodigy felt like he'd known Nina for years. She just had that thing about her that made people comfortable.

This thing called life never ceases to amaze me. Here I am about to spill my guts to someone that I've known for only a couple of hours, yet I can't bring myself to share things with people that I've known all my life, he thought.

He told her the whole story of why Bernard acted the way that he did toward him. She surprised him by agreeing with Bernard. She said that he would eventually come around to forgiving him and that Prodigy should be patient with him.

Prodigy listened and tried to understand what she was saying. But he was still thinking, *Damn Bernard.*

They made it back out to the party and danced. They were in the middle of a song when Poppa Doc came over and took her away. Prodigy shook his head and searched for Mrs. Ethel. When he couldn't find her, he pulled Brittany on the floor and danced to a song by Lil Bow Wow.

Nina gave Prodigy the cue that she was getting tired, so he told Poppa Doc that they'd enjoyed themselves but it was time for them to move on.

Poppa Doc thanked them for coming, then he pulled Prodigy aside and told him that he needed to take Nina and Blake home and come back for a sit-down with Bernard.

Prodigy didn't feel like taking that long drive, but he knew that Poppa Doc only asked for something when it was really important. So he agreed to be back in an hour.

They pulled up to Nina's house a little after nine. It was already dark and Blake must have jumped himself out, because he was in the backseat snoring like a grown man.

Prodigy and Nina sat there speechless for a moment, not knowing what to say. This was not exactly a date, yet they had had fun together. Both of them wanted to see the other again but they were both tired of relationships.

Maybe we could just be really good friends, Prodigy thought.

He never thought he would find himself thinking something like that. Especially about someone as fine as Nina.

He turned in his seat and looked at Blake resting peacefully. He volunteered to carry him into the apartment to keep from waking him.

Nina sat motionless, just staring out into the night.

"Is everything alright?" Prodigy asked.

"Just don't wanna take my son back to this place. Brittany has two rooms in two different houses, and my son has never even had his own room in the one that we have. I've got to make some changes. That's why I work so hard and go to school so much, because he deserves so much more than what we have."

"He has a lot of love, but I understand what you're saying," Prodigy said, hugging Nina for the first time. He saw a tear make its way down her cinnamon-colored cheek. He wanted to hold her longer but decided to let it and her go.

Once they made it to the apartment door with Prodigy carrying Blake, Nina fumbled for her keys. She opened the door and Cathy was sitting on the couch watching video reruns of *Oz.* When they walked in, Nina pointed to her room for him to put Blake on the bed.

When he came out of the room, Cathy said, "I don't remember you being this fine, Mr. Banks," looking at Prodigy from head to toe.

"That's because you were too busy trying to get out the door with that man you were with," he replied.

"What man?" Nina asked.

"Excuse me, unlike you, I go out on dates. Prodigy, I can't believe you got the nun to go out. How'd you do it?" Cathy asked.

Prodigy decided that was a conversation that he'd better leave alone. He said his good-byes and Nina walked him to his truck.

"Thank you for a good time," she said.

"No! Thank you, Nun Nina. I enjoyed you guys," he said, joking with her.

"My sister is right, I haven't been out in quite some time. I need to get out more often, but I have a goal and it's hard to fit in a social schedule."

"I understand."

"But thank you for the outing," Nina said as she walked away.

"Let's do it again sometime. Life is too short to work all the time," he said to her back.

She didn't say anything, just nodded her head.

Prodigy watched her as she walked back to her door; she stopped, turned around, and put her hand up to her ear like it was a telephone, indicating that she wanted him to call her.

No doubt! he thought.

10

Caught
in the Act

s Prodigy headed back over to Poppa Doc's house for the informal roundtable discussion, his cell phone started screaming. He hit the send button.

"Hello."

"Hey, my man! Where've you been?"

"What's up, Unc?" Prodigy said to his Uncle Ray.

"How ya handling ya new roomy over there?"

"I'm about to put him out."

"Already? What did he do?"

"Just being Jermaine, you know. I guess it's just a compatibility thing. Two grown men aren't meant to cohabit for too long. Plus, I've outgrown a lot of the things that he seems to be crazy about."

"Well, you gotta remember that you're a year or two older than him, so be patient."

"It's not just that. He's disrespectful. He drinks all day and all night, and if he's not drunk then he's high. Earlier today I almost lost it. I brought some company over and he was passed out on the floor, inebriated. Then he left some hot grease on the stove and almost burned my house up, not to mention his dumb ass. I wanted to kill him," Prodigy rattled off.

"That's different, he has to respect you in yo' house now. You want me to come and get him?" Uncle Ray asked.

"Nah, that's part of his problem, we've always made allowances for him. I already told him that he has one month to get it together, because he needs his own place."

"Well, good. It seems like you handling things over there. What about a job? Has he found a job yet?"

"Hell no! And that's another thing. One of my dogs is a manager at Best Buy, so I asked him if he could hook Jermaine up with a job. He told me no problem, all Jermaine had to do was come in and fill out the job application. You know, that clown never showed up. When I asked him what happened, he said he went to the wrong store and waited for two hours. And I'm supposed to believe that," Prodigy said, clearly frustrated with his sorry cousin.

"Give him time. I just called to check up on you. Let's get together one day next week. I got some things that I wanna get your opinion on," Uncle Ray said.

"Just give me a call, but make it after eight o'clock in the evening, anything before that is bad for me," Prodigy said, feeling proud that his uncle respected him enough to ask his opinion on something.

"Jermaine told me that you were volunteering up at some youth center. Go ahead, boy, and do ya thing. I like that."

"Yeah, it's kind of cool," Prodigy said modestly.

"I'm not gonna hold ya. We'll talk."

"A'ight, Unc."

Prodigy's uncle's call got him to thinking about Jermaine. He was truly getting tired of his little cousin. He didn't want to put him out in the streets, but something had to give. All Jermaine seemed to want to do was get high and talk about all of the women he was sleeping with. Prodigy could literally feel his own transition into becoming a real man, because in a matter of weeks he went from seeking out the latest concubine to sleeping alone.

He thought about how, in their childhood and all the way up until a couple of years ago when he left Philly, he and Jermaine would do everything together. Now it was as if the only thing they had in common was their last name.

Prodigy decided to think about something a little more pleasant, and Nina's face popped up. Since Prodigy had dropped her and Blake off, she'd been on his mind like clockwork. He couldn't explain it, but something happened between them, something that had never happened to him before. As a matter of fact, he had to stop himself from pretending that she was still sitting in his passenger seat on the way home. He kept looking over there, talking to where she used to be.

This was really unfamiliar territory for him, due to being so spoiled by the ladies of Atlanta. Nina didn't really show that much interest in him. But then again, he didn't try to push up on her either. Nevertheless he found himself riding around in his truck like a kid with a crush on his elementary-school teacher.

He somehow shook the thought as he pulled up into Poppa Doc's driveway. He found Bernard and Poppa Doc sitting out on the deck behind the house. It was obvious that Poppa Doc had been doing some heavy talking, because Bernard greeted Prodigy by standing and offering his hand. Prodigy shook it, nodded, and took a seat.

Poppa Doc spoke. "Y'all want something to drink?" he asked as he got up and walked over to the small outdoor refrigerator that he kept in the hot tub room off of the deck.

"Yeah, I'll take whatever you bring me," Prodigy said.

"No, I must've drank about thirty glasses of fruit punch. What does Momma put in that juice?"

"You don't wanna know," Poppa Doc said as he covered his mouth like a secret had slipped out.

Everyone chuckled. Then they sat down together. Poppa Doc opened the discussion. "Bernard, I know that you've had some issues with Prodigy, and, Prodigy, I know that you've had some issues with Bernard. But tonight all of that will be put to rest, because not only are you two put in an awkward position whenever everyone gets together, everyone that loves the both of you are affected. Now, I think it's time we resolve all of your issues and leave here, if not as friends, at least not as enemies. Is that fair?" Poppa Doc asked as he looked at both of them for confirmation.

Prodigy spoke up. "Well, I understand how Bernard feels, but I want him to know that I've done everything in my power to make that wrong a right. I specifically told all of those guys that women, no matter what age, shape, or size, were off-limits."

"Yeah, but what were you doing out there in the first place?"

"No!" Poppa Doc said. "Bernard, that is not the issue. Let's stick to the issues. That was the past, let's leave it there. Prodigy has made some wonderful strides as a person since then."

"Yeah, I know, and I guess I'm really not upset with Prodigy; it's people who make a living taking from other people. Some of us work real hard, and to have the fruits of our labor snatched away by some lazy bums, it's just not an easy pill to swallow. I think about my little girl and . . . I don't know!"

"Well, Bernard, I can't say that I know how you feel, because it wasn't my child, but when I heard what happened on the news, there was only one thing left for me to do and that's what I did. I shut down my uncle's six-, sometimes seven-figure operation when I returned that car."

"He didn't leave it on the side of the road, Bernard, he drove it up in the yard. That's character. Ain't too many people would have done that," Poppa Doc added.

Bernard nodded his head knowingly.

"I love all kids, man. Hell, I love Brittany, and believe me when I tell you that I don't want anything to happen to her," Prodigy said sincerely.

"Prodigy, I lost a lot of sleep over this thing, not to mention hair. I'm gonna be bald like Pops here in a minute," Bernard said, joking and rubbing his thinning hair.

"That's a good problem, boy. You live long enough, you'll start missing a helluva lot more than hair."

"Man, after I did what I did. I almost lost a couple of family members. Nobody could understand why I had to do what I did, so other than my mother, I was alone for a while."

"You know, Prodigy, I'm learning to never say what you won't do, because given the right situation you just might do anything. So I'm willing to move on if you are," Bernard said honestly.

"Man, you ain't said nothing but a word," Prodigy said as they both stood and gave each other powerful brotherly hugs.

"Oh, sit down, y'all look like two sissies. I didn't know y'all were gonna get all mushy." Poppa Doc tried to bring a little laughter, but he felt like a ton of bricks were lifted from his shoulders. He looked at both men as his children and hated to see the tension between them.

"Lost an enemy, gained a friend. And I hope that my friend can give me a ride home. Diane got mad and took my truck. Prodigy, don't ever get married."

"Now, don't tell the boy that! If I got to put up with a nagging wife—and I know you got one, Bernard, because I spoiled Diane real good for ya—then so does he."

"Spoiled? That woman is impossible."

"Don't you talk about my baby!" Poppa Doc said.

Speaking of babies, Michael walked by with a suitcase. He'd found an efficiency apartment over by the West End. He wasn't happy about the area, but his father had said something that struck a chord. Michael wanted his parents to be proud of him.

"Michael, you moving?"

"Yes, Dad! I know you're happy," Michael said sarcastically. "What's up, Bernard, Prodigy!"

They both nodded in his direction.

"Hell yeah, I'm happy. Aren't you?"

"Yeah, I'm happy. Now I don't have to hear you put me down every hour on the hour," Michael said as he tried to walk by.

"Michael, I want you to know that I put you down to make you walk on your own. And remember, if someone can put you down, then they must've been carrying you! You'll be just fine, son. Just maintain!" Poppa Doc said as he stood up and gave his son a strong handshake.

"Well, we better be getting out of here," Prodigy said.

"Oh, don't rush off. You coming to church tomorrow, Prodigy?"

"Yeah, I'll be there, standing tall and looking good."

"Alright, I look forward to seeing you, and bring that cute little girl and her son with you."

"Will do! Bernard, are you ready?"

"Yeah! And, Pops, I appreciate you letting us use your facilities for the party. Prodigy, let me run in here and kiss Brittany good night."

"I forgot Britt-Britt was staying over. I might win me some money tonight."

"Well, she has plenty of it," Bernard said, remembering his fight with Diane.

Brittany was sitting at the table counting her money. When she realized that she didn't have enough for the special gift that she was saving for, she asked one of the guests for five more

dollars. Bernard snapped at her and told her to stop asking people for money.

Diane, who knew what Brittany was saving for, lost it. "The
money is for your time, Bernard. She's been trying to come up
with enough money to pay you to stay home for a day with
her, because she didn't want you to lose any of your precious
pay, and all you can do is yell at her."

Bernard really felt bad and was left speechless by his daughter's thoughtfulness. He committed to taking weekends off.

"Alright, Poppa Doc, I'll see you tomorrow. Bernard, I'll be
out in the truck," Prodigy said as he snatched the ringing cell
phone from his pocket.

"Hello!"

"What's the haps, baby?" Jermaine said.

"Not a thing, what's up?"

"Yo, P, I need a ride. Can you come scoop me up?"

"Where are you?" Prodigy said, shaking his head. He could
never stay upset for too long with his cousin.

"At the Marriott on Peachtree. This little thing I met got
mad at me for falling asleep on her and left me."

"Alright. When are you gonna get a damn car?"

"Come on, baby, I'm working on that," Jermaine said.
"Hey, P, don't take all day, man."

"Yo, who are you rushing? You're the one that needs a ride.
I'll get there when I get there. I should hang up on your ass and
make you get a cab."

"Alright, dog, calm down. Be getting all mad over the
smallest things. You still coming?"

"Be outside, man. If I have to wait on you for one minute,
I'm dipp'en."

"You know I know, as many times as you done left me."

As Prodigy got in his truck and started the ignition, Bernard
ran up and hopped in on the passenger side.

They backed out of Poppa Doc's driveway and headed toward the highway. Prodigy informed Bernard that they had to make a stop to pick up his cousin before he could drop him off at home.

"I appreciate this, Prodigy. I got left in my own vehicle. I don't know what to say about my wife. It's as if she can't live without fussing and fighting. Hell, everyone makes mistakes, but she finds one and rides it into the ground," Bernard said.

Prodigy didn't say anything, but he was surely thinking, *Isn't that what you did with me for the last two years?*

"Prodigy, tell me about you. I've never taken the time to get to know you. Where are you from?" Bernard asked.

"Philly," Prodigy said.

"What brought you here?"

"Needed a change of scenery. Philly was getting old."

"Look, man, Pops thinks a lot of you. I was just doing what I felt was right for my little girl, but she loves you too. I saw how everyone at the party was coming up to you and walking away with smiles on their faces and . . . I'm just glad that we buried the hatchet. I'm sorry for dragging this thing out for so long."

"No problem, I understand a father's love."

"Was that your son who was with you at the party?" Bernard asked.

"Nah, but he's a real close friend," Prodigy replied, thinking about his little buddy Blake.

"Yeah, kids are something else, man. I never knew my father. That's why I love so hard with Brittany."

"Yeah, I never met mine either, he died in a gang fight while I was still marinating in my mommy's belly."

" 'Mommy'—I haven't heard that word in a long time," Bernard said, thinking about his own mother. He used to call her Mommy until the kids started teasing him, then he changed it to Momma.

"Is your mom still with us?" Prodigy asked, but immediately wished he hadn't.

"I don't know, buddy. She disappeared one day when I was a little boy."

"I'm sorry to hear that," Prodigy said.

"Tell me about it. I still miss her, though. Who was that fox you had with you at the party?"

"Look at ya. Checking out the young folks."

"I ain't too old to look, but that's where it stops with me."

"That's good, Diane seems to be a pretty nice lady!"

"Oh, that definitely ain't the reason, because she really ain't that nice, but I love her. She's family."

"Yeah, family is important, that's why I'm picking this knucklehead up, because he's family."

They talked a little more and realized that they had much more in common than they expected. They even said they would hang out one night together. Then they pulled into the Marriott's parking lot and saw Jermaine standing by the front door. He jumped into the backseat. Prodigy introduced him to Bernard. Just as they were pulling around the curvy driveway, Bernard asked Prodigy to stop for a second. Bernard got out and walked down to the end of the building and came back to Prodigy's side of the truck.

"Prodigy, you ain't gonna believe this. That's my damn truck down there," Bernard said, looking like he didn't know what to think. "Do you have a minute?"

"Yeah, I can wait," Prodigy said, not wanting to leave his newfound friend hanging. Obviously someone had stolen his truck.

Bernard walked into the lobby and spoke with the attendant, then came back out and asked to use Prodigy's cell phone, to call the house to see if Diane noticed that the truck was missing.

No answer! He called her cell phone and got her voice

mail. So he called Poppa Doc's to see if he had heard anything. He dialed 911 and was promptly placed on hold. While he was waiting on Atlanta's Finest, Diane and a tall gentleman walked toward the truck.

Bernard stared hard, as if trying to be sure that that was his wife. After focusing in and realizing it was Diane, he darted down to the end of the parking lot just as Diane had closed the door on the passenger side. The tall gentleman was now in the driver's seat. Seeing what Bernard saw, Prodigy shut the truck's ignition off, and he and Jermaine ran after him.

Bernard ran over to the passenger side and tried to open the door. Diane had locked it. He reached back and broke the window with one huge thrust of his elbow. He grabbed Diane, who was screaming and trying to crawl into the backseat. He snatched her out of the vehicle through the broken window and pulled her to her feet. He slapped her with so much force that she fell back into the truck's door and slid to the ground.

Bernard was livid. His eyes looked like that of a wild beast on the hunt, crazy and deranged.

Diane rolled to her knees and crawled onto the grass, cowering behind a bush.

She was crying, "I'm sorry, I'm sorry," over and over.

Bernard walked after Diane but changed his direction and walked around his truck to get the driver. Then he stopped. He closed his eyes and lifted his head toward the sky, looking for answers. He balled his fingers up into a fist and let out a demonic yell.

The driver held his hands in a defensive posture and spoke: "Now, Bernard, it's not what you think. This was a counseling session ordained by the Lord," Reverend Brooks said.

"What?" Bernard asked as he lifted his head and stared at his pastor of the last five years.

"Why don't you come and see me tomorrow after service, and we can discuss this matter after you've calmed down. Thou shall not speaketh when thou has a troubled heart," Reverend Brooks said in a nervous yet pastoral tone.

Bernard cocked his arm back and caught the pastor with a straight left that made his nose bleed like the Red Sea, then he hit him in the stomach so hard that Reverend Brooks instantly threw up whatever he'd had for dinner. By then the reverend was on his hands and knees, but Bernard wasn't done. He picked him up, grabbed Reverend Brooks around the neck, and pressed him against the truck so hard that it looked like the reverend's eyes were going to pop out of his head. Vomit dripped down the reverend's chin onto his white collar, as Bernard took his free hand and pummeled.

Prodigy realized that Bernard didn't have any plans of letting the reverend go until he was lifeless, so he ran over and pulled Bernard away from a death that was sure to bring him a murder charge. After he released his grip, Bernard hopped in his truck, then jumped back out and snatched his keys from Reverend Brooks's hand. Before he reentered the truck he pulled his leg back as far as it would go and kicked the reverend in the groin. Reverend Brooks let out a yell that was in perfect key with Diane's screaming. He rolled under the truck, and had Prodigy not pulled him out of the way he would have surely been crushed beyond recognition by the roaring ton of steel.

Prodigy and Jermaine helped the badly beaten reverend and the shaken-up Diane to his truck. He agreed to give both of them a ride back to their respective homes.

Diane sat in the backseat of Prodigy's truck sobbing uncontrollably. Reverend Brooks sat on the passenger side, moaning and holding his eye, which was getting blacker by the second.

Jermaine was sitting in the back with Diane, trying to get Prodigy's attention through the rearview mirror. He wanted to laugh at the reverend's moaning, but he knew that Prodigy would put him out. Prodigy thought that the reverend's moaning was hysterical himself and knew that if he looked up into that rearview, he would lose it, so he bit his lip and kept his eyes on the road.

"Hey, Rev, you need to cut all that damn moaning, man," Jermaine said.

Prodigy looked out of the window and didn't say a word. It took every muscle in his face to keep from laughing.

Reverend Brooks gave Prodigy directions to his palatial estate. He got out and walked around to the back door and tapped on Diane's window. Diane ignored him, but he persisted. She opened the back door and went off.

"What! You son of a bitch! What do you want?"

"Diane, just calm down. Give me two minutes."

"For what? You took advantage of me. I trusted you, you sorry, Satan-filled sonofabitch!" Diane screamed. Diane felt that the reverend used her weakness for his own pleasure.

"Diane, it's not like that at all. Let me talk to you alone for just a second," Reverend Brooks said, as he reached out for Diane's arm. Big mistake!

"What for? Some more of your counseling! How many other unsuspecting women have you counseled?" Diane said, as thoughts of how this mistake would change everything filled her head. She decided that since she didn't get in this mess all by herself, she shouldn't suffer all by herself. She took off toward the front door of the reverend's house. He tried to stop her but she turned around and started swinging at him from all directions. Reverend Brooks must have decided that one beatdown was enough for one night. He backed off.

Diane stormed up onto the porch and started ringing the bell, banging on the door like a woman possessed.

A woman in a housecoat answered.

"Diane, is that you?" Mrs. Brooks said, trying to figure out what could bring Diane Charles to her house acting like this.

"Did you know that your husband is running around counseling other women with his little dick?" Diane said, not caring how this news might affect the lady standing in front of her.

"Diane, please go home. This is uncalled for," Reverend Brooks said.

"Thanks to you, I don't have a home," Diane shouted.

"What happened to your eye?" Mrs. Brooks said, looking at her husband's swollen eye and overall terrible condition.

"Tell her what happened to your eye. Oh, you still got hair in ya throat. I'll tell her! My husband came to the hotel where Reverend Lil' Asshole here asked me to meet him and kicked his ass, that's what happened to his goddamn eye."

"That's it. You are no longer welcomed here, Cecil. I've had enough. A dog can only be kicked but so much. I've given you chance after chance after chance, but no more." Mrs. Brooks turned to Diane. "I'm truly sorry, Diane, if you felt you were taken advantage of. Cecil, you wait here, I'll gather you some clothes and a set of keys to one of the cars. I don't want to see you anymore until our divorce hearing," Mrs. Brooks said as she turned and walked into the house, locking the door behind her.

Diane walked back to Prodigy's truck and got into the backseat.

"Prodigy, will you please take me to my mother's house? And how did you get involved in this?" she asked, remembering that he and Bernard were not the best of friends.

"We sat down tonight and resolved our differences at your father's house. He said that he needed a ride home, but I had to pick my cousin up at the hotel and . . ."

"I see," Diane said, and went silent.

For the third time that day, Prodigy found himself headed back out to Alpharetta. When they arrived, Mrs. Ethel was standing on the front porch, rubbing her hands together and looking nervous. Bernard had already called with his findings.

Diane thanked Prodigy for the ride. She got out of the truck, walked into her mother's waiting arms, and began to cry again.

"Come on in, sweetheart," Mrs. Ethel said to her daughter as she lead her into the kitchen.

"How could I have been so stupid?" Diane asked herself. "How could I have been so weak?"

"We all make mistakes, Diane, but life goes on," Mrs. Ethel said, while placing a wet cloth over Diane's bruised face.

The phone rang. Mrs. Ethel picked it up, said a few words, and hung up.

"That was Bernard. He said that he's going away for a couple of days."

"Did he say where?"

Mrs. Ethel shook her head.

"Diane, how long has this been going on?"

"Momma, I swear today was the first time. Bernard made me so mad at the party that I just needed to get away. I didn't want to take you guys away from the party, so I called Reverend Brooks. He asked that I meet him at the hotel. Said that he was getting things ready for some convention that the church was having and . . . oh, Momma, I should've known better. I just wasn't thinking."

"Why don't you go lie down. We'll talk tomorrow," Ethel said, seeing how distraught her daughter was.

Diane got up, headed to one of the guest rooms, and closed the door.

The night seemed darker than normal; even the moon wasn't in the mood to shine. Bernard stopped at the all-night Amoco gas station on the way home and purchased a pack of Newports. He only smoked when something was heavy on his mind, and tonight was about as heavy as it had been in a while.

No matter how he tried, he couldn't shake the memory of

Diane's face when she saw him approaching. He had never hit his wife before, but he didn't feel any remorse. As a matter of fact, he had gotten some satisfaction out of smacking her. All of those years of her self-centered behavior had built up to this.

For the first time in ten years of marriage, he realized that he didn't like his wife. He still loved her, but he didn't like the person she was. It wasn't just this last incident; it was an accumulation of events that led him to feel the way he felt. He couldn't put a finger on what was hurting more: his heart or his pride. *When a man marries a woman, no other man is supposed to enter her body,* he thought.

Bernard found himself sitting in his driveway trying to figure out how had things gone so wrong. He didn't feel like he deserved this. *If she wasn't happy, then all she had to do was say so, but to sneak around with another woman's husband is lower than low,* he said to himself.

The rain started falling hard, but Bernard's window remained down, allowing water to drench his left arm and thigh. Then a pair of headlights pulled up behind him. He was hoping that it wasn't Diane, because if it was, he thought he'd probably leave Brittany without any parents. Because he was going to jail and Diane was going to the mortuary.

The car stopped and the lights went off. Poppa Doc got out and walked up to the driver's side of the truck. He was shielding his face from the rain with his hand when he asked Bernard why was he sitting out in the rain with his window down.

"Trying to get the smell of a whore and a false prophet out of my truck." Bernard's voice was filled with venom.

Poppa Doc asked if he could get in. Bernard nodded in the direction of the passenger door. Poppa Doc walked slowly around the front of the vehicle and opened the door. As he shut the door, the rattle of the broken glass could be heard through the side panel.

Bernard, remembering Poppa Doc's medical condition, tossed

his lit cigarette out of the window onto the pavement. He watched the orange flame as it dodged the raindrops for a few seconds before being extinguished by the falling water. He wondered how long Diane had been dodging before her fire was put out.

Poppa Doc ran his fingers through what hair he had left and gave a long sigh.

"You know, Bernard, I've always tried to teach my kids to do right by all people. Obviously I haven't always succeeded, but that was my goal. Bernard, you are a good man. I could tell that the first day that Diane brought you over to the house. She followed me around like a puppy, trying to see what I thought of you. I told her that I liked you and that I saw a quality in you that any man would feel comfortable trusting his only daughter with. Now I find myself sitting here disappointed with her. But life is like that, Bernard; soon as you think you know someone, they throw you a curveball. We always want what we don't have; you got a million dollars, you want two, you get two, now you won't sleep till you get ten. That's life, Bernard. It's not right, but it's life. We all make mistakes, especially in relationships. It's so hard dealing with someone day in and day out," Poppa Doc said, before continuing. "Now, I know this feels like a kick in the ass, with all that you've done for your family, but this doesn't have to be the end."

Bernard shook his head. He knew this was the end. There was no way he could ever trust her again.

"Pops, that's your daughter, so I—"

"Nah, speak freely. You wanna call her out of her name, go right ahead and vent. I'm not biased in the least. She's always gonna be my daughter and I'll always love her unconditionally, but wrong is wrong no matter who's doing it."

"Pops, I need a favor," Bernard said, as he stared off into space.

"Shoot," Poppa Doc said, studying his son-in-law. He knew

THE HEARTS OF MEN

hurt when he saw it, no matter how much Bernard tried to mask it with his tough-guy act.

"Take care of my baby girl, teach her to do the right thing all the time, no matter how much she feels she has to gain by doing wrong. Teach her to do the right thing."

"Oh, I'm definitely gonna help, Bernard, but that's your job. No one can teach you like your own daddy," Poppa Doc said, trying to give him something to look forward to. Bernard was showing signs of a suicidal person and Poppa Doc was not going to leave him like this.

"I'm tired, Pops!" Bernard said, on the brink of tears. "I'm tired of being unappreciated. I'm tired of being used and made to look like a fool. Do you know who she was in that hotel with?" Bernard asked.

"No, I don't!" Poppa Doc said.

"Reverend Brooks!"

For the first time in a long while, Poppa Doc didn't know what to say, but he knew that he had to underplay this for Bernard's sake. He responded calmly, "The devil works in mysterious ways, Bernard. Just because a man preaches the word doesn't mean he's filled with the Holy Spirit."

"Nah, Pops, you don't understand. I went to that asshole's church for five goddamn years. He ate dinner in my house, baptized my baby girl, and had sex with my goddamn wife. Now, you tell me what the hell is going on."

"He'll get his—"

"You damn right he gone get it, cuz I'm gone give it to him. And when I'm finished with him, I'ma give it to Diane," Bernard said as he got out of his truck and slammed the door. Just the thought of Diane and Reverend Brooks sent him back into a rage.

Poppa Doc didn't call after him. The wounds were too fresh.

Bernard went into the house, walked over to the mantel and picked up their wedding picture. He looked at it hard and long, then threw it up against the marble fireplace so hard that it shattered into a thousand little pieces.

The doorbell rang.

"Go away, Pops! You can't help me! Go and try to save that ungrateful-ass daughter of yours," Bernard said from the living room, loud enough for Poppa Doc to hear him through the front door.

Poppa Doc decided to give him time and not take his threats too seriously at this point. Life had taught him that people say things when they are angry, only to regret them later. He had accomplished his main goal tonight and that was to let Bernard know that he was there for him. That he was still family!

As Bernard paced the living room, he glanced out their bay window and saw Poppa Doc backing out of his driveway. He wondered how such a giving man could have such selfish offspring. Everywhere he turned, his eyes found pictures of Diane. Diane, Diane, Diane, this house had Diane written all over it.

At this point he couldn't remember what it was that had attracted him to her in the first place. She had always been selfish, and always a bitch.

Bernard was feeling a bit destructive, but he didn't want to tear the house down anymore. He didn't want Brittany to see her home destroyed, so he decided to take a drive. After calling a friend of his at Ford to fix his window, Bernard grabbed a suitcase and packed up enough clothes for a couple of days away.

He didn't have any specific destination in mind, but he needed to drive. After packing his toiletries and underclothes he was back in his truck and on the phone with Ethel.

"Mrs. Fuller, I'm—"

"Bernard, I'm still Momma. Call me Momma. I'm so sorry."

"Okay, Momma, I'm going away for a little while. I need to

sort some things out. If I stay I'm gonna hurt somebody and we don't want that."

"No, that won't solve anything. How long will you be gone?"

"I don't know, I don't even know where I'm going, but tell Brittany that I love her," Bernard said, and pushed the end button on his cellular phone.

He was on I-285 when he realized that it wasn't going to do anything but take him around in one big circle, so he exited onto I-20 and headed east.

He drove for hours. All sorts of thoughts crossed his mind and he was tired of thinking. A new day was dawning and he was getting sleepy.

As Bernard searched the highway for the next hotel, he saw a sign that read, FLORENCE 12 MILES. Florence was only ten minutes away from the town he grew up in. He hadn't been back there since he left more than twenty years before. Diane had his mind so thoroughly twisted that he never even remembered crossing the state line into South Carolina.

He decided to pull off on the Florence exit and check into a hotel. Tomorrow he would explore his old stomping grounds.

11

Naked Lady

fter all of the day's drama, Prodigy made it home a little after midnight. He wondered if Nina was still up. He showered and was looking in his closet for something to wear to church the next day when the phone rang. He casually walked over and picked it up.

"Remember me?" a familiar voice said.

"Yeah, I remember you. How've you been?" he said to the seductive voice on the other end of the line.

"I'm fine, but I miss you. When can I see you?" the voice asked.

"I don't know."

"What do you mean, you don't know? Have I slipped that far down the totem pole that I have to take a number now, Mr. Banks?"

"Where are you calling me from?" Prodigy asked.

"Outside your door."

"Hold on." Prodigy walked into Jermaine's room with the cordless phone up to his ear, but he said nothing. He looked out of the window and sure enough, Simone was sitting in her convertible Volvo with the top down. He smiled. He kinda missed that girl—or did he? Maybe it was that level-ten coochie of hers that she could work like a nine-to-five.

Prodigy stood there for a minute and waved at her. She waved back. He walked back to his room and sat on the bed.

"What are you doing in my 'hood?"

"Looking for Mr. Goodbar!"

Just then his other line beeped.

"Hold on, Mrs. Lady."

"Are you gonna let me in or what?" Simone asked.

"Hold on," he said again and clicked over to answer the other line.

"Hello."

"Did you forget to call me?" Nina asked.

"Nah, you wouldn't believe what happened tonight. I didn't know if you were still awake, so I decided not to call. Did you get settled in okay?"

"Yeah we did. I hope everything is alright."

"Oh yeah, this was other people's drama."

"Are you on the other line?" Nina asked.

"Yeah, can you hold on for a second?"

"Sure, or you could just call me back."

"Nah nah, that call's not important," Prodigy said, as he clicked back over to Simone.

"Simone, I'm gonna have to pass."

"Why?"

"Let's just say that I made a promise to a man that I don't wanna break," Prodigy said, and clicked over before she could respond. He didn't trust himself when it came to her and that level ten. She didn't know it, but Nina was already saving him from himself.

"So did Blake wake up?"

"That boy is out like a light. I started to make him get up and take a shower, but I'll give him a pass tonight."

"Yeah, let him sleep. He worked hard and played hard today."

"That was about the worst rake job that I've ever seen. I told you that boy was lazy," Nina said, laughing.

Prodigy liked the way she laughed.

"Yeah, I lost a little bit of money on that job. But he gave it a good try. I just like to see the effort."

"That reminds me! Thank you for taking such an interest in my little pumpkin," Nina said.

"He's a good kid, and he's so funny. He reminds me of myself when I was younger, but he's a whole lot smarter."

"There is never a dull moment with Blake, that's for sure."

They were both silent for a moment. Prodigy was thinking of how soothing her velvety voice was sounding. He thought that he could lay there and fall asleep to the sound of her breathing.

Nina was thinking that it was nice to talk to a man. It had been almost three years since she lay in her bed with a man on the other end of the phone line.

The doorbell rang. Nina heard it.

"Sounds like you have company," she said.

"You wanna hold on? It's probably my cousin. I sent him to the store to get me some milk. He drank all the milk and left the empty container in the refrigerator. I hate that! Then he has to borrow my truck to go get my milk."

"Tell Jermaine hello for me, but I'm a little tired. I just wanted to make sure you got in safely, so I'm gonna—"

"Nah, just . . ." Prodigy said, then he caught himself. *Damn, I can't believe I'm acting like this.* "Okay, if you have to go then I won't hold you up."

Nina went silent for a moment, then said, "Prodigy, go get your door. I'll wait."

"I'll be just a sec." He walked into Jermaine's room again and looked out of the window. No car in the driveway. He ran down the stairs with the cordless in hand, thinking that something had happened to his truck. He was going to kill Jermaine for real this time. He threw the phone on the couch and slung the door open.

What he saw standing on the other side of the door was not Jermaine but Simone.

She was wearing a three-quarter-length raincoat. She untied it and showed Prodigy her perfect figure with more curves than a San Francisco highway.

Damn, this woman is fine, he thought, as he looked at her standing in the doorway in a silk bra and matching thong underwear.

He unconsciously moved back to let her in and looked to see if her husband was peeking out of the window down the street at his late-night creep spot.

"Who are you looking for?" Simone asked.

"Oh, you never know who's lurking around the corners," Prodigy said.

Simone walked in and brushed her hand against his crotch. Instant erection! *Damn!*

"Simone, what's the deal, baby? Why are you acting up? Coming over here all naked."

"Cuz I miss you and I'm horny as hell," she stated frankly.

"Look, I told you I wasn't with that no more. Why are you tripping?"

"You really want me to leave?" Simone said as she stepped closer to him and placed his hand where he could feel the warmth between her legs.

"Damn!" It'd been almost a month since he had his last

sexual episode with Gina, and his jimmy wasn't making this easy at all. He felt like he was gonna burst through his shorts. He felt like praying. Just falling to his knees and asking for this temptation to stop or for someone to come around and tie that coat back up, because he was much too weak at this point to even try.

Damn! he thought.

Simone reached up and put her arms around his neck and pulled his head down to hers and stuck her tongue in his mouth.

He actually felt himself losing it. He put his arms around her and kissed her long and deep. He moved her over to the couch and laid her down. He was about to take off his T-shirt when his prayers were answered by way of a buzzing phone on the couch, making that sound it made when it was left off the hook too long. He disengaged his mind from Simone's seductive grasp, helped her up, and ushered her to the door.

"Simone, you have to leave."

She didn't fight, but turned to him and said, "I'm proud of you. Didn't know that there was such a man that could turn it down, especially when it was staring him right in the face. Whoever she is, she's a lucky lady. You be good, Prodigy, and think about me sometime," she said as she walked out of the door.

Prodigy plopped down on the sofa and remembered that Nina had been on the line. He knew that she had to have heard at least part of his conversation with Simone. He felt like shit. Whatever chance he thought he might have had was definitely gone now. *She's probably thinking I'm the biggest player in Atlanta,* he said to himself. He dialed her number. She answered on the first ring.

"Hello, Prodigy."

"Hi, I'm sorry I left you on hold so long."

"Sounds like you're a busy man. Was that your girlfriend?"

"Nah!" he said, trying not to sound too guilty. He felt as though he were cheating and needed to explain.

"Must have been someone important for you to forget about me like that."

"I didn't forget about you." All of a sudden he didn't feel like playing games. He wanted something with this woman, and whether it was something deep or something shallow, he wanted it to start with honesty.

"Yes, you did," Nina said, sounding like it wasn't a big deal. She had heard the entire conversation and decided to hang up when she didn't hear any more talking.

"Nina, that was this lady who I use to kick it with. I broke it off about a month ago, because what we were doing wasn't right. She's married."

"You don't have to explain, Prodigy."

"I know, but I want to. May I continue?"

"Suit yourself," Nina said.

"When I first moved down here from Philly, I wasn't living a life that I was proud of. I met some people, made some adjustments, and thought I was doing alright. Then I started seeing this lady and something else happened, so I made some more adjustments. But it seems like every time I try to do the right thing, I'm pulled back into doing the wrong thing. Tonight was a test that I knew was coming."

"Sounds like you failed!"

"Nah, I actually think I did alright! Had it not been for you I would've failed miserably."

"What do you mean? What did I have to do with it?" Nina asked, surprised.

"Nina, I like you. I don't know what it is, but I like you. I've been thinking about you since I dropped you off, so that's how you saved me from letting her in when she called earlier. That was her I was on the line with when you called. Then if you hadn't hung up, the phone would have never made that

irritating sound to save me from doing something that I would
have regretted later. So I owe you one. When do you want re-
payment?"

"Thanks for telling me that, but you don't owe me anything.
Some men would've hung up the phone and continued where
they left off, so give yourself some credit," Nina said.

"Yeah, I guess so."

"But I've been thinking about you too, and when I heard
that woman in the background my thoughts of you just drifted
away."

"Well, tell 'em to drift back."

Nina laughed and said, "I don't think that would be a problem. I really appreciate your honesty, and for some reason I believe you."

"I'm glad, because I'm telling the truth."

"I think you are."

"So tell me about you. As beautiful as you are, why don't
you have a man, or do you?" Prodigy asked.

"No, I don't. I have never had a man."

"So Blake's adopted, huh?" Prodigy said sarcastically.

"No, he's mine, but what I mean is, I've never had someone
who takes on the responsibility that is required to call oneself a
man. So I've had boys, but never a man."

"Blake tells me that he doesn't have a father. You feel like
talking about that?"

"Oh, it's no problem. Blake's father pulled a Houdini act
when I informed him that I was pregnant."

"So you mean to tell me that he's never seen Blake?"

"That's right."

"What a loss for him that is. He doesn't know how much
joy he's cheating himself out of."

"I don't worry about him. I used to look out of the window
every day and pray that he'd changed his mind, but when I real-

ized that he wasn't coming back, I made a pact with myself that I would raise my son on my own. My dad helps some, but he's inconsistent."

"You never even heard from Blake's father in all this time?" Prodigy asked, astonished.

"Last I heard he was in prison. I don't mean to put any unnecessary pressure on you, Prodigy, but Blake has never had a positive male influence in his life, so if you plan on leaving the youth center please stop spending time exclusively with him. He's been longing for that father figure for so long that he thinks the world of you. And he gets attached so easily."

"Nina, you don't ever have to worry about me letting Blake down. I really have grown pretty fond of his little tank head."

"Prodigy, we've been let down so much that I've almost lost my faith in men. I just do what I feel is best and pray that my son doesn't fall prey to the streets."

"He's a good kid and I think that you've done a helluva job raising him alone."

"We do what we have to do, Prodigy."

His other line clicked and he started not to answer it, but after tonight's drama he thought that it might be something important.

"Nina, I know you're tired of holding on, but could you, just one more time?"

"Go ahead, just don't forget about me this time," she said, chuckling.

"I won't, I promise," Prodigy said, and clicked over.

"Hello."

"Hey, playa, what you doing?" Jermaine said, calling from inside the truck.

"I'm on the other line, make it snappy."

"Hey, man, I'm sorry about today. It won't happen again."

"I know! It's cool. Where are you?"

"I'm on the way home and I just thought about how I was acting. You doing alright for yourself and I gotta get there," Jermaine said.

"You will, but bring my damn truck home. And you going to church tomorrow, right?"

"Yeah, if I can wake up."

"Oh, you're getting up. Bye! I'm on the other line. One!"

"Peace!"

Prodigy clicked back over to Nina.

"Y'all wanna go to church with me tomorrow?"

"Where do you go?" she asked.

"New Birth, but tomorrow I'm going to Hopewell."

"Sure, we'll go. What time should we get ourselves ready?"

"I'll be there at ten o'clock."

"Blake is gonna be beside himself, seeing you two days in a row."

"It's me who's beside myself, seeing both of you two days in a row."

"Well, Mr. Banks, I have to get some rest. I enjoyed my day, and as you can tell Blake had a ball."

"Me too. And I'm about to retire, myself. I'll see you in the morning."

"Good night, and tell Jermaine to come with you to church in the morning."

"He said he's coming, but we'll see."

"Oh well, all you can do is try," Nina said.

"That's right. Sleep well."

"I will."

The sound of the alarm clock jolted Prodigy from a bad dream. He was dreaming that Bernard had been shot by Diane's lover and that Poppa Doc was chasing him with a brick, thinking that he was the culprit.

He rolled over and looked at the clock on his dresser. It said 8:00. He decided to get up a little earlier in order to get some running in before church. Last night's episode flashed through his mind and he kind of felt sorry for Bernard. Although they'd had their differences in the past, he always knew where his heart was, and that was with his family. Prodigy rolled out of bed and walked into his bathroom. He saw the business card that Bernard had given him hanging out of his wallet. He pulled it completely out and studied it. Bernard had written his cell phone number on the back of the card. Prodigy walked back into his room and picked up the telephone. He didn't know what he was going to say to Bernard, but he just wanted him to know that he had his back.

The phone rang and Bernard's voice mail came on.

"This is Bernard Charles. I'm not available, so please leave a message."

Prodigy started to hang up, then he changed his mind and left a message. "Bernard, this is Prodigy. I just called to see how you were holding up. Although I can't think of anything that you would want from me, here's my number anyway, 555-2860. Just checking on you, my man. Stay strong," Prodigy said as he hung up the phone.

He threw on some Nike running gear and headed to his backyard to stretch. After going through his old Army warm-up routine, he opened his neighbor's fence and called his running buddy, Chocko, his neighbor's chocolate Labrador retriever. He could always count on Chocko to be happy to see him coming. Prodigy rubbed the brown animal on his head and behind his ears. Once they were in accordance with Georgia's leash laws, they were off on their two-mile stress-releasing jog. After last night's fisticuffs between Bernard Balboa and Reverend Apollo Creed, he needed all of the relief that he could get.

Running always cleared his mind. He thought about how much his life had changed since he was a youngster and how much effect a complete stranger could have on you. Blake crossed his mind and he wondered why he was placed in his life. Then Nina's face popped up and he wondered where they were headed with their friendship.

When he and Chocko trotted up Heartbreak Hill at Stone Mountain Park, Prodigy lost all train of thought. All he could think about then was how he was going to get the right foot in front of the left one. Once the huge hill was conquered, they raced back toward his house, with Chocko leading the way. Exhausted, Prodigy stopped running about a full block short of his normal spot and started walking. He made a silent promise to himself to never let another two weeks go by without work- ing out. He walked around the side of his house and gave Chocko some water. He took the hose and ran it over his al- ready sweaty head, allowing the water to instantly cool him off. While he was putting Chocko back on lockdown, his Jamaican neighbor Trevor walked out.

Trevor had dreadlocks hanging down to the middle of his back and a clotted-up salt-and-pepper beard. Trevor owned his own dry-cleaning business and could always be counted on to give Prodigy some flak. He was a good neighbor, whenever he was home, and his wife Geisha's cooking was nothing to be played with. They invited him over for dinner at least once a week, but he only took them up on their offer about once a month.

"What's up, stranger? I didn't know you still lived around here. Thought immigration might've came around and de- ported your ugly ass," Prodigy said jokingly.

"Yuh know, you can kiss a rasta's ass, don't you, mon. And stop fiddling wit' me dog."

"If it wasn't for me, Chocko would have muscular dystro- phy, cuz we know you don't walk him."

"I caah believe yuh got your lazy butt up this early," Trevor said.

"Lazy? I just got back from my morning jog. I haven't seen you on the track in ages. You used to be my running buddy, what happened?" Prodigy said as he shook his neighbor's hand.

"Me cyaat call it. And who in de hell yuh trine fool, mon? Me saw yuh pour de water over yuh ten-gallon head. Waah, yuh got one of yuh many lady friends over and yuh waah impress, huh?" Trevor said, as he peered, like he was looking into Prodigy's window.

Prodigy chuckled at his friend's accent and the way that he butchered words. "Nah, dog, this is all legit. I'm getting a little heavy around the midsection and I can't have that. I'll mess around and start looking like you, beer gut."

"Me got too much work to do to be bouncing up de damn streets wit' the likes of you, mon. And waah yuh mean, beer gut? I'm built for comfort," Trevor said, rubbing his pudgy belly.

"You could find the time if you wanted to. Oh, I forgot y'all Jamaicans have about nine jobs. You would think, as much as you work, that you would invest in a new car. Smoking up the neighborhood in that old-ass Chevy. You're the reason we always having those smog alerts."

"You Americans are much too superficial. Me car works, it's a machine. Kiss me black ass, Podgy," Trevor said, butchering Prodigy's name. He always spoke like he was highly upset, but he actually had a good sense of humor.

"I meet your kinfolk de utter day, tell me he lookin' for work. I offa him a job, cleaning me buildings, but he never call me. I see laziness runs in de blood line, huh?"

"Yeah, now he's lazy," Prodigy agreed, but was interrupted by Mr. Lazy himself.

"Yo, P, telephone," Jermaine yelled from the kitchen window.

"Who is it?" Prodigy shouted back

"Nigga, I don't know," Jermaine said, and slammed the window shut.

"Ain't that something? He lives with me, but I guess my phone calls bother him. Look here, Trev, I'm out. Gotta get ready for church," Prodigy said, as he slapped his friend's hand and walked toward his house.

"Okay, mon, church is a good place for yuh. Don't knock on de door, jus walk in. And there is no cover charge, yuh know. Be easy, mon," Trevor said, and headed back into his own house.

Prodigy walked in his back door, which was off the kitchen, and pulled one of his wrought-iron stools from the island. He sat his sweat-drenched body down and picked up the phone.

"Hello."

"Good morning," Nina said.

"Good morning to you. How's Blake? Is he up?"

"One question at a time, fellow. He's not feeling so hot. He has asthma and it's acting up. So it looks like we're going to have to pass on church today."

"I understand. Does he need anything?"

"Nah, I think we'll be alright."

"Okay, but if you need anything, I'll have my cell with me. I left the number . . ."

"Yeah, I have it."

"Okay, but I must tell you that I was looking forward to see-ing you. Seeing both of you."

"I know, and we were looking forward to it also, but we may still be able to see you later."

"That's cool," Prodigy said.

"Prodigy, will you call us when you get in? We might be able to surprise you with something. That is, if you don't mind."

"Now, why would I mind a surprise from you guys? Oh, wait a minute, as long as it's a good surprise."

"I think it will be. Call us when you get in," Nina said.

"Will do. Bye."

"Bye. Say a prayer for us."

"Consider it done. Talk to you later."

"Bye."

Prodigy hung up the phone feeling a little deflated. He had really been looking forward to seeing Blake and looking into Nina's pretty eyes. As a matter of fact, he'd thought about those pretty eyes all night long. But right now it was not to be, and Poppa Doc and Mrs. Ethel would be waiting at Hopewell Methodist Church for him, so he thought he'd better get a move on. Ironically, Poppa Doc was speaking today on the preservation of the black family.

Prodigy threw on his navy-blue suit, with a light-blue shirt, a power tie, and black alligator shoes. He yelled for Jermaine to hurry up.

Jermaine was stalling like he did when they were kids and he didn't want to go somewhere. He was hoping that Prodigy would get tired of waiting and leave him, but that wasn't going to happen today. He had already conned his way out of going the last couple of Sundays, and today he had to pay the piper. So Prodigy stood in the doorway of Jermaine's room like his mother used to do years ago, and told him if he didn't bring his ass on, that he had better spend the day packing because he was bringing back a one-way bus ticket to Philly.

All of a sudden, it was as if "I Dream of Jeannie" herself dressed him. Jermaine exited the room in a nice blue suit of his own. It wasn't custom-made like Prodigy's, but it hung well and he looked nice.

"Damn, boy, I almost didn't recognize you. I haven't seen you in a suit since you caught that felony charge."

Jermaine, contorting his face, said, "Don't make me curse yo' ass out before I step up in a church."

"When's the last time you been to church?"

"When our homeboy Bozeman died. I was a pallbearer."

"Not a funeral, fool. When is the last time you went to church just to hear the word?"

"Oh, I don't know."

"Well, this will be good for you."

"Church is always full of honeys. Since when did you become so damn holy?"

"I got to be holy, just to go to church. Lock the door behind you."

They jumped into Prodigy's truck and headed to Hopewell. They arrived in time to catch Poppa Doc and Mrs. Ethel walking in. Prodigy yelled for them. They turned around, smiled, and waited. Poppa Doc told Jermaine that he owed him a butt-kicking for it taking so long for them to meet. Jermaine laughed and apologized. After all of the introductions were made, Diane and Brittany walked up and gave Prodigy a hug, and Diane apologized for the night before. They were seated, and waited for the sermon to begin.

A young visiting pastor walked up and said that he wanted to give thanks for the black woman. He asked that everyone close their eyes and bow their heads. As the congregation's chins hit their chests, he launched into a poem:

"Dear Lord, we'd like to give thanks to you today for all that you've given and for all that you will continue to give. And today, Lord, I'd like to thank you for the black woman. For it is she that allows us to be the man. It is the black woman who has been the last to go to sleep and the first to rise. It is that black woman who carried you, who nourished you, who gave you life. It is the black woman who cooked and cleaned to send you to school. It is that same black woman who put the house up and risked being homeless when you got locked up for acting a fool. It is the black woman who raised you, your brothers and sisters all alone. She did it cuz she loved you and because Daddy was gone. I love the black woman, fat, skinny, short, or tall. The way she rolls her neck and sucks her teeth. Thick lips, fat hips and all. So every day is Mother's Day because all respect is due. Black woman, there is no such thing as a family without one of you."

The pastor asked that everyone lift their heads, and told everyone to look to their left and to their right and thank a black woman.

After he exited stage left, Poppa Doc was introduced and called to the podium. He gingerly walked up to the pulpit and a silence fell over the entire congregation as he began to speak.

"People always ask me the key to the longevity of my wife and me. And I used to say things like 'I love her,' or 'We're friends,' and although both of those things are true, it's something more profound that has kept us together for forty-five years. My wife is holding up six fingers, so I guess I'll be sleeping on the couch tonight." The congregation roared with laughter. Poppa Doc tried to recover. "Sorry, honey, time just flies when I'm with you and I lose track of all time." More laughter. "I'm trying, y'all, but I still think I'll be on the couch," Poppa Doc said, before continuing his soliloquy.

"But the one thing that I can honestly say that has kept us together is respect. I respect my wife and she respects me. Because believe me when I tell you that in our forty-six years, we have done every possible thing conceivable except disrespect each other. I don't mean to rain on anyone's parade, but love fades and looks change. So don't focus so much on the way a person looks, because you can buy looks. One trip to the plastic surgeon's office can do wonders. Some of y'all will have to make more than one trip, but what I'm trying to say is, judge people for their character, not their appearance.

"Now, I bet some of you are saying, 'I respect my wife or

my husband, but we still can't go a week without a knock-down-drag-out fight.' Then I will have to say that you don't truly respect your spouse. Because you can't respect someone and call them all kinds of foul names just to hurt that person's feelings. You can't respect someone when you stay out all times of the night in places that you don't have any business in. You can't respect someone when you put your hands on him or her in anger. Men, you don't respect your women when you impregnate them and leave them to fend for themselves. Ladies, you don't respect your man when you've always got your hand out, knowing he's doing all he can. You must respect yourself before you can respect anyone else."

The congregation shook with applause. Poppa Doc continued.

"I was listening to the previous gentleman's poem, and he said something that is crucial to the preservation of the black family, and that's that women have to allow you to be a man. Now, I know some of my hardheads are buffing at that, but it's true. If you want to have harmony in your relationship, then the woman can't be barking at you whenever things don't go her way. Some of you women want your cake and your ice cream. Some of you wanna be old-fashioned when it comes time for paying the bills, but wanna holla, 'I ain't yo' slave!' when it's time to cook and clean. No man can make a woman do anything that she doesn't want to do. So it's the woman who holds the key—this is considering that the man wants to act right—to have a successful marriage. I'm old-fashioned and I believe that the man is the head of the household, but that doesn't mean I run my house. My wife runs our home. We discuss everything. We don't always agree, but that's where respect comes in. I make the final decisions and I take full responsibility when things don't go right, but when those things don't go right, she doesn't say, 'I told you so.' Do you know why she doesn't say things like that? Because we are not in competition to see who is right the most, we are in a partnership. And as many of you know, partnerships take sacrifices." Poppa Doc paused to let the applause die down.

"I'll say one more thing, and then I'll leave you. The black family is in trouble. Black men make up twelve percent of the population, yet we are over sixty percent of the prison population. Something isn't right. Black men, we have to start being accountable for each other. And we have to stop running out on our children. Even if the person that needs your help is not in your immediate family, he is still in the black family. We have to stop selling one another out to look good. I heard of a young man that sold his own mother crack cocaine. Something's not right! Although the scales are still unbalanced, we can't blame the white man for our genocide. Someone told me that blacks don't bring the drugs here. They said it's the white man that preys on the misery of blacks and it's him that floods our communities with drugs and alcohol. I say that may be true, but is the white man putting a gun to your head and making you sniff it, sell it, or smoke it? I've yet to see that happen. We have to start being accountable for our actions, and that means taking care of our women and our children. Men, I challenge each of you to be a father to your children, every day of their lives. May God shine his light on each of you," Poppa Doc said to a standing ovation.

12

Guess Who's Coming to Dinner

here was a rumble outside the door. Then it went away. The telephone rang twice, then stopped. Then the rumble came back. "Twelve o'clock, it's twelve o'clock," a female voice said in a deep southern accent. He could hear other voices outside the door, but he was still a little disoriented. He stared at the ceiling, trying to gather himself. Then the rumble became louder, followed by laughter.

Bernard pulled himself up and sat on the edge of the bed. Thoughts of yesterday were waiting on him. He stood and walked across the carpeted floor to the door. A lady in her early fifties was standing behind a cleaning cart. "You checking out or staying, sir?" she said, smiling.

"I think I'll stay another night," Bernard said.

"You need to tell the front desk, because they got you checking out today! Would you like for me to clean your room?" she asked politely.

"No, thank you, and I'll give the front desk a call," Bernard said, as he pushed the door closed.

He walked over to the desk in the corner of his room and lifted the telephone receiver.

"Front desk!" a female voice said.

"This is Bernard Charles in 306, I'll be extending my stay for another day or so."

"One more day, sir?" the desk clerk asked.

"I don't know. Charge a week to the card, and if I leave before then, I'll just have you credit the difference," Bernard said.

"No problem, and I hope you enjoy your stay at the Fairfield Inn," the clerk said before hanging up.

Bernard showered and got dressed. He walked down to the hotel lobby and ate a quiet meal alone. He really didn't have anyone nearby he could call, because once he left South Carolina he cut all ties. He reached for the cell phone at his hip to check his voice messages. He dialed in and heard Diane crying softly, asking if he could forgive her. He deleted the message before she finished whatever she was saying. Then Fred, his friend from work, left a message saying that he would cover for him as long as he needed to be out of the office. Poppa Doc was next, saying that he was really concerned and for Bernard to at least give him a call to let him know how he was doing. Then, to Bernard's surprise, Prodigy left a message that expressed his concern also. Brittany left a message saying how much she missed her daddy and that she wanted him to come and get her.

After listening to the people who were really close to him, he found himself dialing Poppa Doc's number. Diane picked up. He hung up the phone. He wasn't ready to speak with her. He called his office and left a voice mail for Fred, letting him know that he would probably be out for the following week but would let him know of any change of plans. He wanted to call Prodigy to thank him for calling, but he erased the message before writing down his number. A smile found its way onto his face when he'd heard Prodigy's voice. *He really is a cool guy,* Bernard thought. He felt better after he took his phone away from his ear, but he was still a little uneasy.

After his meal, Bernard found himself back on I-20 east, headed to East Dicksville. He had a hard time remembering the streets, although some things did look familiar. There were a couple of new establishments, but for the most part his birth town hadn't progressed much since he'd left.

He rode slowly, taking in the sights that he never thought he'd see again. Living in Atlanta for almost twenty years made East Dicksville seem so . . . primitive. After a turn here and a turn there he found himself on his old street, looking at the house he was born in. With the exception of the streets now being paved, the area looked exactly as he'd left it. He parked on the street in front of his old home and stared at the place where his foundation was laid. The house looked like it may have had a coat of paint, because he remembered it being darker.

A little boy, who looked to be about the same age as Bernard was when he last lived in the home, stood up on the porch and waved. Bernard waved back. He glanced over at Mrs. Loula Mae's. It looked as if she had added a screen on her porch.

Bernard exited his truck and went over to Mrs. Loula Mae's house. He walked up the six cement steps and knocked on the porch door. He heard some moaning coming from the screened-in porch, but he couldn't decipher it. He opened the screen door to find Mrs. Loula Mae sitting in a rocking chair with her face contorted into a permanent frown, enjoying the sunshine. Her lips were quivering and she was mumbling something. She still wore a nightgown and the pink rollers.

Then an older gentleman who didn't look familiar stumbled out of the house.

"Can I help you?" the man said in his drunken stupor.

"My name is Bernard Charles, and I used to live here," Bernard said as the memories of his growing up in the liquor house came rushing back to him.

The man squinted his eyes and turned his head as if trying to get a better look. "Oh yeah, I 'member you. How you doing? Sit down. You want a drink?" the man said, but Bernard knew he was lying about recognizing him. The man fell back into a rocking chair beside Mrs. Loula Mae and motioned for Bernard to do the same.

"I've been doing well. And your name?" Bernard asked as he took a seat in a folding chair by the door.

"Why? You the law?"

"No, sir, I'm not the police!"

"You wanna drink? Man, you sho' do look like the law. One of them undercover lawmen," the man said again.

"No, sir, I don't drink. And I promise you that I'm not the police."

"You don't drink! Well, what the hell you doin' here? That's a good-lookin' watch ya got there," the man said, admiring the TAG Heuer that Diane had given him for their anniversary.

"Just dropped by to say hello," Bernard said as he stood up to leave, but something in Mrs. Loula Mae's eyes beckoned him to stay. He sat back down.

"Vernon Wells's my name. You bet' not be the law or I'll hafta kill ya fa lyin'," Vernon said, as he smiled. He must have forgotten to use his Dentu-Grip, because his top plate of teeth slipped out of his mouth. He caught it, placed it back in his mouth and acted as if nothing had happened.

"Nice to meet you, Mr. Wells," Bernard said, smiling and shaking his head. He then turned his attention to Mrs. Loula Mae, who hadn't taken her eyes off him since he'd arrived. Her eyes were smiling but her mouth stayed in its deformed shape.

"How are you today, Mrs. Loula Mae?"

She moaned hard and stirred in her seat. Vernon spoke up. "She can't talk, but she can understand you, go ahead and talk. I just got to get her writing pad. She had a stroke about two years ago. I'll be back directly," Vernon said as he staggered to his feet and stumbled back into the house.

It was an awkward moment for Bernard, seeing the woman who was once as strong as a man now sitting there helplessly rocking and unable to speak. She was still a very large woman, but her face seemed smaller. Vernon returned with a yellow legal pad and a blue Magic Marker. He handed the items to Mrs. Loula Mae. She wrote, *How you?*

"I'm fine, and you?" Bernard said.

She nodded her head, eyes still smiling.

"Do you need anything?" Bernard asked.

She shook her head, and wrote the word "Momma" on the pad.

This time Bernard shook his head. Letting her know that he hadn't seen his mother. Mrs. Loula Mae hit the pad with the marker and nodded her head. Bernard looked to Vernon.

"What is she saying, Mr. Wells?"

"I'on know. Loula, what the hell you talkin' 'bout?"

Mrs. Loula Mae wrote the word "Parker's" on the pad.

Vernon looked at it but still couldn't make out what she was talking about. He shook his head. Mrs. Loula Mae obviously still had some fire, because she narrowed her eyes at Vernon as if to say, "You better think hard."

He stared at the paper, then back at her. She pointed toward town. He caught on. "Oh, Parker's is the crazy house. I guess that's what she mean."

Mrs. Loula Mae nodded her head intently. Bernard thought that she wanted to go to the place called Parker's.

"Would you like a ride? Is that what you are asking me?" Bernard said.

Mrs. Loula Mae shook her head and pointed at the word

"Momma," then pointed toward town. She did that over and over.

Bernard finally caught on to what she was trying to say. He couldn't believe it. He jumped to his feet and asked Mrs. Loula Mae if his mother was at this place that she had written on the pad. She nodded her head hard. Bernard leaned down and kissed her on her head. He shook Vernon's hand, ran down the stairs, and jumped into his truck.

Bernard drove like a madman up the main street. He looked for signs that said Parker's. Just as he was about to stop and ask someone, he saw a small green and white sign sitting on a lawn that read, PARKER MENTAL HEALTH FACILITY. Bernard turned his truck into the parking lot and hit the ground running. He walked into the quiet lobby and noticed three older black women watching television. He wondered if one of those women was his mother. He walked over and looked at each one of them, but none of them looked familiar, so he stopped at the desk.

A woman wearing a blue business suit, who looked to be of some mixed heritage, asked if she could help him.

"Yes! I'm here looking for a woman by the name of Susan Charles," Bernard said anxiously, with tears welling up in his eyes.

The woman put down the folder that she was holding and picked up another file.

"And you are?" she asked.

"Bernard Charles!"

The woman stopped looking at the folder and stared at Bernard. She smiled and said, "God is good!" She had long lost hope in ever meeting the man Susan talked about daily. "Yes, your mother is here! Please follow me," the woman said, smiling but almost in tears.

Bernard's heart raced. He pinched himself to make sure he wasn't dreaming. He followed the lady.

"My name is Carolyn St. Jean," she said, extending her hand. "Your mother is a very sweet lady and she has been talking about you for quite sometime now. She said that you would be coming for her one day."

"How long has she been here? Is she alright? Where is she?" Bernard rambled on as they walked down the hall and waited for the elevators.

"She's fine. But she wouldn't talk to the officers, so they did her like they do any other black person who they don't understand, brought her here. She doesn't have a mental disorder, we just had the space available."

"What officers?"

"The correction officers over at the prison."

"What prison?"

Carolyn stopped walking and turned to Bernard. She asked him, "When was the last time you saw your mother?"

"Not since I was a little boy. But what prison are you talking about?"

"Your mother spent nineteen years in a woman's correctional facility. She's been here for the last seven years!" Carolyn said, realizing that this was all new to Bernard.

"Prison! For what?" Bernard asked, astonished.

"I don't know the specifics of her case, but I can gather that information if you would like."

"Can I take her home?"

"Absolutely! The only reason that she's here is because the State could not release her, due to what they considered to be a mental illness. When in fact she just doesn't have much to say to anyone. Since she's been here, I'm the only one she has opened up to. The first thing she told me was that she had a son."

Bernard was speechless. Stunned!

"I put in a request to locate the next of kin, but the system is so backed up, they probably haven't even started the investigation."

"I had no idea. I didn't know where she was."

"She will be overwhelmed to see you, I'm sure."

They made it to the third floor, and Carolyn opened the door. Susan Charles sat with her back to them as she filled a bird feeder. Her hair was still parted in the middle, just as Bernard last remembered it.

"Mrs. Charles, I have a surprise for you."

Bernard could no longer stop the flow of tears. He never thought that he'd see his mother again, yet here she was in the same room with him. He walked slowly over to her as if he might disturb her. "Momma!"

Susan turned around and calmly smiled. She stood up and placed her cinnamon-brown hands together and closed her eyes.

"Thank you, Jesus," she said softly as tears rushed down her face.

"Carolyn, that's my boy I was telling you about."

"I know, Mrs. Charles, I know!"

She had gained some weight, but her perfectly smooth skin had remained the same. Her hair was still long, but time had turned it gray. And due to a slight case of glaucoma she wore a pair of silver wire-rimmed glasses.

Bernard held his mother close and began to cry. He turned to Carolyn and said, "What do I need to do in order to take her home?"

"Just sign the papers," Carolyn said, crying herself.

"Home? I'm going home?" Susan eyes lit up.

"Yes, Momma, we are going home."

Carolyn informed Bernard that she could release his mother that day, but they would have to come back the first thing in the morning to fill out all of the paperwork.

Susan pointed at her suitcase. "I knew you would find me. I never unpacked. Seven years and I never gave up hope. You see what faith can bring!"

Bernard picked up the bag and thanked Carolyn St. Jean for taking such good care of his mother. He gave her a business card, wrote his hotel information on the back, and took Carolyn's card as well. As he and his mother walked hand in hand out of the hospital, all of his problems seemed to have disappeared.

"You look so good. I missed you so much, son," Susan said as she continued to cry. "You have to excuse me, but I've been holding back these tears for a long time."

Bernard cried and smiled as he put his mother's belongings in the back of his truck.

"You look like you're doing good for yourself," Susan said as she ran her hands across the soft leather seats.

Bernard looked at his mother and said, "Now that I have you, I'm doing so much better. Are you hungry?"

"Yes! Let's have dinner."

"What would you like?"

"I don't care, as long as you're there."

Bernard drove over to Florence and found a nice steak house. They sat down, neither of them wanting to take their eyes off of the other. Bernard's cell phone rang. He held up a finger. "Excuse me, Momma," he said, as he answered the phone. "Hello!"

"Daddy! Where are you? When are you coming home?"

Bernard smiled. "I'll be home real soon, and do I have a surprise for you!"

"What did you get me?" Brittany asked, excited.

"I didn't get you anything," Bernard said as he shook his head, looking at his mother. *Was this real?* he thought.

"Okay, then what is my surprise?"

"Would you like to speak to her?"

"Speak to who?"

"It's a surprise! Hold on, Brittany." Bernard handed his cell phone to his mother and made the introduction. "Momma, this is your granddaughter, Brittany."

Susan covered her mouth and began to cry again. She took the phone. "Hello, darling."

"Hi!" Brittany said, not knowing whom she was talking to.

"This is your Grandma Susan."

"Hi, Grandma. You coming home with Daddy?"

"Yes, sweetie, and I can't wait to meet you! How old are you?"

"Nine! My birthday was yesterday."

"Well, Grandma's gonna have to stop and buy you something real nice. I can't wait to see you."

"Me too. I want to see you now."

"Oh, aren't you a darling? How are you doing in school?"

"I made the honor roll last nine weeks, but I missed perfect attendance because I had the chicken pox."

"Well, that's alright, you couldn't help that. I'm so proud of you. I'm gonna give you back to your daddy, okay? And I love you."

"I love you too. Daddy talks about you all the time. He says I look like you."

"Oh, you're much prettier than me. Your daddy just showed me a picture of you and I don't know if I can wait another minute. Looks like we're going to have to get our food to go. I'll see you soon. I love you."

"I love you too, Grandma."

Bernard took the phone back and told Brittany that he would see her sometime tomorrow. He told her to tell everyone that all was well and he would see them when he returned.

Susan bowed her head into her hands and wept softly.

She had been waiting for this moment for more than twenty-five years, but now that it had arrived she was truly overwhelmed.

"Where do you live, son?" Susan said, still looking at the family portrait that Bernard had given her. "May I keep it?"

"Atlanta! And, Momma, you don't have to ask me for anything. Whatever your heart can dream up, I'll provide it."

"You have a beautiful family!"

"Yes, I do!" Bernard said as he nodded his head and looked at his mother. "I really and truly do."

Susan was ready to meet her granddaughter, so she asked if they could take the food with them. Bernard called the number on the card that Carolyn had given him and asked her if they could handle all of the paperwork via fax and Federal Express. She said that she understood and that she was sure something could be worked out. She asked that he tell Susan to write or call her sometime.

As soon as the food arrived, Susan asked the waiter to pack it up. She told him that her grandbaby was waiting on her and she couldn't let her wait another minute. Once he was done wrapping the food, Susan and Bernard headed back to the hotel to gather Bernard's things. Bernard called the front desk and informed them that he would be checking out after all. Susan wanted to go to the mall and buy Brittany a birthday gift, so they headed over to Magnolia Mall.

Susan picked out a gold locket and chain. Bernard reached for his wallet to pay the cashier and Susan slapped his hand. "Now, don't make me cut yo' butt, chile. That's my grandbaby, and I'll buy her gift myself," Susan said quite frankly. She reached in her purse and removed a large roll of hundred-dollar bills.

"Momma, we're gonna have to get you to the bank and open you an account," Bernard said.

"I don't trust those white folks with my money," Susan said, handing the white cashier two hundred-dollar bills.

"Well, we'll go to Capital City Bank or Citizens Trust. Those are black-owned banks."

"Oh, we have black people owning banks now? I like that, but I still don't trust it!" Susan said.

After the shopping was done, they jumped on I-20 and headed back west to Atlanta. Bernard had so many questions for his mother, but he decided to let her rest. He thought that when she wanted to talk she would. He mashed the accelerator until the speedometer read eighty-five, and set the cruise control.

Susan sat quietly on the passenger side, deep within her own thoughts. She had questions of her own, but wanted to bask in their quiet time, just like days of old. She drifted off to sleep, and Bernard couldn't take his eyes off her.

Three and a half hours later they pulled into Bernard's driveway. The garage door was up and Diane's Volvo was backed in. Brittany was on her Rollerblades with her friend Sierra. She rolled up to the passenger side and opened the door. Susan opened her eyes, saw her grandbaby, and couldn't stop smiling. She got out of the vehicle and kneeled down and hugged Brittany tight. Brittany smiled, turned to Sierra, and said, "This is my grandmother Susan, isn't she pretty?"

Bernard unloaded the bags and left his mother to play with his daughter and her friend. Diane walked out and gave Susan a hug and introduced herself as her daughter-in-law, Diane. Susan stopped smiling at Brittany long enough to give Diane a hug.

Diane asked her if she needed anything, and Susan said that all she ever needed was right in this driveway. Diane asked her to come on in the house, but Susan declined and stayed outside to play with her grandbaby. Diane excused herself and walked back into the house. She nervously walked toward Bernard, but he walked right past her without saying a word. He trotted upstairs to the guest bedroom at the end of the hall and placed his mother's things in there. Diane followed.

"My mother will be living here forever. If you don't like it, then you can find somewhere else to go!" Bernard said.

"Bernard, please don't treat me like that. You know I welcome your mother with open arms. I cried when you cried. I've been praying for this day just as you have."

"You been doing a helluva lot more than praying."

"Can we go to counseling? I really want our marriage. I just made a mistake."

"Yeah, uh-huh!" Bernard said sarcastically as he walked out of the room.

Diane went back into the kitchen and continued cooking. Susan had just about played herself out, so she told Brittany that they could catch up on playing later. Susan went into the house and asked Diane if she needed any help. She was immediately impressed with her son's home.

"I think I've died and gone to heaven!" Susan said to Diane.

"Why do you say that?"

"This home is so lovely! May I have a tour?"

"Sure!" Diane said, as she removed a pot from one of the burners, but Bernard intervened.

"I'll show her," he said as took his mother's hand and lead her through the four bedrooms that were upstairs, the bonus room that Diane had turned into a study, the living room that Diane had decorated with Swedish furnishings and Italian marble, and the den, which was also nicely decorated. They walked through the kitchen and Susan noticed Diane crying, but she didn't say anything. Bernard led her downstairs to the basement, which housed a hand-carved pool table, a television set bigger than any Susan had ever laid eyes on, and a collection of African-American art. She ran her fingers over the black leather theater chairs in the entertainment room and smiled at her son's prosperity.

They walked outside through the basement's sliding doors. They strolled around the lawn until they came upon the deck out back, which sat in a nice shaded area of the house off the kitchen.

They sat out on the deck furniture and talked.

"Son, you all have such a lovely home."

"It's your home too, Momma!" Bernard said.

"Oh no, I'm not gonna live here. You have a family. I'll find someplace close, but families need their space."

Bernard was hurt and it showed. "No, Momma, I won't have it any other way. Now, if you want the basement, then you can have it, but you are staying here. Now, that's final!"

"If you insist! Now, why is my daughter-in-law in there crying?"

Bernard looked down and frustration came over his face. He looked away as if he was trying to find the words to explain.

"Momma, the reason I was in South Carolina was because I needed to get away. Our marriage is in shambles."

Susan was far too wise a woman to form an opinion based on one side of the story, so she calmly nodded her head. She reached over and grabbed her son's hand and said, "Son, God works in mysterious ways! Are you happy to see me?"

"Yes, this ranks up there with the birth of my child," Bernard said.

"Well, believe it or not, I got pretty discouraged that you'd never show up. So I started praying that something would happen to you that would make you have to come home."

"I'm glad that I have you, but our marriage has been falling apart for a long time."

"Now, son, don't take this the wrong way. Hear me out before you respond. I see this beautiful little girl, a very pretty

183

lady in the house with tears in her eyes, and this lovely home, right?"

"I guess!"

"To me, that's enough to fight for. No relationship is without its problems. So work on whatever it is and move forward."

"That's gonna be hard! She's a very selfish woman."

"That's a learned behavior, and just like it was learned it can be unlearned."

"Momma, you don't know her. She's so difficult. I work so hard to give my family everything they need, and she threw it back in my face."

"I understand your pain, but look at the big picture. Sometimes you have to lose in order to win. Son, I hate to sound selfish, but tonight will be the first time in over twenty-five years that I will sleep in a bed that was not issued by the state of South Carolina. And had your wife not done what she did, I would've been sleeping in a state-owned bed tonight. Forgiveness is very important. For the longest time, Bernard, I thought that you could never forgive me for leaving you. But here we are together again."

"Momma, that's different."

"You're right. I did you worse than she ever could do."

"Momma, why did you leave?"

Susan took a long breath as the memories of those hard days crept back into her mind. She turned her chair to face Bernard. She didn't want to talk about it, but she felt she at least owed him an explanation.

"Son, I hated my life, but I loved you so much! I made some mistakes with alcohol and heroin and I hated for you to see me like that. Every time I took a drink or wrapped a belt around my arm, I would think of how far I was pulling myself away from you. So one night Loula asked me to drive her somewhere to get a package of liquor for her shop. I drove and the police pulled us over. Loula had already been arrested a number of times, so I took the blame, thinking that all I would get was maybe a year, which is what she got the first time that she was arrested. I wanted to go to jail, anywhere to clean myself up so that I could be a better person for you. Well, the judge wanted to send a message and sentenced me to twenty-five years. I didn't want them to take you and place you in one of them homes, so I asked Loula Mae to look after you. Son, I'm so sorry. I never meant to leave you like that."

"It's okay, Momma," Bernard said as he stood up and walked behind her to rub her neck.

"The only thing that kept me sane were the letters and cards that you wrote. Loula Mae sent them no sooner than they arrived at her house. Kind of funny how I still ended up in the crazy house, ain't it?" Susan said, trying to smile though her ever-flowing tears.

Bernard reached over the table and wiped the tears from her face. He told her that he loved her and that he respected her more now than he had anyone else in his life. They disengaged themselves from each other when Brittany walked up the stairs to the deck and told them that dinner was ready.

13

Just Like a Daddy

Usually after Sunday church service, Prodigy would have dinner with the Fullers, but today he declined their invitation and headed home. Poppa Doc's speech had touched something personal in him. He always wondered why men had babies and left the mother to be the father. His thoughts drifted to Blake, whose father left him out in this evil world to figure out how to be a man without so much as ever laying eyes on his son. Then he thought about a little fellow closer to home—Kahlil, Jermaine's kid in Philly. He wondered what Jermaine's plans were for his own flesh and blood.

As they piled into the truck and said their good-byes to Poppa Doc and his crew, Prodigy hit Jermaine for some answers. "Jermaine, what are you going to do about Kahlil?"

"What do you mean, what am I gonna do about him?"

"Just what I said. What are you going to do about him? Are you going to send for him once you get your place?"

"P, my son's not even a year old yet. He don't even know I'm gone. Plus he's all up under my moms. Lil' cat don't want no part of me right now."

"Why do you think he's all up under your mom? Because she spends time with him. If you were doing that then he'd be all up under you. Man, this is bonding time. What, you gonna just show up when he's three or four?"

"Oh you done listen to Reverend Ike up there, now you wanna get on my case."

"I'm just saying, dog, neither one of us had our fathers growing up. Don't you think it would be a little unfair to send your seed through that same thing?"

"I'm gonna take care of mine. Why you tryna shine on me?"

"How are you gonna do that, Jermaine? Hustling ain't all that stable. When is the last time you sent some loot up the way for your son?"

"I don't need to, my moms got that."

"Your moms wasn't the one that bust a nut. It was you! Stop putting shit on your moms all the time with your spoiled ass," Prodigy said.

"Nigga, you got lucky and ripped off a wanna-be Gandhi or some damn body. So now you wanna preach that shit to me. Save it, baby! I knew I shouldn't have come down this piece. Now I got to hear what I ain't doing just because you think you straight. Got me going to church and shit."

"I ain't forcing you to stay. You wanna catch an attitude because you living fucked up. Yeah, you'd rather continue doing nothing, cuz it's easy. You gonna be thirty before you know it. All I'm trying to do is save your son from going through the same shit that we went through. You selfish muthafuckas make me sick!"

"P, my son is not out there like that! He's at my mom's house right now! You acting like I just neglected all my responsibilities," Jermaine said, trying to defend his case.

"How you figure you handling your business when you ain't there to raise him? You keep talking about your mom. It should be you!"

"Whatever! P, you always thought you were the shit! Just because I live with you don't mean I gotta square up like yo' ass."

"You sound like a fool. What the fuck does squaring up have to do with taking care of your child? And what the hell you mean 'squaring up,' anyway? Oh, I'm square just because I got a job? Just because I don't wanna be ducking every time I see a police car? Because I'm tired of getting over on people and want to take care of my damn self? You got that stupid nigga mentality."

"Whatever, P! I mean Mr. Perfect!"

"Yo, I'm not that patient with grown-ass men. If you don't like the way I run my ship, you can leave the same way you came. Lazy muthafucka! You need to get off your ass and do something with your life. Start living and stop existing."

They rode the rest of the way home in silence. Jermaine was pissed because he thought that Prodigy was taking this parenting thing too far. As far as he was concerned, his son was being taken care of and Prodigy was blowing this whole thing out of proportion.

Prodigy, on the other hand, was debating whether he was being fair to his cousin. Was he taking his frustrations for all deadbeat dads out on Jermaine? Ever since Nina had told him about the disappearing act that Blake's father pulled, he had been quite sensitive about a man's job to raise his child.

He hated the way his own mother had had to work two or three jobs and was never home, because his own father wanted to run the streets and be a gangbanger. And the way Jermaine's father would show up from time to time with another woman on his arm, looking fly but not offering his Aunt Nettie any money, made him mad. He knew Jermaine like a book, and if he wasn't careful he was going to be the same way that his father was, trifling!

Once they made it home, Jermaine jumped out of the truck and stormed up to his room. Prodigy checked his messages. His mom had called, and Simone had called, saying she needed to talk to him, it was an emergency. He called his mother back.

"Hey, Mom! How are you?"

"I'm fine! I take it that you all went to church?"

"Yes, we did. You should have been there. Poppa Doc spoke today. He was talking about maintaining relationships and thangs."

"Oh yeah! Jermaine went with you?"

"Yeah, he drug his butt up in there."

"How are you and Jermaine making out?"

"We a'ight! I just went off on him about leaving his son for his mom to take care of."

"Nettie said he calls him every night."

"Oh yeah, I didn't know that. I guess I owe him an apology."

"Yeah, I think he really loves the little guy. He's so cute, doesn't look anything like Jermaine. I'm gonna go and pick him up some things in a little while. I got to go over there to help Nettie with some legal troubles she's having with one of her tenants."

"Send me a picture of Kahlil. Jermaine only has Polaroids. When are you coming down again?"

"Do you wanna have Thanksgiving dinner at your place?"

"That's cool. Just don't invite Uncle Ray's clan. I don't feel like putting up hidden cameras or installing metal detectors. That reminds me, he said that Lynette was supposed to be in town."

"I think she's doing hair now. The other three are probably locked up somewhere. It's a shame when you can't trust your own family. I had to stop taking their cases. Of course all of them were pro bono. Soon as I asked for a retainer all I got was 'Aunt Liza, you know I'm on empty.' Funny how they find some money for a lawyer when they can't get in contact with me. Thank God for caller I.D."

"Yeah, sometimes your family can be your worst enemy."

"Well, sweetie, I must be running now. I told Nettie that I'd be there over an hour ago. Tell Jermaine hi for me, and you leave him alone."

"Okay, and don't forget to send the pictures of Kahlil. I want to frame 'em and sit them on my mantel."

"Will do. Love you."

"I love you too," Prodigy said, as he hung up the phone. He decided to give Nina and Blake a call.

Cathy answered on the first ring. "Hello!" she said in a rushed tone.

"Hello! May I speak to Nina or Blake? This is Prodigy!"

"Oh, hi, Prodigy. I thought you were Nina calling. She's at the hospital. Blake had a bad asthma attack."

"Is he alright?" Prodigy asked, concerned.

"I don't know! I'm just sitting here worried to death. I came home from the library and the neighbor told me that an ambulance came and picked him up."

"What hospital did they go to?"

"She said Grady. I was on the phone trying to find out for sure when you called."

"Well, I'm going up there."

"Will you pick me up?" Cathy asked.

"Yeah, I'm on my way."

Prodigy didn't even change his clothes; he headed right back out to his truck, made it onto Memorial Drive, and drove toward Nina's home near East Lake Meadows. Cathy was standing on the corner at the MARTA bus stop waiting for him. She hopped in the truck, looking edgy. Prodigy could tell that she really loved Blake. After all of the time they'd spent together, there was no doubt in his mind that she loved him like he was her own son.

"Thank you, Prodigy. You got here quick!"

"You guys aren't that far from me, and I left soon as I got off the phone with you."

Cathy folded her arms and rocked back and forth as if that would make the truck move faster. "I hope my baby is alright. It drives me crazy thinking about him not being able to breathe. I don't know nothing," Cathy said as tears ran down her coffee-brown face. She looked identical to her sister, Nina, but was about two shades darker. They shared the same big dark eyes.

"Yeah, I'm pretty worried about him myself," Prodigy said as he drove through red lights and stops signs like it was no big deal.

"So you and Blake are pretty close, huh?" Prodigy asked.

"Oh, that's my baby! He's bad, but he's a sweetheart. Ya know!"

"Oh, do I ever! Are you guys from here?"

"No, we're from Seattle, but Blake was born here."

"What brought you guys all the way to the Right Coast?"

"Our dad! He's retired Air Force. Our mother passed away of pneumonia about seven years ago, so we came over here to stay with our dad."

"Does he still live here?" Prodigy asked.

"Yeah, he comes around when he's not drinking. Nina won't open the door for him if he's had a drink. He's pretty abusive, verbally, that is."

"That's too bad."

"Yeah. He's a good man. Always took care of us, but he just can't seem to shake that alcohol. And when he's drinking he's a totally different person. We got tired of the Jekyll and Hyde routine and moved out of his house to over there," Cathy said, pointing back at Lil' Vietnam.

"You gotta do what you gotta do."

"Ya know! We're working on getting a better place."

"Yeah, Nina told me. You guys will be a'ight."

"Got to." Cathy was quiet for a moment, then she turned to Prodigy and said, "So do you like my sister?"

"I think she's sweet."

"That's not what I asked you."

"Yeah, I like her. I think she's sweet," Prodigy said, smiling as he repeated his words.

"She hasn't dated in a long time. After Blake's punk for a daddy ran out on her she kind of lost her faith in men. She used to be bad, but now she's a pretty good judge of character. My sister has a trifling-man-o-meter equipped with a death ray."

"Yeah, she doesn't seem to have time for a lot of foolishness, but she's still a sweetie."

"She can't afford to, but she's a really nice person. So you better treat her nice or I'll have to hunt you down and take you out."

"You must really love your sister to up and snuff somebody out like that."

"I love her, but I respect her so much. She's been my mother for the last seven years. You know that we don't have to live out there, but she wants me to go to college instead of working full-time. So she's paying her way and my way through school. She only has one more class and she'll have her master's, then we're out of there."

"How old are you, Cathy?"

"I'm twenty-one!"

"You seem to be pretty mature for a twenty-one-year-old."

"Yeah. Nina preaches that we have no time for games. She said we can play when we're paid."

"I'd have to agree! I wish I would've got that lesson a little sooner."

"Nina said that you have a nice house, so you must've done something right."

"God has been looking out for me. I had absolutely nothing to do with it," Prodigy said, thinking about how many times he had come close to adding to the criminal population.

"I'll tell you a secret."

"What's that?"

"Nina likes you too. She hasn't said anything, it's just the way she lights up when Blake is running around there hollering your name fifty-five times a minute." Cathy smiled, then her worry lines returned as they approached the hospital.

They pulled into the emergency-room parking lot of Grady Memorial Hospital. Prodigy let Cathy out at the big sliding doors. He told her not to wait on him and that he had to try and find somewhere to park. Once he made it inside, all he saw were a thousand people, some in white outfits and some in blue, running a thousand different places. He walked up to a female desk clerk, who was on the phone, typing on a PC, and looking at a chart, and asked her where he could find Blake Laws. She must have just given Cathy the same information because without even looking at anything she blurted, "Two-oh-two," and went back to her million and one tasks. He decided to take a chance and try to find 202 on his own. She didn't look like she wanted to be disturbed again. He was in luck. Just as he turned down the hallway he saw a sign leading him to his destination. He ran into Cathy as he was walking toward Blake's room. She said that Nina was hungry, so she was going to get something from the cafeteria. She asked Prodigy if he wanted anything and he declined.

Prodigy walked into the room and noticed Blake lying on the bed with tubes running from his mouth. He thought the worst, and a painful feeling came over him that he couldn't explain. He hadn't felt this way since his grandmother passed away a year ago. Why was he so attached to this child? All of this had happened within a month's time. He looked at Nina, who sat in a chair with her legs folded Indian-style, reading a book. She looked up at him and smiled.

"Thanks for bringing my sister," Nina said.

"Actually she just caught a ride. I called and she told me what happened, so I was on my way."

"That's awfully sweet of you."

"How's he doing?"

"He'll be fine. It looks worse than it is. They have to stabilize his breathing before they can remove the tubes. How was church? You look nice!"

"It was good, and thank you. What happened?" Prodigy asked, genuinely concerned about Blake's health.

"A little too much running and jumping. He aggravated his asthma."

"At the party, huh? I'm sorry," Prodigy said as he removed his suit coat and placed it on the back of the door.

"Oh no, it's not your fault. You know how kids are—if it's not one thing then it's another," Nina said calmly.

"Nah, I don't know how kids are. I don't have any, remember?"

"Do you ever want any kids, Prodigy?"

"Sure, I love kids. I'm just concerned about what kind of father I would be. Kids are a lifetime commitment."

"Nothing's wrong with commitment. Or is there?"

"No! I don't have a problem with commitment; it's just that when I have a child, I want to be there with him or her every day of every year. The one thing that I fear is breaking up with my spouse and only being allowed to see my child every other weekend. I've got a friend going through that and he's miserable. He calculated the days that he has his son and came up with sixty-one for the year. That's ten months that he didn't see his child. I couldn't live with that. How can you be an effective parent four days out of the month and two weeks in the summer? Whoever made up that law had to be a deadbeat dad."

"Just to hear you say that lets me know that you'll be a wonderful father! Any child will be lucky to have you," Nina said, as she stood up and walked over to Blake. He was still sleeping. Prodigy walked over and stood beside her. She leaned back into his chest. He responded by placing his arm around her shoulders.

She whispered, "Thank you, Prodigy."

"For what?" he whispered back.

"For being you," Nina said as she nudged him with her elbow.

"Thank you, but you deserve all the praise. I learned a lot about you on the way over here."

"Cathy?" Nina said as she smiled a proud smile. "That girl can't hold water, but I love her."

"How old are you, Nina?"

"Twenty-six! And you?"

"Twenty-eight," Prodigy replied. He was happy that she didn't give him one of those "Don't you know it's not polite to ask a woman her age?" comments. *Why not?* He thought. *How in the hell are you supposed to know how old the person is you are dealing with? You can't tell these days, not with the way some of the young girls' asses are sticking out.*

Prodigy took a chance on his feelings. He turned Nina's body around so that she was facing him. He ran his fingers through her long, straight black hair and looked into her narcoticlike dark eyes. He tilted her head slightly and lowered his head to her level. Nina closed her eyes and waited to be kissed. At the last second he changed the course of his lips and pecked her on her forehead. Something about this woman said forever, and he didn't want to ruin it by moving too fast. He decided to change the subject.

"What were you reading?" he said as he removed a black book from her hand.

"*Thunderland*! It's a horror novel, written by the only black horror writer that I've ever heard of."

"Brandon Massey!" Prodigy said, reading the author's name on the cover.

"Is it any good?"

"Uh-huh, it's real good. It's got all black characters. Do you read, Mr. Banks? I didn't see any books when I visited your place."

"Oh yeah! All of my books are on a shelf in my bedroom. My mother used to read all the time when I was growing up, so it's something that I picked up trying to act grown."

"At least her influences were positive. What types of books do you read?"

"Mostly African-American writers. You know, Eric Jerome Dickey, J. California Cooper, Walter Mosley. Every now and then I'll pick up an autobiography. I liked the Geronimo Pratt book and Nathan McCall's *Makes Me Wanna Holler.*"

"Why does he name all of his books after Marvin Gaye's songs?"

"Want me to call and ask him?"

"Do you know him?"

"Nah, I was just kidding."

"I think he lives in Atlanta. What about E. Lynn Harris, ever read any of his work?" Nina asked, wanting to get his take on homosexuality.

"I read one of his books. It was pretty good. It's some pretty hard reading for a heterosexual like myself, but he definitely has the gift of telling a good tale. As a matter of fact, I'm reading this book now called *Lookin' for Luv.*"

"Who wrote it?"

"Cat name Carl Weber."

"Is it any good? I can't stand to see folks waste paper."

"Yeah, it's hot."

Nina was impressed. She couldn't think of one thing that she disliked about this man, but she knew that she had to be careful. She once felt this way about Blake's father. Yet there was still something about this man named Prodigy that she liked. He was obviously a very caring individual, with him volunteering his time at the youth center coupled with the fact that he was sitting here with her and he didn't have to be. He seemed to be responsible. He was gainfully employed, and most of all he took an interest in her son that no other man had. All of this and he never once tried to come on to her. Either he was really caring or really cunning. She figured she'd take her chances as she nestled back in his arms to watch over Blake.

Cathy walked back in, carrying a McDonald's bag. She looked at them all hugged up and gave an obvious wink to Nina, who only shook her head.

"Prodigy, I bought you a Quarter Pounder Value Meal."

"I said I didn't—"

"I don't wanna hear it. Eat and be merry," Cathy said, as she waved his comment off.

"Here!" Prodigy said as he reached in his pants pocket and handed her a twenty-dollar bill.

"It's okay. I got it," Cathy said, waving off his offering.

"No, take it!" Prodigy insisted.

"Okay, if you insist. Thank you."

"No problem."

They gathered around Blake's feeding tray, said their blessings, and got their grub on.

The doctor came in and said that all of Blake's test results looked good, but that they wanted to monitor him overnight.

Prodigy was at a loss as to what to do. He didn't want to

leave them there, but he couldn't miss any more days of work. He was just starting to get used to everyone not saying anything when he arrived on time, plus Craig surprised everyone by selecting Prodigy as one of the candidates for promotion to supervisor. After all, his job performance had always been exceptional, he just had a problem making it to work on time. Just this last Friday, Craig pulled him aside and told him not to miss work for any reason or he would probably not be selected. He knew that with all of the excuses that he'd come up with in the past no one would believe that he truly had a real emergency. He looked at Blake and wished that he'd never cried wolf.

He excused himself and walked out into the hallway to make a call to Jermaine. He wanted to apologize and let him know that he probably wouldn't be in tonight, but his cell phone started ringing before he could dial the number.

"Hello!"

"I need to talk to you. Why didn't you call me back?" Simone asked.

"I'm gonna have to call you back. I can't talk right now," he said, not interested in what she had to say. Prodigy didn't dislike Simone, he just felt it was time for a change.

"Well, when can you talk? This is important."

"Is tomorrow too late?"

"That's fine, but I need to be the first call you make. Bye!"

"Bye!" Prodigy hung up, wondering what she was all up in arms about. Her tone was a little too serious for his liking, but oh well! He dialed the number to his house.

"Holla, holla!" Jermaine answered.

"What's up, dog?"

"Nothing. I'm about to go out with Uncle Ray."

"Is he there?"

"Nah, not yet."

"Where y'all going?"

"He wants me to help him move some stuff. He said he bought a new house."

"Oh yeah. Tell him I said what's up. Hey, dog, I owe you an apology for what I said earlier, or maybe for the way I said it."

"Nah, you cool. I do need to check myself with putting everything on Moms."

"I asked my mom to send us a picture of Kahlil so we can put it up. She was on her way over to your mom's spot."

"She over there now, I just got off of the phone with 'em. Troy won't pay his rent. I wish I was up there. I'd knock 'em the fuck out. You see how people act when you try to help them. They would have been at some shelter if Moms didn't look. With his badass credit!"

"Yeah, my moms told me something about that earlier, but I didn't know it was Troy she was talking about," Prodigy said, alarmed that their childhood friend would do his aunt like that.

"He only actin' up cuz I'm down here."

"We might have to take a trip. I ain't feelin' that at all." Prodigy frowned at the thought of someone taking advantage of his aunt.

"I'm hip!"

"Look here, dog, I gotta roll. I just called to get straight."

"You straight! Peace."

Prodigy hung up and went back into the room. He sat in one of the hospital recliners and kicked his feet up.

Cathy stood over Blake and looked just as worried as Nina.

"Nina, do you want me to stay with you?" Cathy asked.

"You don't have to, we'll be fine."

"Are you sure?"

"Yeah, go ahead and go to work."

"Okay, but call me if you need anything," Cathy said as she gathered her bags.

"I will."

"Hey, Cathy, do you need a ride to work?"

"Oh no, I work right around the corner."

"Where?"

"At Graphic Mountain. I design Web pages," Cathy said proudly. Since her major was computer engineering, she was happy to land a paying job, especially when most of her classmates were still interning.

After Cathy left, Prodigy looked at Nina, who had snuggled into bed beside Blake. Right then and there, he decided that there was no way that he was leaving them up here alone. He called his job and explained his situation to Brenda's voice mail. He figured that he wouldn't get the promotion, but being there for someone was much more gratifying.

Nina overheard him leaving the message and mouthed a thank-you. She closed her eyes and dozed off to sleep. He picked up her novel and read until he too dozed off.

14

Stop Crying!

As the Charles family gobbled down tender roast beef, collard greens, mashed potatoes, and corn bread, Bernard couldn't take his eyes off of his mother. Susan would look up every now and then and catch him staring, but all she did was smile. He would smile too, then turn away as to not be rude and continue feasting. But when his eyes met Diane's, the smile flipped upside down into a repulsive frown. His mother made him feel like a child who'd just met his hero for the first time. Diane made him feel like he was looking into the face of the bully that just stole his bike.

After they finished the feast fit for a king that Diane had prepared, Susan insisted on helping Diane and Brittany with the cleaning. Bernard looked at Diane and nodded a courteous thank-you. He pulled his overly stuffed tummy up and walked around to the den to catch the rest of the basketball game. As he watched the Hawks take it to the Knicks, he kept glancing back into the kitchen, sneaking a peek at the three women that were responsible for nearly all of the joy and pain that had taken place in his life. He was sure that he and Diane's relationship was over; it was just a matter of figuring out which one of them was going to make the move first. There were some things that he just could not forgive, and infidelity was one of them.

Susan finished her meal and went straight toward the kitchen for cleanup. She was an old-fashioned woman and would not allow Diane to load the dishwasher. She said that maybe one day she would get used to it, but today she wanted to wash them by hand with her granddaughter. She prepared the hot soapy water and pulled a bar stool up to the sink so that Brittany could rinse while she washed.

Diane was putting the leftovers in plastic containers for Bernard's lunch and wiping down the countertops. She still wore a look of hurt and desperation. The last thing that she ever wanted to do was hurt her husband. But after years of not being loved the way that she thought she should be loved, she got weak and made the mistake that would forever change her life. Every time she looked at the hurt in Bernard's eyes she wanted to cry, but the blame was not hers alone, she thought.

After Diane finished up what she was doing, she asked Susan if she needed for her to take over. Susan, who was enjoying her conversation with her granddaughter so much, smiled, politely shook her head, and continued washing.

Diane walked into the living room and sat in a chair across from Bernard. She wanted to say something but didn't know where to start.

Bernard tensed up when Diane walked into the room and sat down. He knew that he could no longer enjoy the game in peace. He looked at her, but all he felt for her was disdain. He tightened his gaze on the television and tried to watch the Knicks/Hawks game.

"Can we talk about it?" Diane asked.

"No!" Bernard growled.

Diane didn't want to push the issue, but she could no longer hold back the tears. She stood up and hurried upstairs to their bedroom. Bernard was unmoved by her stream of what he considered to be crocodile tears. As far as he was concerned, Diane was a spoiled brat who would play whoever to get whatever she wanted.

It was halftime and he needed to take a bathroom break. He tried the bathroom by the kitchen, but his mother was in there, so he ran upstairs to use the one in the hallway. As he was leaving he noticed Diane packing her clothes. They made eye contact briefly, but he didn't mumble a word.

Diane dropped the garment that she was placing in a bag and lowered her head. She was hoping that he would say something. And now she too was sure that their ten years as husband and wife had come to an abrupt end. He didn't even care that she was leaving. Didn't even ask her where she was going. *Obviously, he doesn't care for me,* she thought.

Susan and Brittany were coming up the stairs as Bernard was turning to go back down. Susan saw what Diane was doing. She reached down and gave Brittany a big hug. She told her to go get herself ready for bed and that she would be in shortly. During their dishwashing bonding session, Brittany made her promise that she would sleep with her tonight.

Susan walked into the room that Diane was in and stood beside her daughter-in-law. She placed her hand on Diane's hand.

"I don't know everything, but maybe I can help," Susan said as she took a seat on the end of the bed and tapped her hand on the comforter beside her for Diane to take a seat.

"Oh, Mrs. Charles, I messed up so bad," Diane said, sitting down as the tears rushed down her face. She fell into Susan's waiting arms.

"Mrs. Charles, I'm sorry that you had to come into our home when it's like this."

"Don't you go worrying about that now, chile," Susan said as she rubbed her hand up and down Diane's back.

"I messed up so bad. I don't know if he'll ever be able to forgive me."

"He will! Just give him some time. Healing takes time."

"I don't know! I did something that I don't know if he can heal from."

"Chile, you ain't done nothin' that hasn't been done before. But I understand men tend to look at women a little differently when the woman messes up. But your issue is not with Bernard, it's with God. Pray for Him to forgive you and He will. Once that's taken care of, everything else will fall in place."

"But he won't even talk to me."

"Who won't talk to you?"

"Bernard!"

"Baby you're not listening. Diane, do you believe in God?"

Diane thought about her episode with the pastor that got her in all this mess and said, "Did Bernard tell you what I did?"

"No, he didn't, and unless it was blasphemy then it's not important."

"It wasn't God, but he was supposed to be a man of God. I had an affair with the pastor of our church."

"Okay, but what does that have to do with God? That pastor was a man, and men makes mistakes."

"I know, but I trusted him."

"What about yourself? Did you trust yourself? Because he couldn't have done anything that you didn't let him do, unless he forced himself on you."

Diane started crying again. She stood up and said, "No he didn't force himself on me and that's why I think it would be better if I left."

"Try talking first."

"I tried, but he won't talk to me."

"Take it slow. Remember, time heals all wounds. God may not come when you call, but he's always on time," Susan said, then stood up because she heard Brittany calling out to her. "Diane, he's a forgiving person; he forgave me."

Susan walked toward the door but stopped when she heard Diane call her name. "Yes!"

"Thank you! Bernard is very lucky to have an understanding mother like you."

"He has a very good wife too, we just got to get him to realize it," Susan said as she smiled and turned to answer her granddaughter's call.

Bernard fell asleep on the sofa and was awakened by Diane.

"Bernard, what can I do to make it right?"

Bernard woke up. He looked into his wife's eyes, swollen from crying for two days. He pulled himself upright on the sofa.

"Diane, the only thing that you can do for me is leave me alone," Bernard said, as he stood up and slowly walked up the stairs. "And stop all that damn crying. It was you who stepped outside our marriage. Now you want somebody to feel sorry for you. Go cry to your preacher man."

"He's not my man."

"Could've fooled me. Or maybe you just go frolicking around to hotels with just any ol' body?" Bernard asked as he stopped halfway up the stairs.

"No! Bernard, please!" Diane cried.

"Please what? You should have thought about whatever it is that's on your mind when you gapped ya damn legs open. Now leave me alone," Bernard said as he continued up the stairs.

Diane followed Bernard up the stairs and into their bedroom, and started packing again. She walked over to the nightstand and called Poppa Doc.

"Hey, Momma, may I speak to Daddy?" Diane said through her sniffles.

"Is everything alright?" a concerned Ethel asked her daughter.

"No! But I need to speak with Daddy."

"Alright, well, hold on," Ethel said as she pressed the intercom button that would alert him down in the basement. "Winston, Diane's on the phone for you."

Poppa Doc picked up. "I have it," Poppa Doc said, but he didn't hear the phone that Ethel was on hang up. He spoke anyway; he knew that Ethel was just as concerned as he was about their daughter. "Hey, baby girl, how are you?"

"Daddy, I'm going to need a truck."

"Why?"

"Because I'm leaving. He doesn't want to talk to me and I can't live like this."

"Are you sure this is what you want to do? I mean it doesn't seem like you gave it any time."

"I'm sure. I think it would be best if I just left."

"Well, if that's what you want to do, then I'll get you a truck tomorrow."

"Thank you!"

"You're welcome. Is Bernard there?"

"Yeah, he's sitting right here."

"Okay, well, tell him that I'll call him tomorrow."

"What for?"

"Because I'm grown and I can call whoever I want to call, Diane," Poppa Doc snapped. Although he loved his daughter with all of his heart, he sometimes hated her selfish ways. He coughed a hard cough and told Diane that he had to go, it was time for his dialysis treatment.

"When did they put you on dialysis, Daddy?"

"Last night!"

"What happened last night?"

"I just had a little bout with this thing, so I called Dr. Beck. He thought that this might help, but it's getting on my nerves, amongst other things."

"Don't worry about the truck, Daddy, I didn't know. I'll do it myself. If you need me for anything call me," Diane said, picking up on the fact that her daddy was tired and not in the mood for the whining daughter.

"Are you sure?"

"Yeah, I'm sure. Get you some rest."

"Okay, bye."

Diane hung up the phone with Poppa Doc and walked into the bathroom to take a hot shower, which always helped to relieve some of the stress.

Just as the door closed to the bathroom, Bernard picked up the phone and called Poppa Doc. This time he answered the phone. "Yes, Diane," Poppa Doc said, assuming that it was his daughter.

"No, it's me," Bernard said.

"Hey, Bernard," Poppa Doc said pulling himself upright on the sofa. "How are you doing?"

"I'm fine. I overheard Diane say something about a dialysis. What's going on?"

"This cancer is kicking my butt, and now my kidney is acting up. But I got something for it in round two."

"Is there anything that I can do? Do you need anything?"

"As a matter of fact, there is."

"What's that?"

"Talk to your wife."

"Come on, Pops."

"I didn't say now, but just don't wash your hands of the relationship. Keep an open mind. Brittany needs the both of you."

"Hey, I need to apologize about the way I acted the other night."

"That's alright! Where did you go?"

"I went to South Carolina. I brought my momma home."

"You did what? I thought . . . Hold on . . . Ethel . . . ," Poppa Doc called out.

"Yeah, I know, but she's here now. I'm still coming to grips with it myself," Bernard said as he smiled at the memory of his mother sitting at the dinner table.

"Is she still up?" Poppa Doc sounded like he was about to meet a long-lost friend.

"Naw, she's in the bed with Brittany. She done conned her into sleeping with her."

Ethel walked into the room. "What is it?" she asked, worried that something had happened to him.

"Bernard's mother is over there," Poppa Doc said to his wife.

"Really! When did she get here?" Ethel said in the background.

"When did she get here, Bernard?"

"I brought her home today."

"Why in the hell didn't you call me, boy?"

"I don't know. Just excited and got a little caught up."

"Well, I'll be. We'll be over there tomorrow to meet her."

"That's fine. We'll be looking for ya. Hey, what's Prodigy's number? I erased it off my voice mail."

"You got a pen?" Poppa Doc rattled off the number.

"I've got to give him a call. You were right about him; he's a nice guy. He left me a message expressing his concern."

"Yeah, he's a good kid. When you talk to him, tell him to call me."

"I'll do that, and we'll see you tomorrow."

Diane walked out of the shower wearing a formfitting pink nightgown. She was drying her hair with a towel that had Bernard's initials on it. Her eyes were locked onto his, trying desperately for some sort of sign that he might open the lines of communication. He glanced at her, shook his head, and walked into the bathroom for his shower before he went to bed.

When Bernard exited the bathroom, all of the lights were out and Diane was in bed. He stood there contemplating whether or not to join her. He sure did like the good night's sleep that that eleven-hundred-dollar mattress provided. But he never wanted to be that close to her again. So he grabbed a pillow and headed down the hall to the unused guest room.

15

Your Past
Is Gonna Getcha

rodigy awakened about six A.M. to a loud ringing in his pants pocket. He quickly grabbed the cell phone and pushed the green send button before he woke Nina and Blake. He jumped up from the hospital recliner, placed his feet back into his unlaced shoes, and exited the room.

"Hello?" he said, his voice still filled with sleep.

"When were you going to call me?"

"Simone, it's six o'clock in the morning," Prodigy said, looking at his watch.

"I know that. I've been up all night packing."

"Why are you packing?"

"He wants me to leave, so I'm leaving. Anyway! I need to see you."

"When?"

"Now!"

"Can't! I have to stay here until they release Blake."

"Who's Blake? One of your criminal-minded friends?"

"Don't worry about it. Why do you need to see me in such a hurry?"

"If I wanted to talk about it over the phone, don't you think I would have done so by now? Are you going to work?"

"No, not today."

"What is it this time?" Simone said, breathing hard like she was lifting something heavy. "Your dog died?"

"Simone, I'll call you later," Prodigy said, ignoring her sarcasm.

"Prodigy, when will that be? This is important."

"Ten o'clock." Prodigy just picked a time out of nowhere. He didn't fall off to sleep until after three. Even then he didn't get any consistent rest, due to the doctors and nurses coming in and out of the room to check on Blake.

"I need to see you, Prodigy. So make me a priority today, okay?" Simone said as the phone slammed down into its cradle.

Prodigy stood there in the busy hallway, a little baffled. While they were together, she never acted like that.

He saw the young black doctor, Dr. Rogers, who looked to be in his late twenties, administering to Blake. "How's he coming along, Doc?"

"He's doing just fine. I'm about to disconnect him from the tubes. Then we'll monitor him for the next four to five hours and if all is well, we'll release him. But I need for you to speak with Admissions, at some point before discharge, in reference to the insurance," Dr. Rogers said, assuming that Prodigy was Blake's father. Prodigy never corrected him. He followed the doctor into the room.

Nina had gotten up and was in the rest room when the doctor unhooked Blake from his breathing machine.

Blake looked around, saw Prodigy, and smiled. He tossed his head back as if to say, "What's up?"

Prodigy winked in response.

"How do you feel, big guy?" Dr. Rogers asked Blake.

"I'm okay. I can breathe," Blake said, taking in a big breath.

"That's good. Your breathing has been stabilized, and if it remains that way you'll be in your own bed tonight."

"I sleep with my momma," Blake said.

"Well, you'll be in your mother's bed tonight."

"Okay!"

Dr. Rogers was listening to the stethoscope that was placed against Blake's chest and was looking at his watch.

Nina walked out of the rest room and stood beside Prodigy. "What did he say?" she asked him.

"He said it looks good, but they are going to monitor him for about five hours."

"Yeah, I figured that. Hey, you can still make it to work. I think we'll be fine."

"How are you going to get home?"

"We'll catch a cab. Go ahead, we'll be fine."

Prodigy looked at his watch, which now read six-thirty, and figured that he could make it, but only if he left now. He still had to drive all the way back to Stone Mountain, shower, and change clothes.

He looked at Blake. "You gonna be alright, my man?"

"Yeah, I'm okay. You coming back?"

"Yeah, I'll be back over to check on you." He turned to Nina. "Are you sure you're okay?"

"Of course. Go to work."

"Alright, I'm out," Prodigy said as awkwardness came over him. He wanted to kiss her, but it wasn't time for that yet. Plus both of them had morning breath. So he rubbed Blake on his head and gave Nina a light hug.

"Take my numbers again. I'm sure you left them at home," Prodigy said as he looked for some paper to scribble on.

"I have them with me," Nina said, pulling the paper

that he'd written his information on out of her blue jeans pocket.

"Call me the minute you guys get the okay to leave."

"I'll call you when we get home."

"Nah, when you are about to leave. I'll come back on my lunch break and take you guys home. No cabs," Prodigy said, holding up his index finger to hold off any response as he exited the door.

Remembering what the doctor had said about an insurance issue, he headed down to Admissions. Once he found where he needed to be, he inquired about the bill for the young man in 202. A lady with graying hair and a bad attitude told him that the insurance information that Nina had provided was not valid. She said that they would be receiving a bill.

Prodigy gave the lady his address and told her to bill it to him. She wanted to know if he was the child's father. He wanted to ask her what difference it made, but he shook his head and told her that he was his uncle. After providing her with all of the information that was required, he headed back out to his truck.

He made it home and showered, changed into another suit, and was sitting at his desk at eight-thirty sharp.

Brenda walked over and sat across from his desk. "This is odd, you coming to work when you said you wouldn't be. So, what was the emergency?"

"One of my kids from the youth center was ill, so I went to the hospital with him," Prodigy said dryly.

She shook her head. "That's a new one."

"Brenda, what can I do for you?" Prodigy asked, not interested in her sarcastic chatter.

"Today is your final interview, and it's with Craig. So you should be a shoe-in. Congratulations."

"I haven't had the interview yet," Prodigy said as he swiveled around in his chair, sending her a message that their conversation was over.

Brenda started to say something else but changed her mind when she heard his phone ring. She stood and walked away.

Prodigy answered the phone and heard Craig's raspy voice on the other end of the line.

"Prodigy? I was just about to leave a message with your voice mail. Brenda told me that you weren't coming in today."

"Yeah, I had a family emergency, but it worked itself out."

"Is everything alright?"

"Yeah, everything is everything."

"The board of human resources reviewed your file; your attendance really hurt you. Everything else was exceptional. Two more months of getting to work on time and maintaining your performance and I'll promise you a supervisor position. Even if I have to create one," Craig said.

"I understand! And I appreciate you looking out, CB," Prodigy said, a little disappointed. He really didn't expect to get promoted this soon after pulling a stunt like he pulled on the stairwell, but it would've been nice.

"I'm not going to hold you. Tell Winston I'm sorry that I missed his granddaughter's party, but I . . . Oh hell, I'll give him a call."

"Yeah, he'll be happy to hear from you. Take it easy."

"You too."

Prodigy stood and looked over to give Debra the news. "I didn't get it."

"That's alright. Ya can't work nights anyway. Those kids at the youth center would cause a riot," Debra said, remembering the time that she accompanied him there and the response that he got from them.

"Damn. I didn't think about that."

"See there! Po' baby was about to cry, wasn't you?"

"Anyway!" Prodigy said as he sat back down. Debra walked around to his area and sat down.

"What's up with Simone?"

"I don't know. You know I don't mess with her no more."

"I called her last night and her husband said, 'The Jezebel don't live here no more.' I'm like, okay."

"Oh yeah! I need to give her a call. She called me a couple of times, but I wasn't able to talk with her."

"Call her and put her on speaker phone," Debra said, edging the chair closer to the desk.

"No! Stop being newsy."

"Newsy! You've been down here long enough to lose that Philly crap. It's nosy. Simone's gonna tell me anyway. Ya know that's my girl."

"Go sit down, you're bothering me."

"When you gonna call Simone? Her husband sounded mad. I thought he done caught you over there and beat the hell out of ya," Debra said, standing up to leave.

"Bye, Debra."

Prodigy checked his e-mail and Meeting Maker. After scanning the screen he didn't notice anything pressing, so he worked on the project he'd started last Friday.

Around noon, his desk phone rang and it was Nina.

"Hi, Prodigy, it's me!"

"Hey there. Are you guys ready?"

"Yeah, but I was thinking. Didn't you say that you worked in the Dunwoody area?"

"And?"

"That's pretty far. Why don't we catch a cab and call you later."

"No! I'm on my way."

"Prodigy!" Nina whined.

He could tell that she was used to doing things on her own.

He figured that was a good trait in a woman. He never did like a woman who always needed him to do this and that. That got old real quick!

"It's no big deal, I'm on my way, okay?"

"Okay, we'll be waiting outside by the front entrance."

"See you in a few."

"Okay, and thank you, Prodigy."

He loved that way she said his name. He closed out of his system and headed out to his truck. Thirty minutes later he pulled up to Grady Memorial Hospital and found Nina and Blake waiting. Nina was carrying his suit jacket.

"You left your jacket," Nina said, handing it to him.

"Thank you. I'm careless like that sometimes."

"It's okay."

They made it back to Nina's place and were met at the door by a sweltering heat. Nina flicked on the light switch but nothing came on. She walked next door to ask her neighbor if her electricity was on but got the answer to her question in the form of a big square fan blowing in their window. She returned to her dark apartment and grabbed the telephone. She called Georgia Power's automated line and found out that she was behind on her bill. She was about to call Cathy but realized her sister was probably in class. The lights had been turned off before but never while they had a guest. It was embarrassing.

Nina plopped down on the sofa and looked like she wanted to cry.

"Grab a couple of things and come on. Leave my number for Cathy," Prodigy said as he caught on to what had happened.

"No! You've done enough," Nina replied.

"Look. It's hot in here, and it's hard for me to breathe, so it can't be good for Blake," Prodigy said as he walked over and sat down beside her. "Things like this happen. That's why God gave you friends, to lean on. Now, come on. I have to go back to work."

Nina leaned over, pecked Prodigy on his lips, and stood. As she gathered some things for her and Blake in an overnight bag, she smiled to herself at his take-charge attitude. She walked back into the kitchen and left a note for Cathy to call them over at Prodigy's. Prodigy read her unsure expression as to what Cathy was going to do. Nina didn't want her sister staying in a hot, dark house, and based on the Georgia Power automated response, three hundred and twenty dollars was past due. It wasn't getting any brighter or cooler anytime soon.

Prodigy told Nina that he would come and pick Cathy up once he got off work. Nina's faced relaxed. She walked into the bathroom to get their toiletries and Prodigy picked up a piece of mail from the counter and put it in his suit pocket.

All the while, Blake was sitting on the sofa fanning himself with his eyes closed. Prodigy yelled to Nina that he was taking Blake out to the truck. She said that she would be out shortly. Once he'd situated Blake in the backseat, he blasted the air conditioner. Nina walked out carrying a small suitcase and a book bag.

Prodigy jumped out of the truck when he saw her, lifted the bags from her hand, and opened her door. He put their things in the backseat beside Blake and jumped back into the driver's seat.

"Prodigy, I don't know how I'm going to repay you."

"I do! Grass! You're cutting the grass and raking leaves. Oh, I have all kinds of stuff planned for you."

Nina smiled that pretty smile, showing off her pearly whites and shaking her head. "You're something else." She looked back to check on Blake. He had already fallen off to sleep.

"I feel like a tape recorder, but thank you, thank you, thank you!"

"It's no problem."

Nina closed her eyes and stole a nap. Prodigy woke her up when they turned onto his quiet street.

"We're here," he said as he patted her on her leg.

"I'm sorry for falling asleep on you."

"Gotta sleep sometime," Prodigy said frankly as he exited the vehicle and picked Blake up. He opened the door to his place, carried Blake upstairs to the guest bedroom, and laid him on the bed. Nina followed them and put their bags down. Prodigy looked at his watch and realized that he had already used more than his hour lunch break.

"Nina, you guys make yourselves at home. I have to run. I should be home around five-thirty or so. I'll call you, so answer the phone."

That is a first. A guy telling you to answer his phone. Usually they do everything in their power to keep your ear from ever touching their receiver, Nina thought.

He walked across the hall and into Jermaine's room, but his cousin wasn't there.

"Nina, my cousin might be showing up at any time but I'll try to get in contact with him before I get home."

"Okay, and thank you again."

"Get the rake. Bye!" he said, smiling. "I don't have any food, but there are some menus of delivery places in the drawer beside the refrigerator. A fifty-dollar bill is in the Bible on the mantel."

Prodigy ran back downstairs and headed out to his truck. Just as he was closing the door, Simone pulled up with suitcases and boxes in her passenger seat and backseat. She pulled in front of him so that he couldn't drive forward. She exited the car wearing warm-up pants and a tank top.

"Why are you avoiding me?" she said as she walked up to his driver-side window.

"I'm not avoiding you, but I'm late for work. So move your car," Prodigy said, hoping that Nina was not looking out a window.

"I thought you said you weren't going to work today."

"I changed my mind. Now, will you please move your car, Simone."

"No! I've been asking you to call me for two damn days now. What's your problem?"

"Okay! Talk!"

"Why didn't you call me back?"

"Do you wanna talk or not, because I have someplace to be."

"Let's go inside."

"Didn't I just tell you that I have to go to work?"

"Didn't I ask you two days ago to call me?"

"Spit it out, Simone."

"I'm pregnant!"

"Okay, but what does that have to do with me?"

"It's yours."

"How you figure?"

"Because I've only been with two men. You and him."

"It must be him because I don't recall any condoms breaking. And I damn sure never went there without one. So how you figure?"

"It's yours, and I'm not having an abortion, so don't even think about it," Simone said as she walked back to her car. She turned before she got in and said, "Tell your new lady friend that you'll be having a new addition to the family."

Prodigy sat looking as her car disappeared around the corner. His mind raced over the last couple of years, trying to find a time when he was a roughrider. He kept drawing a blank!

Simone's trippin', he thought. He pulled himself together and pulled off toward the expressway that would deliver him to GMAC. All the way there he could not shake those two words: *I'm pregnant!*

Simone never could be alone, and since her husband gave her the boot, she's crying pregnant. I'm not falling for the trap, he thought, as he parked his truck and walked back toward his office building, two and a half hours after he'd left.

Prodigy thought that he'd better run this by Debra. She and Simone were good friends, and knowing the way that women talk, maybe she could shed some light on this crazy situation.

He walked directly to her desk and slid his chair up close to her. She could tell by his expression that something was on his mind.

"Simone just came by my house and said that she was pregnant."

Debra gave a quick sigh as if she was saying, "It figures." Then she said, "Well, that can happen if ya do the nasty. That's why her husband was pissed, huh?"

"What do you mean?"

"Ya know she always wanted kids, right?"

"No! She never said anything to me about any kids."

"Well, she talks to me about 'em all the time. Hell, I told her that she could have all three of my badass kids."

"First I ever heard about it."

"Well, it damn sure ain't the last."

"Where are you going with this?"

"Her husband is sterile. He couldn't bust a grape with Welch's permission. You gone be a daaaaadeee," she said in a singsong fashion.

"Stop playin'! But we never did anything without protection."

"You must've done something!"

Prodigy stood and walked back around to his desk. He sat and brainstormed. He decided to call Simone. He called her car phone and got her voice mail. He left a message for her to call him. Ten minutes later he left another message. An hour later she finally called him back.

"Oh, you can't wait to call me now, huh?"

"Simone, how far along are you?"

"Probably about eight weeks. I just took a pregnancy test and it came back positive."

"How do you know it's mine?"

"Prodigy, don't insult me. It could only be yours, because you're the only one that I slept with."

"Oh, so you didn't sleep with your husband?"

"It's yours. Are you going to help me or not?"

"Answer my question. Did you not sleep with your husband?"

"Think, Prodigy! Why would he snap and put me out if he didn't know for sure that this was not his child growing inside of me?"

"Alright, but I still say that we never had sex without a condom."

"Condoms obviously aren't one hundred percent protection."

"This just doesn't sound right."

"Well, you have about seven more months to make it sound right. I have to go. I'm meeting a realtor in five minutes. I'll call you soon."

Prodigy leaned back in his chair and ran his fingers over his bald head. He decided that he wasn't going to worry anymore about this thing. Besides, Simone might be lying. He reached in his pocket and pulled out the letter that he'd taken from Nina's apartment. He dialed the number to Georgia Power, gave them the address off the letter, and paid the electric bill account with a credit card. He called Nina at his place.

"Hello!" Blake said.

"What's up, my man. You finally woke up?"

"Yeah. When you coming home?"

Prodigy got chills when he heard "When you coming home?" Was his carefree world coming to a screeching halt?

"I'll be there shortly, my man. You need anything?"

"We going to the center tonight?"

"Nah, I think you should take a break. I don't want you to take on too much too soon. You scared me, boy."

"I'm alright, I can go."

"Let's take this week off. Where's your mom?"

"Right here, hold on," Blake said as he handed Nina the phone.

"Hello."

"Hi! Is everything alright?"

"Yeah. We're fine. I'm waiting on Cathy to get here. I have a test tonight. What time will you be here?"

"In about an hour. Do you need me to pick up anything?"

"No, unless you want me to have Cathy cook something for you."

"Well, Blake should probably have a home-cooked meal. So what should I get?"

"It's up to you. Get whatever you like. I've been on the phone with Georgia Power trying to get this power back on, but they keep telling me that the account is not past due."

"I paid it! But they said that they might not be able to get it on until in the morning. So it looks like you guys are going to be there for the night."

"You paid the bill?"

"That's right!"

"I'm going to give you your money back. That's too much money to be throwing away."

"I'm not throwing it away. I'm helping a friend."

"Are you sure you don't mind?"

"Positive!"

"What about your girlfriend, does she mind?"

"Don't have one."

"What about that woman who was screaming at you outside."

"She's not my girlfriend."

"Okay! Well, I probably won't be here when you get in because I need to go by the library before my class. I got a little behind this weekend."

"How are you getting to school?"

"I'll call a taxi."

"I'm leaving here in about an hour. So if you want to wait, then I'll give you a ride."

"No! You've already done too much. I'll call a taxi."

"Stop blocking your blessing. Did Jermaine ever show up?"

"Not yet."

"Alright, I'll see you in a little while. Bye."

16

Sleep with Me

rodigy pulled into his driveway and saw Cathy sitting on the front steps. She seemed to be into some heavy studying while Blake played in the front yard. He was throwing a football up in the air and watching it slip through his hands as he tried to catch it. Prodigy exited his truck and walked over to her.

"How's it going?" he asked.

"It's okay, how are you?"

"I'm good. What are you doing, studying for a big test too?"

"Yeah, it's time for finals again. Nina just left. She said that she had to get up to the school and register for graduation or something."

"I told her that I was going to take her."

"Sometimes she a little too independent."

"Catch, Mr. P," Blake said as he threw the ball at Prodigy.

Prodigy reached up and caught the ball with one hand. He

threw it back underhanded and told Blake that he needed to change clothes before he played with him. As he walked up the stone stairs leading to his front door, he held up a finger to Blake letting him know that he'd be right back. Cathy stood and followed him into the house.

"I'm not the best cook in the world, but I picked up some shrimp, and I'm attempting shrimp jambalaya," Cathy said.

"It smells good. That's a start," Prodigy said as he thumbed through the day's mail. "I'm gonna change clothes and go play catch with my little buddy. Hold up! Why is he outside playing?" he said, thinking about Blake's all-night stay in the hospital.

"You can't tell him anything. He started whining about being cooped up in the house all day, so I just let him play."

"How long has he been out there?"

"About an hour."

"That's long enough," Prodigy said as he walked to the front door and called for Blake to come in.

"Aw, Mr. P, I'm tired of staying in the house. Ain't nuttin' to do," Blake whined.

"Come on in," Prodigy said, not bothering to try to negotiate with him.

Surprisingly, Blake frowned a little and walked up the stairs back into the house without any back talk.

"Are we going to the center today?"

"You asked me that already."

"What did you say?"

"I said not today."

"Why?"

"Because, my man, you're on injured reserve and we need for you to be a hundred percent before we put you back into the game."

"Like Kordell Stewart?"

"Yeah, just like Kordell. So relax and turn on the *Power Rangers* or something. I'm going to change clothes," Prodigy said as he headed upstairs to his room.

Cathy smiled at the smooth approach Prodigy used for handling Blake. So far, he had been the only one able to pull off telling Blake to stop doing something without Blake throwing a fit. She walked back out front, retrieved her books from the steps, and went back into the kitchen to check on the food. She then took a seat at the island and continued studying.

Prodigy changed out of his suit and trotted back downstairs wearing knee-length basketball shorts, a tank top, and flip-flops. He sat down on the floor in the living room beside Blake and quizzed him about the Power Rangers.

"Which one is your favorite?" Prodigy asked.

"The blue one."

"But you said that your favorite color was green."

"It is, but the blue Power Ranger is the man. I'm telling you."

"If you say so. So what did you do all day?"

"I watched TV and did my homework."

"Did your mom or aunt check it?"

"My mom said that she would when she got back."

"Go and get it, I'll check it for you."

Blake rolled over and pulled a green book bag from the side of the sofa. He pulled out some papers and a book.

"I'm doing adding. I'm not too good at math, but I think I got most of them right."

"First, let's not say that you're not good at math, because you can be good at anything if you put in the work. If you say it, you might start thinking it. Right?"

"Right!"

"Okay, let's see here. Two plus three equals what?"

Blake closed his eyes, tilted his head back, and said, "Four."

"Okay! Let's cheat," Prodigy said as he held up his hand, "How many fingers on this hand?"

"Three!" Blake said.

"Okay. Now how many fingers are up on this hand?" Prodigy said as he held up a peace sign.

"Two!" Blake said.

"So three plus two is what?"

"Five!"

"That's right. Don't worry about doing it in your head. It's easier if you do it on paper. Use these stick figures to count," Prodigy said as he drew some straight lines and some adding problems on the paper. "Each one of these lines represents a one. Use these to add. Okay! You work on these and I'll check with you in a minute," Prodigy said as he pressed the off button on the remote control.

"Why you turn the TV off?"

"Your schoolwork is more important. You can watch TV later," Prodigy said as he pointed at his writing pad. Once again, Blake didn't give him a response.

Prodigy walked into the kitchen, where Cathy was deeply engrossed in her own schoolwork. A pot on the stove was boiling over. He walked over and removed it from the hot burner. Cathy looked up and said, "Oh, my goodness. I wasn't paying attention. I'm sorry, Prodigy."

"No problem. Want me to take over from here?"

"Oh no. I have it," Cathy said, closing her book and walking over to the stove.

"Prodigy, can I ask you a question?"

"Shoot."

"Why are you so nice to us? Nina told me what you did about the electric thing. You've opened up your house to us. You like my sister that much?"

"Cathy, I've been blessed, and I believe in passing on your blessings. So that's all I'm doing. Nothing more, nothing less."

"So you tryna say that you're not interested in Nina?"

"I didn't say that at all, but that's not why I'm helping you guys."

"Well, thank you. And don't think that we don't handle our business, because of the blackout over at the house."

"I didn't say a thing."

"Nina thinks that she can save the world, and sometimes people take advantage of that."

"What do you mean?"

"One of our father's children, Carla, was in a bind, so Nina let her come and stay with us for a few days. Well, anyway, she stole some checks and cashed them. So the check that Nina wrote to Georgia Power bounced. And guess what? Nina said she's not pressing charges against her."

"There's no need to. She'll need you guys again."

"And Nina will help her again. That's just the point, she's too nice. I ain't having it."

"Well, let it go," Prodigy said, cutting their conversation short because he heard the doorbell. Prodigy walked into the living room and looked out of the bay window, but he didn't see a car.

"Who is it?"

"Me!"

"Boy, where's your key?"

"I got it. I just didn't want to put all this stuff down. What's up, lil' man?" Jermaine said, speaking to Blake and handing Prodigy a grocery bag.

"Hello, I'm doing my homework," Blake said.

"Okay, well, I won't disturb you. I'm Jermaine, what's your name?" Jermaine said, reaching out to give Blake five.

"Blake."

"Nice to meet you, Blake. I heard a lot about you, but go ahead and finish your work."

"Okay."

"Uh-oh, what came over you? Buying groceries."

"I started working today too. Damn, who dat?" Jermaine said as he caught a glimpse of Cathy in the kitchen.

"Pick yo' lip up. Where are you working?"

"Wit' Trevor. Dude lazy! I guess since I'm the new guy, he wanna put everything on me. But that's cool, cuz I wanna open me up a cleaning joint one day. Move on up like George and Weezy."

"I hear you."

"Oh, Uncle Ray called you last night while you were out. Said for you to give him a call."

"Did he say what for?"

"Nah, he's probably just lonely. Yo, let me go shower. Who that, ya new girl?"

"Nah, that's Cathy, Nina's sister. You remember Nina, don't ya? Or were you too drunk to remember?" Prodigy said.

"I remember speaking to her in my drawls. I'm about to quit drinking too."

"What!" Prodigy said, placing his hand on Jermaine's forehead. "Boy, are you sick?"

"Back up. Introduce me to the dime piece. Stop being rude," Jermaine said as he walked into the kitchen. Prodigy followed and made the introductions. Jermaine must not have gotten the eye contact that he wanted, because he said a few things and made a quick exit.

Prodigy walked back into the living room and sat down on the floor beside Blake.

"Did you finish?"

"Yep, and I got 'em all right this time."

"Let's see," Prodigy said as he removed the paper from Blake's hand. "Looks good. Four out of five ain't bad. Check on number four and tell me what's the problem."

Blake took the paper, frowning. He just knew all of his answers were right. He studied the problem, counted on his fingers, and smiled. "Your nine looks like a seven. Mr. P, you can't write."

"Oh, but I can fight," Prodigy said as he leaned down, grabbed Blake, and picked him up over his head.

Blake laughed and tried to fight back, but Prodigy's reach was too long for him. Blake managed to playfully smack Prodigy's bald head. Prodigy put him down, rolled onto his side, and covered up his head. Blake did his impression of a WWF and dropped down on Prodigy with his elbow. Prodigy made a sound like he was being beaten to death. Blake jumped up and started hitting the floor for the count-out.

"One, two, three. Ring the bell. Mr. P, you ain't got nothing for these pythons," Blake said, holding his scrawny arms up and showing off his microscopic muscles.

"Okay, Goldberg, I need to make a call or two. You can turn the television back on."

"Can we fight again later?"

"Did you think that you could just beat me up and get away with it? Give me a few minutes. It's on."

"Yeah, you're on injured reserve," Blake said.

"I think I am, my man," Prodigy said, holding his back.

Prodigy walked out onto his deck and called Uncle Ray.

"Talk to me," Uncle Ray answered.

"What's going on, Unc?"

"Hey, fella, you got a minute?"

"Yeah, what's up?"

"I wanted to talk to you about a business venture."

"I'm listening."

"I'm thinking about opening a bonding company and a DUI school. Now I got a couple of prior DUIs myself, so I can't open the school in my name. But if you do it I'll cut you in on thirty percent of the profits from both companies."

"What do they need from me?"

"A clean driving record and that's all. Everything will be in your name, and you can have all of the paperwork sent to your house. All I need is your squeaky-clean signature."

"When do you need your answer?"

"Take your time, just don't take forever."

"Alright, I'll get back with you in a couple of days."

Prodigy hung up the cordless and walked back into the house. By now Cathy had finished cooking, and Jermaine and Blake were sitting at the table.

"Is there enough in there for Nina? She'll probably be hungry when she gets home."

"Oh, so this is home now," Cathy said.

"You know what I mean. Home from school."

"Yeah! Okay!" Cathy said sarcastically.

"P, you done went domestic on me and ain't tell me?" Jermaine said.

"Whatever! Cathy, what color is white rice supposed to be?"

"She always burns the rice," Blake said, standing up and looking in the rice pot. "Oh, light brown ain't that bad for Aunt Cathy. She'll make you eat that."

"You hush and sit down and eat."

"I told you," Blake said, taking his seat.

"Cathy, I ain't hungry," Prodigy said after Cathy put some hard, gooey-looking shrimp mixed with some greenish-colored sauce on his plate.

"Me either," Jermaine said. "I just ate before I got here."

"I don't feel good," Blake said, pushing his plate away and holding his stomach.

"Oh, y'all gonna do me like that? It's good. I ate a whole plateful. See if I cook for y'all again."

"Don't cook no more," Blake said, frowning as if he had a bad taste in his mouth. Prodigy and Jermaine could not control their laughter.

"Alright, take ya lil' big head around there and watch TV.

And I better not see none y'all in these pots," Cathy said pointing at Jermaine and Prodigy.

"Cathy, it's a good thing that you're cute."

"What are you trying to say, Jermaine?" Cathy said, acting like she was a member of the family.

"Nothing! I got some work to do upstairs, so I'll holla atcha."

"What are you laughing at, Prodigy?" Cathy said, smiling herself.

"Cathy, I'll give you ten dollars if Chocko will eat this food."

"Who's Chocko?"

"My neighbor's dog."

Cathy put her hands on her hips and peered at Prodigy like "No you didn't."

"Prodigy, if I used profanity I'd tell you to go to somewhere south of the dirt," Cathy said as she removed the untouched plates off the table.

Prodigy liked her sense of humor.

A lot of people's feelings would've been hurt for sure if no one wanted to eat their cooking, he thought.

He walked into the living room and stretched out, down on the floor. Blake was already stretched out on the sofa. Blake asked, "Mr. P, you hungry?"

"Starving! What about you?" Prodigy whispered.

Blake nodded his head.

"You thinking what I'm thinking?"

Blake nodded as both of them got up and started putting on their shoes.

Prodigy told Blake to run upstairs and ask Jermaine if he was hungry. He figured Cathy's stomach couldn't take much more, so he decided not to ask her.

"Cathy, we'll be right back, we're going to the store."

"Bye," Cathy said, acting like she was upset.

"You need anything?"

"No. I already ate," Cathy said, letting Prodigy know that she knew where he was going.

Blake came back downstairs and said that Jermaine was going to pass. They headed out to the truck and were off to McDonald's.

"Now, you know we have to eat our food before we get back home, don't you?"

"Oh, me and my momma sneak off and eat all the time. Aunt Cathy just can't cook."

"Boy, you're something else."

Prodigy drove the scenic route to McDonald's. As they drove down Memorial Drive, Prodigy noticed that Blake looked to be in good spirits. That made him feel good.

Kids should always be happy, he thought.

"Mr. P, do you like my momma?"

"I do. I think she's a very nice lady."

"No, I mean *like* like," Blake said, nodding his head as if to say, "You know what I mean."

"Why?"

"Because that's my momma, and I'll have to hurt you if you make her cry."

"Well, I don't want that, so I'll be careful."

Prodigy and Blake finished eating, got up from the outside dining area, and tossed their wrappings in the trash. They headed back to the truck when Prodigy's cell phone rang.

"Hello."

"Do you want me to have an abortion?" Simone said.

"Did I say that? I thought that wasn't even an option."

"Well, I thought about it and I don't want to have a baby by someone who doesn't want to be a part of his or her life."

"I never said that either," Prodigy said as he buckled Blake into the front seat belt.

"Well, what do you want me to do?"

"Can we talk about it tomorrow?"

"What's with you? You're always putting me off until tomorrow, then you don't even call me. I'm not interested in messing up your little action with your new lady. I just want to resolve some things."

"I'll call you tomorrow. I promise."

"You better! Or I'm getting an abortion and you won't have to worry about ducking me anymore," Simone said.

"I'm not ducking you. I've just been a little busy, but tomorrow we'll talk for sure."

"Alright. I'll talk to you then."

Prodigy said his good-byes to Simone, and then they took the quickest route home, but not before he stopped at the cleaners to pick up six suits and ten handmade shirts. When he and Blake arrived back at his place, it was almost eight o'clock.

"Blake, what's your bedtime?"

"My momma lets me stay up until nine, but Aunt Cathy makes me go at eight-thirty."

"Well, when we get in you can start taking your bath and getting ready for bed. Did your mom say if you were going to school or not?"

"No. I don't wanna go."

"Why?"

"Cuz, I just don't."

"Do you like school?"

"Yeah."

"Okay! If you're well enough to play football and beat up on me, then you're well enough for school. So school it is."

"Wait, how am I gonna get to school? The bus don't run over here."

"I'll take you."

"Yay," Blake said as he pumped his fist.

Prodigy rubbed him on his head as they walked into his house. He sent Blake upstairs to take a bath in his bedroom.

Cathy was seated on the couch, still enthralled with her schoolwork.

"Y'all full?" Cathy said, smiling.

"What are you talking about? I had to go and get my clothes out of the cleaners."

"Don't act up, you know what I'm talking about."

"What?" Prodigy said, acting clueless. "What time does Nina get out of school?"

"Your wife should be here any minute."

"Oh, so now she's my wife? Jermaine still cooped upstairs?"

"No, he went somewhere with the guy from next door."

"Alright, I'll leave you to your studying. Thanks for cleaning up the kitchen," Prodigy said.

"You're welcome."

Prodigy ran upstairs and put his clothes into his closet. He heard Blake in the bathroom doing an a cappella version of one of the latest rap songs. Prodigy smiled and shook his head, reminiscing on the days when he did the same thing. After he put away his custom-made clothes, he went into the laundry room in the hallway, pulled some clothes out of the dryer, and dumped them on his bed. As he was folding his clothes, he turned and saw Nina peeking in on him. A broad smile took over his face; he couldn't hide how he felt.

"Well, that's a pleasant thing to see after a long and hard day."

"What is?" Prodigy said, still smiling.

"All thirty-two of those things between your lips."

"I've got thirty. I had two extractions."

"Okay," Nina said. "Where's my son?"

"Taking his bath." Prodigy nodded toward the bathroom door. "How was your class?"

"Long, but it's almost over. One more test and I'm out of there."

"I'm impressed. We'll have to celebrate."

"Now, that I'll take you up on," Nina said as she opened the door to the bathroom and caught Blake drying off.

"Hey, Mom." Blake moved his arms a little faster with the towel, threw on his underwear, and ran to give his mother a hug.

"How was your day, young man?"

"Good."

"Did you eat all of your food and do your homework?"

"Aunt Cathy cooked," Blake said, frowning. "And Mr. P checked my homework."

"Homework is taken care of and you're hungry?" Nina said, smiling. She knew that if Cathy cooked, then Blake didn't eat.

"Me and Mr. P went to McDonald's."

"I'm going to have to stop you from eating all of that fast food. Go on and get yourself ready for bed," Nina said as she leaned down and gave him a kiss on his lips.

"Let's save the Mr. P for when we go to the center, okay?"

"Can I call you Dad?" Blake said.

Nina and Prodigy looked at each other, completely caught off guard.

"Anything except Mr. P," Prodigy said.

Nina thought about what was just said and felt a little un-comfortable, but decided not to say anything. She pulled her bag off her shoulder and placed it on the floor. She sat down in a recliner in the corner of Prodigy's room, put her feet up, and released a long sigh.

"You sound tired."

"I am. Those hospital beds don't provide the best night's sleep."

"At least you had a bed."

"You sounded like you had a good night's sleep, with all of that snoring you were doing."

"I don't snore."

"I know, you call hogs."

They laughed. Nina stood, walked to the other side of the bed, and started helping him fold clothes.

"So you tasted one of Cathy's concoctions?"

"Nah, we never got past the visual."

Nina laughed. "That girl has to be the worst cook I've ever seen. You would think that she would've given up by now, but no, she keeps thinking her next meal will be her best meal."

"So she's testing her skills on y'all, huh?"

"She tries. So how was your day?"

"Just fine. I can't complain."

"I thought about you today and how nice you've been to us all. Thank you."

"No problem, and stop thanking me."

"Okay."

Just then, Cathy walked upstairs and called out from the hallway. "Hello."

"Come on in," Prodigy said.

Cathy walked in, grabbed a garment, and joined in on the folding. "Jermaine just called and said that he won't be home tonight. Said that he and the guy next door will be working down in Macon."

"I didn't even hear the phone ring."

"Oh, I was on the other line, sorry."

"You guys are the politest people I've ever met. If one more person tells me sorry or thank you I'm going to lose it."

"Thank you, Mr. P, I mean Dad," Blake said as he exited the bathroom and stole a look at Prodigy from the corner of his eye.

Everyone laughed at Blake's timely humor. Cathy looked at the T-shirt that she was folding, then threw it back on the bed. "I ain't folding up nothing. Nina, did they tell you what they did to me today?"

"No. What did they do?"

"They wouldn't eat my cooking, wouldn't even try it. And this one here was talking about he'd bet me ten dollars that the mutt next door wouldn't eat it."

"No, they didn't! What did you cook?"

"It was shrimp jambalaya. It was good. I ate it."

"You don't have anymore, do you?" Nina asked, twisting her face as if to say, "Please say no."

"Forget you, Nina," Cathy said as she playfully threw a shirt at her sister.

"Prodigy, where will I be camping out tonight?"

"Cathy, you can take the guest room, and Nina and Blake can have my room. I guess I'll sleep in Jermaine's room."

"That's cool. I'll see you lovebirds later," Cathy said as she headed back downstairs.

Nina and Prodigy both smiled as they watched Cathy leave the room.

"Prodigy, don't take this the wrong way, but why don't we let Blake sleep in Jermaine's room and you sleep in your own bed," Nina said. She had been thinking about him all day. And although she knew her mind was moving a bit too fast, her heart told her something different. She didn't want to have sex with him; she just wanted to feel the closeness of his body.

"With you?" Prodigy asked, smiling.

"Yeah, with me, as long as you stay on your side of the bed."

"All of it's my side. I got a receipt for that bed."

"Well, I'm renting a side of it tonight."

"Don't be tryna sneak you a feel when I fall asleep, either."

Nina smiled a shy smile and shook her head.

Blake fell asleep on the sofa. Cathy came up and waved and said that she was turning in. Nina changed the sheets on Jermaine's bed, and Prodigy picked up a sleeping Blake and placed him on the fresh sheets.

Nina returned from the guest room with her overnight bag and headed for the shower. Prodigy laid some thick cotton towels on the bathroom counter for her and headed for the hallway bathroom for his shower.

When Nina exited the bathroom wearing a white satin bathrobe, Prodigy had already finished his shower. He was lying in bed on top of the covers and reading an issue of *Code* magazine. All of the lights were out, with the exception of a reading lamp that sat beside his bed, giving the room a much too romantic glow.

Nina paused when she noticed Prodigy lying on the bed with only a pair of FUBU pajama bottoms on. She tried her best not to stare at the model-like chest, sculpted abs, and smooth dark skin, but her eyes kept betraying her. She walked to her rented side of the bed and quietly sat down. With her back to Prodigy, Nina pulled her hair up and wrapped it with a yellow scarf.

"Alright, Aunt Jemima."

Nina turned and shot him a look. She finished wrapping her head and removed her robe. She now only wore a long white satin gown.

Prodigy couldn't take his eyes off what he thought to be the sexiest woman that he'd ever laid eyes on.

Nina lay down on her side, reached over, and removed the magazine from Prodigy's hand. She thumbed through a couple of pages then tossed it on the floor on her side of the bed.

"How did we get here so quickly?" Nina asked.

"Fate. I believe in fate. Do you?" Prodigy said.

"I'm starting to. You know, the funny thing is, I don't even feel uncomfortable."

"Good, you're not supposed to be uncomfortable around me." Prodigy smiled.

"It's not you. I haven't been with a man since Blake's father.

I know you might find that hard to believe, being that he's six years old, but it's true. So I thought that I'd at least be a little uncomfortable."

"Your ass is horny," Prodigy said, laughing. "I'm just kidding. Why has it been so long since you've been with a man?"

"Did I tell you that Blake has never met his father?"

"Yeah, you told me."

"Well, after I informed him of my pregnancy, he really broke my heart by disappearing and not being there for me. We were so close. I mean, we dated for two years, then all of a sudden he was gone. I guess it's true that you never fully know someone," Nina said.

"Responsibility scares a lot of people. But if he did that, then you were better off without him."

"What about you, are you afraid of responsibility?"

"No, not at all."

"Simone called here today. You told me to answer the phone, so I did."

Prodigy closed his eyes and shook his head. He really didn't want Simone to come between what he was feeling for Nina.

"She told me about her pregnancy. What are you going to do?"

Prodigy ran both of his hands over his bald head and let out what seemed like a week's worth of breath.

"She wants to meet with me tomorrow to talk about it, but I can't get with that abortion crap that she's talking."

"That's good. You knew the chances when you were taking them, so it's best to just deal with it. Besides, I think that you'll be a wonderful father."

"I don't mean to get too personal, but I never had sex with her without a condom."

"And?"

"And, how in the hell is she pregnant by me?"

"Every adult knows that condoms aren't foolproof. Just take a DNA test if you have doubts."

"Most definitely!"

"Was she sleeping around?"

"She's married."

"Oh, so what is her husband saying about all of this?"

"I don't know. I heard that he put her out. Something about he can't have kids, so how is she pregnant. I'm thinking the same thing."

"Just wait and see. Children are gifts from God. It's a shame how we act like it's a bad thing when it's actually a blessing."

"I don't think it's a bad thing. I just want to make sure that the baby is mine if she's saying that it is."

"So if you find out that it's not your child, then what?"

"If she still needs my help then I'll bend over backward for her, but I need to know these things up front. I think it's only right."

"That's fair."

They both were quiet for a moment. Prodigy reached over and turned the light out.

"Nina, if the baby does turn out to be mine, will you disappear out of my life?"

"Not in a million years. Let's just hope for a girl."

"You're a special lady, Ms. Laws," Prodigy said as he rolled over and kissed her lips.

Nina slid as close as she could get and placed her head on Prodigy's chest. She let her hand glide across his rippled stomach and whispered, "Good night."

"Good night, sweetie," Prodigy said as he kissed the top of her head.

17

I'm Tryna Be a Man

Poppa Doc was moving slow but feeling good. He was sitting on a sofa in Michael's living room, holding little Winston's head in his lap while he took his afternoon nap. Christina and Crystal, Michael's two other kids, were also over visiting with their father at his new place.

Poppa Doc had called Michael that morning to solicit help in moving Diane's things and was pleasantly surprised to hear the joy of children's laughter in the background. All of a sudden he felt a surge of joyfulness take over his weakening body. And to add icing to the cake, when he arrived at his son's apartment, Samantha, little Winston's mother, answered the door.

"Hey, Daddy. How've you been?" Samantha said in her Georgia-peach accent. Samantha was a full-figured woman who wore it well. She always greeted everyone with a warm smile.

"Hey, Granddaddy," Crystal and Christina said as they ran over from the television to hug Poppa Doc.

"Hello, darlings. Woo, y'all growin' like weeds. Look at my babies." Poppa Doc held them at arm's length and smiled from ear to ear.

"Okay, y'all, let your granddaddy in the door. How you doing, Daddy?" Samantha said as she took the girls' hands and led them back over to the living room.

"I'm doing just fine, and you?"

"I'm alright. Come on in and have a seat. Michael is changing clothes."

"How old are you now, Christina?"

"Six."

"What about you, Crystal?"

"I'm six and a half, but I'm about to be seven next month."

"Well, alright then." Poppa Doc turned his attention back to Samantha. "I see y'all got the whole clan over, huh?"

"Yeah, we were all over Atlanta this morning picking up siblings."

"That's not ideal, but it's still a good thing."

"Oh yeah, I've been waiting on Michael to do this for a long time. He must've fell and bumped his head on a 'do right' rock or something."

"It looks like he's trying to come around," Poppa Doc said as he sat on the sofa and lifted little Winston to see how he'd grown.

"Well, Daddy, I have to finish fixing Crystal's hair. I don't know what her momma called herself doing."

"Go ahead, do your thing. I'ma just sit and wait on slow-poke."

"Ain't he slow. Move like a snail," Samantha said as she and Crystal headed into the bathroom.

While waiting on Michael to get dressed, Poppa Doc realized that today would be the first time in his life that all of his grandkids would be under the same roof. All of the previous Christmases and Thanksgivings, at least one of them was always missing. Today he would finally get to take a picture with all of his grandkids. The way that he had been feeling lately he wasn't sure if this day would ever come again. Michael entered the living room from the back of his one-bedroom apartment.

"Okay, Dad, I think I'm ready," Michael said, lifting little Winston from his father's lap.

"It's about time. I almost fell asleep."

"You tired?"

"Nah, I'm just talking. Don't you feel better about yourself?"

"Yeah, Dad, I do. But what's going on with Diane? Ain't nobody telling me nothing."

"It's not anything anyone wants to talk about."

"Oh, so you gonna keep me in the dark too, huh?"

"Come on out here," Poppa Doc said as he walked out onto the balcony with Michael on his heels.

"Your sister had an affair, and Bernard has decided that he doesn't want to try to make it work."

"Dag. Why Diane do that?"

"Who knows, but that's what we're dealing with."

"That's messed up. Where is she going to stay?"

"I'm hoping some time away from each other will do them both some good."

"Yeah, Bernard's alright. A little uptight, but there was never a question about him working hard for his family."

"From what Ethel tells me, that was the problem. Too much work, not enough play," Poppa Doc said.

"I can't believe Diane stepped out like that. All the times she got on my case, now she out there sneaking around," Michael said, smiling and shaking his head.

"Alright, Michael, this situation is not to be used as ammunition for one of y'all's foolish spats. Y'all too old to be acting like children anyway. Now, she's very sorry for what she did and she could use our support. So if you can't act right, then don't even go."

"Nah, I ain't gonna say nothin'."

"Good, because it's not funny, it's a very serious issue. Now, come on. I wanna get a picture of all my grands."

"How you gonna do that? Brittany ain't here and I didn't plan on taking mine wit' us."

"Well, they don't have to stay long. Have Samantha follow us so I can take my picture."

"Okay, you're the boss," Michael said as he followed Poppa Doc back into the house.

"Hey, Sam, put lil' Winston on some more clothes. Daddy wanna take the kids to take a picture."

"Where y'all taking my babies?" Samantha asked as she walked out of the bathroom. Although only Winston was her biological child, she treated the girls as if she gave birth to them also.

"I wanna get a picture with all my grands. I don't have any with everyone together."

"Oh, that would be nice. Give us a few minutes and we'll be on our way."

"You know, Sam, you can follow us. That way you don't have to stay."

"Okay. I promised the kids that I would take them to a movie—maybe Brittany would like to come."

"Well, we'll be outside waiting on you," Poppa Doc said as he and Michael walked out to the car.

"So, Dad, how do you like the place?"

"I like it, son. I'm proud of you. It does my heart good to be able to come and hang out with you at your place sometimes. Keep doing right by your kids and the blessings will rain down on you." Ever the positive soul, Poppa Doc didn't tell him what he was really thinking: *I'll be proud when you prove that you can keep it for more than three months.* This wasn't the first time that Michael had moved out on his own, only to return home to his parents' house after a couple of months. But Poppa Doc decided to try a new method of motivation this time and not knock him. He wanted Michael to think that he really believed in him this time.

Samantha walked out of the house holding little Winston, with the girls following close behind. The kids said they wanted to ride with Poppa Doc, and of course he let them. So Michael and Samantha pulled off behind him, headed over to Diane's house.

When they arrived, they saw Diane sitting on the front porch, talking to Susan.

Diane and Susan stood when Poppa Doc approached holding his grandson's hand. A puffy-eyed Diane made the introductions.

Poppa Doc hugged Susan like she was a long-lost sister. "I can't even begin to tell you how happy I am to meet you. I feel like I already know you, as much as that son of yours talks about you."

"And I've only heard good things about you since I've been here. And aren't these some beautiful little ones?" Susan said as she leaned down to give all of Michael's kids hugs.

"Where's Brittany?" Poppa Doc asked.

"She went somewhere with Bernard," Susan said. "They should be back shortly."

"Okay. So, Mrs. Charles, how are you enjoying the city so far?"

"Well, I haven't done anything yet, but to be honest, I'm just fine here with my family."

"Well, God is good all the time, and we're glad to have you."

"Yes, He is. I just wish these two could work out their differences."

"Oh, they will, just give them some time," Poppa Doc said. "Love is just like anything else, it needs to breathe."

Susan nodded her head in agreement. They all walked into the house, and the girls headed straight for Brittany's room to play, leaving little Winston behind.

"You don't want to go and play, young man?" Susan asked little Winston.

"Nothing but girl toys in there," the four-year-old replied.

"I'm sure you can find something in there to play with, Winston," Samantha said.

"Come on, I'll take you outside," Michael said as he led his son back out the door.

"You have yourself a good-looking set of grandbabies there, Mr. Fuller."

"Oh, let's drop the titles. Call me Winston."

"Only if you call me Susan."

"It's a deal," Poppa Doc said.

Diane fixed them a pot of coffee and went back up to her room to finish packing. Just as they sat down at the kitchen table, Bernard walked in.

"Hey, Sam, Winston. Good morning, Momma." Bernard gave Samantha a hug and shook Poppa Doc's hand.

"Where's Brittany?" Poppa Doc asked.

"She wanted to stay over her friend's house so I let her. I didn't know that you were bringing lil' Winston over, though. She's gonna hate that she missed him."

"The girls are here too. They're upstairs in her room."

"Oh yeah? Well, I know I'm in trouble with her now," Bernard said. He seemed to be in good spirits, which was not a good sign. It only meant that he was satisfied with the decision that he'd made about his inevitable break up.

"How far away is she? I wanted to take a picture with all my grands."

"She's out in Marietta."

"Oh well, I guess we'll have to do it another day," Poppa Doc said, calculating the distance in his head.

"I saw Michael out front playing with lil' Winston. That boy is almost as big as Brittany!"

"Oh, he eats enough," Samantha said.

"That's a'ight, let him eat. He gone be a football player."

"After he graduates from med school, he can play all the football he wants to play," Samantha said.

"I can see it now, lil' Winston tryna set the arm he just broke out there on the football field," Poppa Doc said.

They all laughed, but abruptly stopped when Diane returned to the kitchen. Bernard picked up a five-gallon water bottle and headed down to the basement.

"Daddy, I'm ready whenever you are," Diane said.

"Well, Susan, I'll give you a call tomorrow and maybe Ethel and I can come and take you on a tour of Atlanta," Poppa Doc said, standing up.

"Now, Ethel is your wife, right?"

"Yeah, she's the boss."

"I'd like that very much," Susan said.

"Brittany!" Diane called out.

"Bernard left her at her friend's house," Poppa Doc said.

"He did what? Bernard!" Diane called out.

"What!" Bernard said as he came up from the basement.

"Where is Brittany?"

"She's at Martin and Nel's house, playing with Jada."

"You knew that we were moving today. Why would you take her out there?"

"You're moving, my daughter is not going anywhere. This is her home, and this is where she is staying."

"Bernard, what I did was wrong, and you have no idea how I'm paying for it, but you've got to be out of your mind if you think I'm going anywhere without my baby."

"You must be out of your mind if you think I'm letting you take my baby anywhere."

"Oh, she's your baby now. Before, you couldn't even find the time to take her to the store, let alone Six Flags. But now you can't live without her."

"She was always my baby, and always will be."

"Okay now, y'all cut it out," Poppa Doc said. "No one gets anywhere with all that fussing and carrying on. Now, y'all didn't talk about this?"

"Nah, she just assumed that she was taking Brittany. As usual everyone has to cater to Diane."

"No one has to cater to me."

"Oh, you don't call uprooting Brittany in the middle of school catering to you? You don't call me and my momma having to live without our daughter and granddaughter because of something you did catering to you? Of course you don't, because the world revolves around you. She ain't going nowhere!" Bernard said.

"Yes, she is . . . ," Diane said in a defeated tone as his words stung like she had been attacked by a thousand yellow jackets. She broke down crying all over again.

"Diane, do you want to stay?" Susan interrupted.

"Not if he doesn't want me here."

"That wasn't the question. Now, do you want to stay?"

"Of course I do, but—"

"Then stay," Susan said, cutting off her response.

Bernard turned to leave, but Poppa Doc blocked his path to the doorway. He stopped and turned around to face his mother.

"Momma, you can't just make two people stay together. I don't know what y'all are trying to pull, but it's not going to work."

"Bernard, God knows y'all love that chile, and it's not fair to have her shuffled back and forth because you too bullheaded to forgive. Now, we've had enough breakups in the family, so let's fight to keep this one together," Susan said with tears streaming down her cheeks.

Bernard thought about his childhood and the nights of longing. He didn't want that for Brittany. Then he had to admit to himself that he still loved Diane. He was a family man, and part of that meant dealing with the ups and downs of having a family. This was one of the down times. With his mind racing a hundred miles an hour, he reached out and grabbed Diane's hand. He led her out onto the deck.

"Diane, my mother is right. If I did something like that, then I would want you to forgive me, so it's only fair that I try to do the same. Please don't try and talk to me anymore about this. When I'm ready to talk, then we'll talk. That time may never come, but I'm not ready to throw my family away."

"We can try counseling. Bernard, I didn't realize how much you meant to us until you was almost gone. I love you, and I'm so sorry that I ever hurt you," Diane said.

"Yeah, well, I'll see if I can't get some information on a marriage counselor or something from Ford's family assistance."

"Thank you, Bernard. All I want is a chance to prove to you how good of a wife I can be," Diane said. She wanted to hug him badly but he didn't open that door yet. So she rubbed her hands together just like her mother did when she was worried, savoring that touch when he held her hand while they walked outside. Holding on to what was the first touch since he dragged her out of the window of his truck on that infamous night.

Bernard turned away and walked back into the house, with Diane following close behind. Everyone who was crowded around the kitchen window, looking to see what was going on, scurried back to their seats and tried to pretend that they were not eavesdropping.

"We have decided to try a marriage counselor," Diane said thankfully.

Bernard walked through the kitchen and down into the basement without saying anything.

Susan and Poppa Doc walked over to a happy Diane, who was this time crying tears of joy.

"Nothing worth having is easy, baby girl, so just take it a day at a time," Poppa Doc said as he rubbed his daughter's back.

"I'm happy for you, and I know things will be better now than ever before—you mark my words," Susan said.

Michael and little Winston walked in the kitchen.

"Diane, hurry up. I got some things to do today. You sitting around here lollygagging."

"Hush, boy, your sister is staying here."

"Oh, good, let me borrow that Rahsaan Patterson CD."

"No, stop begging. And when are you going to invite me over to your place? What, you're afraid of me finding half of my stuff?" Diane said.

"You see that, Mrs. Charles? I come over here to help her, and she treats me like a thief."

"It's just love," Susan said.

"Well, I'd sure hate to see how she would treat me if she hated me."

For the first time in a long time, Diane's laughter was sincere.

18

Good-bye!

One Year Later

hanksgiving dinner came and went. Prodigy remembered it as one of the best days of his life; all the people that he cared for and loved were all gathered under the roof of his town house. From Poppa Doc's crew to his Uncle Ray and Ray's new lady friend. Even Diane and Bernard were smiling at each other. His mother and his Aunt Nettie teamed up with Mrs. Susan, Nina, and Mrs. Ethel to create a meal that would forever be remembered. The guys and Cathy gathered around the big-screen television to watch the Dallas Cowboys take on the Washington Redskins. Even though everyone was from a different lineage, they sat at the table and bowed their heads to ask that God continue to bless them as a family.

Prodigy was awakened that Sunday morning by the sweet

252

smell of French toast. It had been nine months since Nina and Blake moved in, and with the exception of Saturdays, Nina made sure that her men were fed a good breakfast every morning. Saturdays were supposed to be Prodigy's day to cook, but he would usually cop out to a breakfast at IHOP.

As Prodigy brushed his teeth, Blake ran into the room and told him that Uncle Jermaine was on the phone. Prodigy finished his morning grooming, walked back over to the nightstand, and picked up the phone.

"What's up, dog? How's everything in Philly?"

"The same, still dirty as hell. I just called you to give you my new number. I put Troy's nonpaying ass out of my mom's rental, and me, my girl, and Kahlil moved in."

"Oh yeah, that's cool. How's my little man doing, anyway?"

"Getting big. He can run now. I have 'em up at the courts out in North Philly taking notes."

"Now, see, that's where you messing up. If you gonna teach him the game, make sure I'm around."

"Anyway! I got major skills, son. Sixers on the other line right now."

"What's your number? I gotta go. My baby is cooking and my other line is beeping. And stay out of trouble or I'll have to assassinate you."

"I ain't been locked up since I left country-ass Georgia. Grab a pen."

Prodigy took Jermaine's new number, said his good-byes, and clicked over to the other line.

"Hello."

"What's up, playboy!"

"Who is this?"

"Oh, a brother go across the water to shoot a little hoop and everyone forgets about him."

"Genesis Styles, what's the haps, baby?"

"Can't call it, dog. I'm back in Atlanta now."

"Oh yeah?"

"Yeah, man. We're going to get together real soon and run some ho's."

"I'ma have to let you have that one, dog. I'm out the game."

"Oh, hell no! How am I supposed to handle all these chicken-heads by myself?"

"I don't know, but I'm sure you'll figure out a way. As a matter of fact, I might be needing your services soon."

"Oh yeah? What's that?"

"I'll fill you in when we talk."

"Okay, I'll holla at you."

Prodigy smiled as he hung up the phone with his old Philly running mate. Genesis was from Atlanta, but he spent a lot of his childhood in Philly hanging out with Prodigy and his crew. He remembered laughing until his stomach hurt as Genesis told joke after joke in his deep southern drawl. Prodigy was a year older, but they had always been close.

Prodigy walked downstairs into the kitchen and sat at the island. Nina had prepared French toast, chicken sausage, and a mushroom omelette with tomatoes and onions. Nina and Blake joined Prodigy at the island and said their blessing.

"Your mother wants you to give her a call," Nina said as she pulled her housecoat straps tighter around her waist.

"When did she call?"

"This morning. She didn't want me to wake you."

"Did she talk you to death?"

"No! She called with your Aunt Nettie on three-way."

"Oh, they ganging up on you, huh?"

"You know you have a wonderful family, don't you? Makes me miss my sister."

"How is my girl Cathy doing, anyway?"

"Still getting used to North Carolina. I don't think she likes it, but she'll never say, since it was our mom's wish that we all share the same alma mater. You know she has a new little man now."

"She told me. I just hope she doesn't drive him away with that cooking."

"Leave my baby sister alone. She tries, isn't that right, Blake?"

"Yeah. She can make cereal real good."

The ringing phone on the wall broke the conversation. Nina slid back and answered it.

"Hello."

"Hey, Nina, this is Diane. Is Prodigy there?" Diane said abruptly. Nina could tell that something was wrong, because she usually spent a little while chitchatting.

"Yes, he's here, hold on," Nina said as she passed the phone to Prodigy.

Prodigy's face quickly turned into a worried frown. "I'm on my way." He hung up the phone and jumped up from his untouched breakfast.

"Nina, Poppa Doc was just rushed to the emergency room and Diane is in no condition to drive. I'll call you guys when I get there."

"Do you want us to go?"

"I don't have time to wait for y'all to get dressed. He's at Northside Hospital, and I got to go all the way out to Fayette County because Diane can't reach Bernard."

Prodigy ran upstairs and threw on a T-shirt, sweatpants, and some FUBU boots. He ran back downstairs, kissed Nina and Blake on the head, and was in his truck headed toward I-285 south.

He arrived at Diane's house in what seemed like minutes. She was waiting on the front porch, pacing. When she saw Prodigy, she grabbed her purse and hurried to the truck.

They arrived at the hospital and made it to Poppa Doc's room down in the emergency area. The doctors stopped Prodigy at the door and told him that only immediate family could enter. He was hurt but he understood, so he took a seat in the hallway and waited. Michael exited the room and walked over.

"Hey, Mike! How's he doing?" Prodigy asked worriedly.

"Don't know! He's still unconscious." A teary-eyed Michael took a seat and slowly started pulling out strands of his hair. "Man, I can't lose my dad. I gotta make him proud of me," Michael said, as he feared the worst.

Prodigy placed his hand on Michael's shoulder and tried his best to comfort him. "Let's think positive. He'll pull through, you know Poppa Doc."

Michael cried harder. Prodigy could only try to relate. He knew how his feelings for Poppa Doc had grown over the last four years, so he could only imagine how Michael felt. Poppa Doc showed him what being a man was all about. He loved him just like a father. As a matter of fact, at this point he felt like he *was* his father. So he stood up and walked into the room, and when the same doctor tried to stop him, he responded, "I am family, let me by."

When Bernard showed up, he suggested that everyone join hands and say a prayer. Miraculously, after the last amen Poppa Doc opened his eyes, took a deep breath, and closed them again, giving the whole room renewed hope.

A little after midnight, the doctors came in and said that they were moving Poppa Doc to a new room upstairs. They suggested that everyone go home and come back the next day. With the exception of Michael and Mrs. Ethel, everyone took his advice.

Bernard opened the door to his truck for his wife. The counseling over the last year had helped tremendously.

He'd learned a lot about his wife and how he took a lot of the things that she did for granted. It was rough going at first, but the changing point came when they were asked to write a list of everything that each thought they brought to their relationship. After everything was written down, Diane's list more than tripled his. It was then that he started appreciating the things that his wife did, from cooking and cleaning to making sure that everyone's needs were met before hers.

He was sorry that the word "selfish" ever came out of his mouth when referring to her. It was hard for him to admit, but her affair had changed everyone's life for the better. He would've never gone to South Carolina and found his mother had he not needed to get away. He probably would've never fully appreciated what his wife meant to the family had they not gone to a marriage counselor. Yet he still felt slighted by her infidelity. He decided that only time would heal that wound. They even made love again. The counselor pointed out that his erectile problems were probably mental, not physical. She said that it was common when couples argued a lot that the stress would affect their sex life.

Diane learned to accept Bernard for the hardworking, God-fearing man that he was. She no longer hounded him about working so much, and it paid off. Bernard was happier, therefore he took the initiative more often to do things together as a family.

Prodigy couldn't sleep. He sat up on the side of the bed and stared out the window at the streetlight. Nina woke up and asked him if he was okay. He turned to her, looked into her eyes, and saw someone really special. She hadn't tripped when she found out about Simone being pregnant by him, nor did she trip when she found out about his shady past. He wondered what it was about her that made her so special, so he asked her.

Nina propped herself up on one elbow. "Prodigy, I used to judge people. I probably would've chalked you up to being a drug dealer or something when I first saw you with your nice clothes and fancy truck. But when I was an undergrad, I used to walk by this homeless guy every day. He would always ask me for some change, and I would always give him a dime or a quarter. I assumed that he was a drunk, trying to get his next drink. But one day he saw me with my statistics book and asked me, 'Do you know standard deviation? What about how to calculate your variance?' Those are statistics terms, so I looked at him and said, 'What do you know about statistics?' and he said that he has probably forgotten more than I'll ever know. Well, I soon found out that he'd lost his wife and daughter in a house fire while he took an emergency call to perform brain surgery. After that, he lost his will to live. What I learned from that man is that life is precious and to never let a moment be taken for granted. He still regrets taking that call to save someone else's life while he lost his own family. I could always see that you were special. You're not perfect, but you're perfect for me and my child."

"Nina, I'll be back. I'm going to the hospital to see my friend."

Before he knew it, Prodigy was walking through the doors of Poppa Doc's room. Mrs. Ethel and Michael had gone home to freshen up, so Poppa Doc lay there all alone. To Prodigy's surprise, he opened his eyes and smiled up at him.

"Hey, boy, what time is it?" Poppa Doc said in a very soft voice.

"A little after two A.M."

"What are you doing out here this time of morning?"

"Worried about you. How are you feeling?"

"I don't know, this cancer thing is something else. And they got me on dialysis for my kidney, and that just makes everything worse."

Prodigy stood over his fatherlike friend as Poppa Doc nodded off to sleep and woke back up. Tears flowed freely from his eyes. Prodigy closed his eyes and asked God to spare Winston Fuller. He never thought that he could feel this way about a man who wasn't his blood relative.

"Looks like I done dozed off on you, Prodigy," Poppa Doc said as he came to.

"That's alright. Get some rest."

"That medication don't do nothing but make me sleepy. What's on your mind that got you up this time of morning?"

"Everything. Simone. Nina. You."

"Well, don't you worry about me. I'm gonna be just fine. Tell me what's going on with your baby girl."

"She's a doll. I just hate the fact that Simone moved back to New Jersey. I'm exactly where I didn't want to be, living with my child in another state."

"What are you doing about it?"

"Mike hooked me up with this lawyer. I'm trying to get joint custody, but that's like pulling teeth with her being in another state. Legitimization laws are different. It's a mess."

"Well, fight until you get what you want. I'm proud of you and Michael for fighting for y'all kids. It doesn't always have to work out with the child's mother, but the child should not suffer in the process. How's my boy Blake?"

"He's doing just fine. He wants to play football this year."

"Man, I'm so proud of you. You've finally realized that life is about being a servant. It's never about you. You and Simone work something out with that baby. It's important."

Prodigy nodded knowingly.

"Poppa Doc, I think Nina is the one."

"I know. I saw that at Thanksgiving dinner. The way your mother smiled at her. She likes her, and you're a momma's boy." Poppa Doc tried to smile but was cut short by a deep cough.

"You get you some rest. I'ma get on home. I'll be back tomorrow after work."

"Alright. Kiss Nina for me and hug Blake."

"I'll do it." Prodigy reached down and rubbed the top of Poppa Doc's hand as Poppa Doc drifted back off to sleep.

Prodigy had a bad feeling in his stomach as he headed home. He woke up Nina by sliding a two-carat diamond ring down onto her ring finger.

"Nina, I don't want to take the chance of you ever slipping away from me. I didn't know that a woman like you existed. Since I met you, my life means more to me than it ever did. You make me wanna be a better man. I prayed and asked God to send me a sign to let me know if we were meant to be together, and He placed a feeling in my heart that I've never felt before. I want you to stay with me forever. Nina, will you—"

"Yes, yes, yes," Nina said, with eyes filled with tears but still shining bright enough to light up the dark room.

Prodigy smiled and held her close. That night they made love for the very first time. And for the first time in his life, Prodigy felt what it was like to love a woman.

But his joy was short-lived. He heard the phone ring and looked at the 6:45 on the digital clock that sat on his nightstand. He couldn't bring himself to answer it. Nina asked him if he wanted her to get it, but he couldn't respond. Tears came by the pint. Nina picked up the phone and Michael's teary voice came on the line.

"Nina, this is Michael. We lost Daddy. Can you tell Prodigy?"

"Oh no! Is there anything that we can do?" Nina started to cry. Prodigy knew what the call was about. He walked into the bathroom and closed the door.

"No, not right now. If you could just tell Prodigy what happened, we'd appreciate it," Michael said before he hung up the phone.

Poppa Doc had touched so many lives in his sixty-nine years on this earth, and it was obvious by the people who showed up at the funeral. Cars stretched for miles as everyone from the mayor of New York City, whom he befriended during his twenty-five years as a city employee, to the inner-city neighborhood hobo made their way out to the mausoleum.

Prodigy, Blake, and Nina rode with the family in one of the limousines up front. Blake and Prodigy wore black suits while Nina wore a black dress with a black hat.

Michael wanted to give Poppa Doc his last wish and take a picture of all of his grandchildren. So he gathered Brittany and his kids in front of the church. Once all of the children were gathered, he stopped and called for Prodigy to bring his and Simone's infant daughter, Arielle, and Blake over to join in the picture. Once he snapped that one, he handed the camera to a friend and asked that all of the family members join together to take a picture so his father could always have his family near. Michael's friend snapped the picture. Mrs. Ethel walked over and placed it in her husband's casket. Oddly, Mrs. Ethel was the pillar of strength as she comforted everyone around her, letting them know that she was sure her husband was in God's hands, and who could argue or feel sad about that. She walked over to Michael and told him that his father was very proud of him, which eased his mind a little. Prodigy walked over to his friend and confidant. He wiped his tears away with a white handkerchief and placed it in Poppa Doc's casket. He then leaned over, kissed him on the forehead, and whispered, "You gave me the heart of a man. I'm going to miss you, Poppa Doc."

A Conversation with Travis Hunter, Author of *The Hearts of Men*

Q: Why did you decide to write a "relationship" novel?

A: I can only write about what I know. I've always been interested in the human psyche and what makes some relationships work and others fail. So I researched by observing relationships. I listened to people's gripes about their spouses and what they were expecting out of their relationships but never took the time to communicate to their spouses. People love drama, and some of the things that I've encountered in my unofficial research are enough to fill ten novels. My goal is to help women understand men better—why we do what we do. But I want to reach men as well, because it takes more than just being over the age of eighteen to make someone a man.

Q: Are you any of the characters in *The Hearts of Men*?

A: I have a bit of all of them in me, but if I had to choose it would be Prodigy Banks. We're very similar. There were a few things that I changed to add to the drama of the book, but I pretty much captured the essence of Travis in the character Prodigy. We have the same heart and the same giving nature but we also have a street edge that says, "Don't make me lose my mind up in here."

Q: What advice would give to someone who dreams of becoming an author?

A: Write something every day. And every rejection letter brings you one step closer to realizing your dream. Be realistic with your expectations; this is not a get-rich-quick business. It's not all glamour; it might seem that way, but you have to put the work in. Surround yourself with positive people; you can't keep the creative juices flowing in a negative environment. Find yourself a mentor if possible. Most of the authors that I met were very helpful. Get a self-publishing manual, even if you don't plan to self-publish. There is a ton of information in those manuals that will educate you on the business side of publishing. And last but not least: Keep God first and everything will work out.

Q: In *The Hearts of Men,* Poppa Doc eases himself into the lives of the male characters to dispense a little wisdom and guidance. How important do you think it is to have a male presence in your life?

A: I think it is extremely important to have a male role model, but not just any male. You need a positive male who thinks first and knows the meaning of sacrifice. I blame a lot of the negativity that is going on in our communities on men. If more men were being men, then black men wouldn't make up 46 percent of the prison population even though we're only 13 percent of the nation's population. If more black men were home raising their daughters, then the teen pregnancy rate wouldn't be so high among our young sisters. I'm not placing all of the blame on black men, but we have to take care of our own and stop running away from our responsibilities. At the rate that this country is shipping our young men off to prison, we're headed for genocide. I wrote *The Hearts of Men* to entertain readers but at the same time make them think what a difference a positive man can make in their lives.

Q: How are you doing your part?

A: I practice what I preach. I take care of my son, financially, emotionally, and physically. My son's mother and I have gone our separate ways, but I made sure that I remained a major part of his life. He lives with me for the same amount of time that he lives with his mother. I'm also the executive director of The Hearts of Men Foundation. It's a nonprofit organization that mentors young boys. The men in THOMF make unannounced visits to our youngsters' schools and homes to speak with their teachers and parents. We ask them to set goals for themselves, and when they meet their objectives, we go out and celebrate. I realize that I don't have all the answers, but if I can touch a few lives, then my mission will be accomplished. I also speak at high schools and prisons. I'm the only male in my entire family over the age of eighteen who has never been to jail. I think God had a higher purpose for me.

Reading-Group Guide

The questions and discussion topics that follow are intended to enhance your group's reading of Travis Hunter's *The Hearts of Men*. We hope they will provide new insights and ways of looking at this funny and moving novel.

Questions for Discussion

1. After Prodigy sleeps with his new coworker, Gina, he tells her that a woman who sleeps with many men is judged by a different standard than a man who does the same thing. Are there different standards for men and women? Does Prodigy believe in them? Does Bernard judge Diane's brief affair with her pastor more harshly because of this?

2. The antipathy Bernard feels for Prodigy is rooted in his role in the theft of Bernard's car some time ago. Bernard persists in punishing him even though Poppa Doc has for-

given him. Is Bernard right? Why does Poppa Doc forgive Prodigy's transgressions? Is it possible to make wrongs right again?

3. Prodigy, Jermaine, and Bernard all grew up without fathers in their lives. How does their lack of father figures affect their ability to become successful fathers? Even with a strong father, Michael finds it difficult to accept responsibility for his own children. Why is this?

4. For much of his past, Prodigy has dated all the wrong women, including his married boss. It is only when he decides to stop dating that he encounters a woman who seems right for him. How is Nina different from Gina or Simone? Has Prodigy changed what he wants in a woman?

5. In some ways Bernard could not change or forgive his wife until he found his mother and let his childhood go. Likewise, Prodigy could not change his life until he gave up crime and encountered Poppa Doc. Would these personal transformations have occurred without Poppa Doc or Susan? What is Hunter saying about parents or parental figures here?

6. Poppa Doc and his wife disagree on how much they should support their son; Poppa Doc thinks that they've spoiled Michael and that he should learn the hard lessons of self-reliance. Why does his wife find it so hard to let go? How do parents help and hinder their children? What are the differences between mothers and fathers?

7. Bernard is trying so hard to compensate for his own childhood that he often loses sight of what is important to his family. Did his own childhood affect his ability to be a father

and a husband? Is his bitterness toward his mother and his childhood justified?

8. When Prodigy's cousin Jermaine comes to Atlanta for a break from fast-paced Philadelphia, Prodigy tries to influence him in a more positive direction. In some ways, Jermaine's presence reminds Prodigy of who he used to be. Is Prodigy successful in helping him? What does Prodigy come to realize about himself and how he has changed?

9. Poppa Doc is the father figure Prodigy never had, and it is a role Prodigy steps into for Blake. How important are fathers and role models? What changes do we see in Blake after Prodigy comes into his life? What does Prodigy provide that his mother cannot?

10. Diane is so angry with Bernard because he doesn't spend enough time with her or their child that she seeks fulfillment elsewhere. Is Diane right? Is she justified in challenging Bernard to be home more? Does Bernard bear any of the blame for her actions?

11. In many ways, *The Hearts of Men* is about men growing and accepting more responsibility in their lives. When Poppa Doc gives his sermon about respect and responsibility, he challenges the men to become real fathers to their children and good husbands to their wives. Do men lack responsibility and respect in real life? What about women?

ABOUT THE AUTHOR

Travis Hunter is an author, songwriter, and motivational speaker. He lives in an Atlanta suburb with his son, Rashaad. He is the founder of The Hearts of Men Foundation, through which he mentors underprivileged children. He is currently working on his second novel, *Married but Still Looking*.

Travis would love to hear from you. Please visit his website at www.travishunter.com or e-mail him at thunter142@aol.com.